Six Bronx Men

Six Bronx Men

Gus Constantine

ISBN: Hardcover 978-1-7960-3507-0
Softcover 978-1-7960-3506-3
eBook 978-1-7960-3505-6

This is a work of fiction. All of the characters, names, incidents, organizations, and dialogue in this novel are either the products of the author's imagination or are used fictitiously.

Any people depicted in stock imagery provided by Getty Images are models, and such images are being used for illustrative purposes only.

Print information available on the last page.

Rev. date: 05/28/2019

To order additional copies of this book, contact:
Xlibris
1-888-795-4274
www.Xlibris.com
Orders@Xlibris.com
791627

To Gus Leodas.
Gus, you discovered me.
You encouraged me.
You educated me.
I never could have done it without you.
I love you like a brother.

The first day of school . . .

Nikos walked into the homeroom class of his new high school, wanting to keep a low profile. He walked directly to the back of the room and sat between two empty seats.

A moment later, three tough-looking guys who clearly had an attitude came into the classroom.

They were loud and disruptive.

As they entered the classroom, Carmine Costello, the leader of the group, knocked the books out of the hands of a much smaller and weaker kid named Irving Feldman as Carmine's two friends laughed.

"Come on, Carmine. Cut it out," said Irving.

"Oh yeah?" said Carmine as he pushed Irving onto the floor. "Who's going to make me? You? I don't think so." He kicked Irving's books.

"You've matured a lot over the summer, I see."

"You better shut the fuck up, you little Jew. You want me to pull your pants off and have you run up and down the halls in your underwear like I did last year? Huh?"

Irving could only look up in embarrassment and reply, "No," as many in the class laughed as they remembered.

Carmine laughed as he walked to the back of the room, with his two friends following. "What the fuck are *you* doing?" Carmine asked Nikos.

Nikos looked up and saw Carmine looking down at him as his two friends stood there, smiling.

"You talking to me?" asked Nikos.

"No, asshole, I'm talking to the person next to you."

"Really? So why you looking at me?" Nikos asked arrogantly.

"Don't be a wise guy, asshole. Get up. We're sitting here. These three seats belong to us."

Nikos thought for a moment as the entire class looked on.

Here I am, my first day of school in a new city, and these three assholes want to disrespect me in front of the whole class. I don't think so.

Nikos was slouched in his seat. The way he was sitting, his 6'-3" 210-pound frame was not totally visible. Finally, as the entire class was looking back, he saw the teacher come into the room and tell everyone to take their seats and turn around for attendance.

"It's your lucky day, asshole," said Carmine as he and his friends took random seats.

2

After class, Carmine turned to Nikos and watched him stand. Nikos towered over the 5'-7" Carmine and both his friends, who were even an inch or two shorter. Nikos didn't say anything. He just walked away but not before deliberately bumping into Carmine. Carmine was shocked, as was the entire class, especially Irving Feldman.

"Hey, wise guy," said Carmine.

Nikos continued walking, not paying any attention to Carmine.

"Hey, asshole. I'm talking to you."

Nikos continued walking.

"Come on, guys, let's go after him."

Carmine's two buddies hesitated. They weren't sure they wanted to tangle with someone who showed no fear when they confronted him, especially since Nikos was obviously bigger and stronger than them individually, but Carmine had a reputation of being a tough guy.

The entire class saw this guy intentionally bump into me, thought Carmine.

"Let's go, guys. We'll grab him in the hall."

One of Carmine's friends, Salvatore Russo spoke first. Salvatore was an inch shorter than Carmine but weighed 220 pounds. He was nicknamed Fat Sal.

"Carmine," said Fat Sal, "let's let him go for now. All three of us are on probation. We got into enough trouble last year, remember? My father told me he'll kick my ass from one end of the Bronx to the other if I get into any trouble this year. Let's wait until after school. If he walks home, we can kick his ass *off* school property."

"Yeah, he's right," added Philip Caputo, Carmine's other friend, who was nicknamed Capo. Capo also showed concern about getting into trouble on the first day of school. Deep down, Capo was nervous tangling with the likes of Nikos.

"All right," said Carmine. "We'll wait. Let's go. I'll see you guys at lunch."

The three walked out of the classroom but not before knocking down Irving Feldman's books for the second time.

Nikos's younger sister, Lilly, sat nervously in her first-period class. A popular girl in her school back in Connecticut, she wasn't sure what to expect at her new school in the Bronx. In Connecticut, she had plenty of friends to start the new school year together. Now she was all alone in a new school without any friends. Two other girls sat next to Lilly and said hello. Lilly smiled back and said hi.

After class, the two girls introduced themselves to Lilly. Lilly felt a little relief as she spoke with Maryann and Teresa. She told them about her recent move from Connecticut. After they went their separate ways, Lilly felt a little better.

At lunch, Nikos walked into the cafeteria and found an empty table. He set his books down and walked over to the food line. Being 6'-3" and good looking, Nikos couldn't help noticing people looking at him. Most guys nodded when they made eye contact. The girls smiled. Nikos was used to the attention.

Nikos picked up a cheeseburger, french fries, and a Coke. When he returned to his table, he noticed his books on the floor. He looked around and saw some of the students looking. Some had their heads down, with their eyes up at him. Some of the girls looked upset.

Suddenly, Nikos looked over to the far end of the cafeteria and saw Irving Feldman sitting at a table, looking at Nikos. On his right were Fat Sal and Capo. On his left was Carmine. The four of them were sitting in a row. Three were laughing, and one looked scared. At a second glance, Nikos noticed Irving's food tray empty while the other three were full. Carmine had two soda cups, Fat Sal had two hamburgers, and Capo had two desserts.

Nikos took a breath and smiled. He gathered his books, walked over to Carmine's table, sat across from them, took a bite of his cheeseburger, and sipped his Coke.

You could hear a pin drop.

"You want my fries?" Nikos asked Irving as he put the fries on Irving's tray. "It's okay. Take them. Here. Take this soda," he continued as he took one of the sodas off Carmine's tray and gave it to Irving.

Irving sat in shock. He didn't know what to say.

"Oh, real wise guy," said Carmine. "Who the fuck do you think you are, coming over to my table uninvited?"

"Your table? I didn't know it was your table. How would I know it's your table? I didn't see your name on it."

"You know what, asshole? You're right. My name is *not* on it. Hey, Fat Sal, give me a magic marker."

"A magic marker? I don't have a magic marker."

"Check Irving's backpack. The Jew's got everything in there."

Fat Sal opened Irving's backpack as though it were his own.

"I found one."

"Good. Give it to me."

Fat Sal reached across Irving's face and deliberately elbowed him in the head as he handed Carmine the magic marker.

Carmine removed the cap and wrote his name on the table with large letters.

"See, asshole? It's my table."

"I see. Now I know it's your table. Now since you don't want me on *your* table, I guess I can't stay."

"That's right, asshole. Get going if you know what's good for you."

Nikos thought a moment as he noticed everyone watching.

"Can I ask you guys your names?"

"Sure, asshole. You obviously need to learn who we are. On the end over there is Capo. Next to him is Fat Sal. Next to me is Irving. Irving's the best. Anything you need, he has it—homework, lunch money, or just lunch. Irving's the man. And me, as you saw me write, I'm Carmine. And let me remind you *again* that you are on *my* table."

"My name is Nikos. Nikos Ioannis. I just moved here. You three—sorry, you four are the first four guys in school I've met so far. You know something? I like you guys. I'm not crazy about the way you don't want to share your table with me. But I love the way you share your lunch with me."

Nikos took the untouched hamburger off Fat Sal's tray and took a bite out of it.

"Ewww, this hamburger's cold," Nikos said as he put it back. Then he took one of the chocolate cakes off Capo's tray, took a bite out of it, and put it back.

"Don't like chocolate. You finish it."

"You just crossed the line, asshole," said Capo as he stood, followed by Fat Sal and Carmine.

Quick as a cat, Nikos stood. He picked up the chocolate cake and shoved it in Capo's face. Then he shoved the hamburger in Fat Sal's face as he picked up the soda cup from Irving's food tray and threw it in Carmine's face.

Then Nikos grabbed Fat Sal by the hair and smashed his face on the table. Capo came around the table and was met by Nikos's fist as he went down.

Carmine jumped onto the table, looked down at Nikos, and jumped on him. Big mistake. Nikos caught him and held him in midair like he was pressing weights. He held him a few seconds and threw him onto Fat Sal as he was wiping the blood from his nose. They both ended up on the floor.

Nikos stood over the three defeated guys, looked down, gathered his books, and walked away as the entire cafeteria watched.

5

That night, Fat Sal, Capo, and Carmine met at the schoolyard of P.S. 14. The three sat against the handball court, totally dumbfounded. They couldn't believe what had happened to them. Fat Sal was in pain with a swollen nose. Capo had a black eye. Carmine had no visible damage, although his back was killing him.

"Carmine, what are we going to do about this guy Nikos?" asked Fat Sal. "Are we going to let him get away with this shit?"

"No way. He has to pay."

"So what are we going to do?" asked Capo.

"I'm not sure. I called Skelly and Vito. I'm waiting for them to get back to me. This Nikos guy really made us look bad. We can't let it go. We can't just kick his ass. He needs to be made an example of. I saw him talking to some kids after school. We need to stop him before he becomes too popular."

Carmine's phone rang. It was Tony Scorzelli. Scorzelli always went by his nickname, Skelly.

"Skelly, where are you?"

"I'm walking to fourteen now. I got Vito with me. I got your message earlier. What happened? Who is this guy? It sounds like he needs to be taught a lesson."

"Yeah, that's why I called you. Get here as soon as you can so we can figure out what we're going to do with this asshole."

"We'll be there in ten minutes."

Fifteen minutes later, Skelly and Vito showed up at the schoolyard. All five guys fist-pounded.

"Talk to me, Carmine. What happened?" asked Skelly.

Carmine spent the next few minutes explaining to Skelly and Vito what had happened in homeroom class and in the cafeteria.

"He did what?" snapped Skelly. "How could you let him get away with that? There were three of you. You mean to tell me this one guy kicked all three of your asses?"

"Skelly," Carmine said, "this guy's huge. He has to be over six feet tall and muscular. Built like a brick shithouse. I'm telling you. He caught me in midair and threw me like I was nothing."

"Don't worry," said Vito. "He's not kicking all five of our asses. We'll take care of him."

"Good," said Carmine. "Between the five of us, we should be able to take him down."

"Don't worry," said Skelly. "He's going down."

The next morning, Nikos and Lilly were up at seven o'clock. Their mother, Maria, made them a hearty breakfast of french toast and bacon. The three spoke briefly about their upcoming school year.

Their father, Michael, had been forced to close his restaurant in Connecticut because of the Hartford Highway Department purchasing eight miles of roadway through Eminent Domain. Michael didn't own his restaurant's property, so he had been compensated nothing. His landlord had made all the money. He was fortunate enough that his business had done well for several years and that he had put a substantial amount of his profits into his saving account. Nonetheless, he had still lost his business.

While all this was happening, Michael's brother, Charlie, had lost his chef's job in a Manhattan restaurant and asked Michael if he wanted to become partners in a diner. Michael wasn't happy about moving to the Bronx, but at fifty years old, he needed to own his own place, as did his fifty-five-year-old brother. Restaurant work was too difficult to work for someone else. Besides, restaurant owners wanted younger men.

So Michael and Charlie bought the Westchester Square Diner, two blocks from Herbert H. Lehman High School, where Nikos and Lilly were enrolled.

* * *

"Nikos, you were a little quiet last night," said Maria. "I know you're not happy about moving to the Bronx, but in time, you'll adjust."

"I know, Mom. It's just not easy. A new school in a new neighborhood with no friends isn't fun. But in time, I'm sure I'll be fine."

"I know you will be, son. Please give it some time. It's only been one day. Lilly met a couple of girls yesterday, and they plan on getting together for lunch today. In time, I'm sure you'll have a lunch crowd too."

Nikos thought about his lunch crowd from yesterday and smiled. "Yes, Mom, I'm sure you're right."

* * *

Nikos and Lilly were three years apart. Lilly was a freshman and Nikos a senior. They were extremely close. Many teenage brothers and sisters didn't like to travel together to school, but Nikos knew after yesterday, he needed to keep an eye on his sister. He was always protective of her.

But now, in the Bronx, he knew he had to be extra protective.

For the second day in a row, Nikos and Lilly left their house on Balcom Avenue, walked eight blocks to East Tremont Avenue, and got onto the number 40 bus. They rode the 40 for six miles to Lehman.

When they reached Lehman, they were like a herd of cattle exiting the bus.

Nikos and Lilly, being from the small town of Glastonbury, Connecticut, were overwhelmed by the amount of students at Lehman.

As they approached Lehman's main entrance, Nikos noticed Fat Sal leaning on the wall, with Capo next to him. Not too far away from them were Carmine, Skelly, and Vito.

"That's him over there," Carmine said to Skelly.

"Holy shit. He *is* big. Who's that girl walking next to him?"

"I don't know."

"You think it might be his girlfriend?"

"I don't know. He said he's new here. He can't have a girlfriend already, can he?"

"I don't know."

"I'll tell you what," said Vito. "I'll follow him to homeroom. Skelly, why don't you follow his girlfriend or whoever the fuck she is to her homeroom?"

"Good idea," said Skelly. "She's kind of cute. She's got a nice ass on her too."

"Yeah, I noticed that," said Carmine.

"Oooh yeah," said Vito. "A real piece of ass."

All three separated. Skelly followed Lilly into the school while she spoke with Nikos. Once inside, Nikos and Lilly went in opposite directions. As Skelly followed Lilly down the hall, he noticed Maryann and Teresa approach Lilly. Lilly looked happy and innocent. Unknown to her, Skelly had other plans for her as he watched her walk away.

"Teresa!" Skelly called out. "Hold on a second."

Both Teresa and Maryann turned and faced Skelly. Both girls had known Skelly since grade school. Neither one of them liked him. Teresa had actually gone out with Skelly in middle school. It was a terrible experience. They had gone to the movies. While Skelly was taking her home, he had made a detour through the park and was all over her. Teresa had ended up running away and crying all the way home.

"What do you want?" Teresa asked arrogantly.

"Nothing. I just wanted to say hi."

"Hi," Teresa said and walked away.

"Hey, wait a minute. Can't we talk?"

"Why don't you go find someone else to talk to?"

"Do you want me to call security?" asked Maryann.

"Oh, come on," said Skelly. "I just wanna talk."

"It's all right, Maryann," said Teresa. "You go to class. I can handle this. What do you want?"

"How was your summer?"

"How was my summer? Is that what you want to ask me?"

"Yeah, I just want to see how you're doing and ask you how your summer was."

"I'm fine, and so was my summer."

"Can I ask you another question?"

"What?"

"Who was that girl you were talking to?"

"Oh, so that's it."

"So that's what? What are you talking about?"

"Don't give me that bullshit. You know what you're talking about. Stay away from her. She's a nice girl."

"What's her name? Does she have a boyfriend?"

"Goodbye, Skelly. And stay away from her."

That afternoon at lunch, Skelly walked into the cafeteria and instantly noticed Lilly sitting at a table with Teresa and several other girls. Skelly was mesmerized by Lilly's beauty. He knew nothing about her but knew he wanted to get to know her. He didn't care if she was Nikos's girlfriend.

Skelly walked directly to their table and sat.

"Good afternoon, girls," said Skelly. "How was your summer? Are you ready for another year of learning?"

"Get lost," Teresa replied while Lilly smiled at what she thought was a sincere question. Skelly instantly noticed the innocent smile and introduced himself.

"Hi, I'm Tony, Tony Scorzelli. My friends call me Skelly."

"Hi, Skelly. My name's Lilly, Lilly Ioannis."

"It's nice to meet you, Lilly. I've never seen you before. Are you new in the neighborhood?"

"Yes, my family and I just moved here from Connecticut."

"Well, Lilly, welcome to the Bronx."

"Thank you, Skelly. So far, everyone's been real nice."

"I'm glad. Anyway, I have to get going. Biology awaits. It was a pleasure meeting you." "It was a pleasure meeting you too, Skelly."

"Hope to see you around sometime."

"Me too."

Lilly smiled as she watched Skelly walk away. She looked toward Teresa. Lilly didn't have a chance to speak.

"Lilly, don't even think about him. He's no good. Don't fall for his charms."

"Really? He seems so nice and sincere."

"He's a real piece of shit. Stay away from him."

9

That night, Skelly met up with Carmine and Fat Sal in the schoolyard of P.S. 14. When Skelly explained the conversation he had had with Lilly to Carmine and Fat Sal, it all came together.

"She must be his sister," said Carmine. "They have the same last name."

"All right now," said Skelly. "At least we know who she is. I have an idea."

"Oh yeah, what's your idea?" asked Carmine.

"I'm going to befriend her. It looked like she took a liking to me. I'm going to ask her out."

"Really?" asked Fat Sal.

"Yeah, really. I'm going to lay on the charm. I'm going to get close to her and her entire family. Yes, even her brother. Then I'm dropping the bomb."

"Just be careful, Skelly," said Carmine. "You really don't want to get Nikos pissed off."

"Fuck him and his sister."

Skelly wasn't afraid of Nikos. Although Nikos was bigger, it wasn't by much. Skelly was 6'-0" and 190 pounds of solid wiry muscle. Besides, fighting was Skelly's thing.

He was always the one to kick ass.

Never the one to get his ass kicked.

"And believe me, I will fuck his sister. Now we need a plan. I'm going to also have to befriend Nikos. I'm going to need his trust. And right now, the only way to do that is to not be friends with you guys. Tomorrow in school, I need to have a confrontation with you."

"Who, me?" asked Carmine.

"Yes, you, Carmine. Also with Fat Sal, Capo, and Vito. If I'm ever going to have Nikos's total trust, I'm going to need him to think I don't like you guys. And, Carmine, don't be a dick. I need you to play it up."

"Don't worry about me. I'll play it real good."

For the next fifteen minutes, all three discussed their plan.

They couldn't wait until tomorrow.

The next morning, Carmine and Fat Sal were up bright and early, waited for Irving in the school courtyard, and took him off to the side. They knew Irving showed up thirty minutes early every morning for the math team. They held him there, talking. Irving was insisting they let him go. Carmine just held him by his collar and kept talking to him.

"Come on, Carmine, let me go."

"Hold on, Irving. I just wanna talk. Can't we talk?"

"Talk about what?"

"About anything. You're my friend, aren't you?"

"Yeah, I'm your friend," Irving said sarcastically. "That's why you pick on me all the time."

"Come on, Irving. I kid around. That's what friends do. They kid around."

"Well, I don't like that kind of kidding. You've been picking on me since grade school. And it's not fun. So why don't you just leave me alone?"

Meanwhile, Skelly was on the other side of the courtyard, watching Carmine. They needed to time it right. Suddenly, Skelly waved to Fat Sal, giving him the signal. On cue, Fat Sal tapped Carmine on the shoulder. Carmine looked up and saw Skelly give him a quick wave.

Carmine looked left as Skelly looked right. They saw Nikos walking into the courtyard with Lilly. As they approached, Skelly started walking toward the middle of the courtyard.

"Hi, Lilly," said Skelly.

"Oh, hi, Skelly. How are you this morning?"

"I'm fine, thanks. Just another day at school, that's all."

"Skelly, this is my brother, Nikos. Nikos, this is Skelly."

"Hi, Nikos," said Skelly as he extended his hand to shake.

"Hi, Skelly. Nice to meet you too," Nikos said as he also extended his hand.

Skelly suddenly noticed Nikos look toward his right as Carmine pulled Irving by his collar. *Perfect timing*, thought Skelly.

"Hey, Carmine!" called out Skelly.

"What's up, Skelly?"

"What are you doing? Why don't you leave him alone?"

Nikos and Lilly just watched.

"Come on, Skelly, I'm just having a little fun with the Jew."

"Come on, let him go. It's a new year. Being a bully is kid's stuff. Irving, go to class. Carmine, I said let him go."

Carmine looked at Skelly.

"Don't look at me like that, Carmine. I said let him go. I'm sure he hasn't done anything to you."

"Carmine," said Nikos. "Listen to Skelly, unless you want to go skydiving again."

Carmine looked at Skelly and then back at Nikos, thought for a moment, and let go of Irving.

"Irving, go to class," repeated Skelly.

Irving walked away embarrassed, as he always did.

"Carmine, I suggest you go to class too."

Again, Carmine looked at Skelly and Nikos, hesitated, and walked away.

"Skydiving?" Skelly asked, looking up at Nikos.

"It's nothing," said Nikos. "I met Carmine yesterday. He and his two friends gave me some trouble. I took care of it. But what's the deal with Irving? He seems to be Carmine's punching bag."

"Yeah, it's always been like that. Carmine's been picking on him for the longest time. Carmine's a bully. He'll pick on anyone he can. Anyway, Lilly told me yesterday you just moved here from Connecticut. When did you move here?"

"A couple of weeks ago," Lilly answered, wanting to move the conversation her way.

Skelly took the hint that Lilly wanted him to talk to her. So he took the ball and ran with it.

"Nikos, it's still a little early. Would you mind if I show Lilly around the school before classes start?"

"Sure, Skelly, as long as you keep her away from Carmine and his friends."

"Don't worry about those guys. I can handle them. Look at me . . ." said Skelly to Lilly. "I asked your brother if it was okay, but I didn't ask you. Lilly, can I show you around the school?"

"Yes, I would like that."

"All right then. Let's go."

Nikos watched Lilly walk away with Skelly.

Skelly spent the next fifteen minutes showing Lilly around. Lilly really didn't pay much attention to the school. She knew she liked Skelly and wanted to get to know him better. They talked about things to do and places to go in the Bronx.

However, Skelly was smart.

He wanted to get to know Lilly but not for the same reasons Lilly wanted to get to know him. The more he knew about her likes and dislikes, the more he would conquer. So he turned the subject over to her. He asked her questions about her old school and her town of Glastonbury.

"Lilly, by your last name, you're Greek, aren't you?"

"Well, I'm actually half Greek and half Cypriot."

"Cypriot?"

"Yes, Cypriot, on my father's side. Cyprus is an island in the Mediterranean. It's independent from Greece, but the religion is Greek Orthodox. But basically, yes, my family's Greek."

"My cousin married a Greek girl. Your last names are similar," he lied. The only Greek wedding he had ever seen was in the movie *My Big Fat Greek Wedding*. "It was a beautiful affair. And the Greek church, it's so beautiful. I wish the Catholic churches were as beautiful."

"Thank you for the compliment. I'm extremely proud of my religion and heritage."

"You should be. All my cousin's Greek relatives are wonderful people."

At fifteen years old, Lilly was really taking a liking to Skelly.

As they were walking through the halls, most of the guys gave Skelly a respectful nod.

What Lilly didn't notice was the way most of the girls looked away.

As Skelly was escorting Lilly to homeroom, they both noticed Teresa looking at them.

"Lilly, your friend Teresa doesn't like me."

"I got that impression yesterday. Why is that?"

"It's a long story, and I really don't want to talk about it. You don't know me, but I'm not the type of person who badmouths people."

"Is it something *she* did?"

"Like I said, I'm not badmouthing anyone, even if they badmouth me."

"All right then. I respect that. I really do."

"Thanks, Lilly. Most girls would try to pry it out of me. Anyway, since we both have the same lunch period, may I take you for a slice of pizza today?"

"Yes, I would like that."

That same day, Nikos walked into the cafeteria. He had no idea Lilly was going out for pizza with Skelly since they had different lunch periods.

Just like the previous two days, he put his books on an empty table and went for his lunch. In his old school, he had never eaten in the cafeteria. He always went out for lunch with his friends. Because of his size, he appeared older. Many of his friends were older than him. Some drove to school. Other friends had already graduated high school. Now in his new school, he had no ride or friends, although his father had promised to get him a car soon.

As he sat, he noticed Irving standing with his food tray, undecided on where to sit. He noticed Carmine sitting alone and waved at Irving to go sit with him.

"Irving!" Nikos called out. "How you doing?"

"I'm okay," Irving said, walking over to Nikos. "How about you? Are you adjusting to the new school?"

"Not really. Here." Nikos pointed to the empty seat across from him. "Have a seat."

"Sure, thanks. Give it some time," Irving said as he sat. "It's only been three days. It's not the greatest school, but it's a lot better than some of the assholes around here."

"Yeah, what is it with those assholes?" Nikos asked as he motioned toward Carmine's table as he watched Fat Sal and Capo approach Carmine.

"Those guys? Forget them. They're bad news. They're always pushing people around. Sometimes they even grope the girls."

"Are you kidding?"

"I wish I was."

"And they get away with it?"

"Yes, they do. You saw the way they push me around. I can't wait to get the hell out of here."

"Where you going?"

"I'm going away to college next year. By the way, I want to thank you for the other day. I don't know if you know it or not, but you're becoming the talk of the school."

"Why?"

"The way you kicked their asses is spreading like wildfire."

"Really?" Nikos smiled. "I haven't noticed. Besides, I'm not the only one to stand up to those guys. That guy Skelly stood up to Carmine this morning."

"Yeah, that was strange."

"What do you mean?"

"What do I mean? I mean Skelly is worse than all those guys combined. That's what I mean."

"Really?"

"Yes, really."

"But he was trying to help you."

"I know. That's why I said it was strange. Last year, it was Skelly who told Carmine to pull my pants off and throw me into the hall. I'm telling you, Nikos, Skelly's bad news."

"Well, he was real nice to me this morning and to my sister."

"Nikos, I would not trust him. Keep your sister away from him."

"Are you sure?"

"Positive."

"All right, Irving. I'll keep an eye on him."

"Lilly, you *do* like pizza, I hope?" asked Skelly.

"Of course, I do. Who doesn't?"

"To tell you the truth, I don't know anyone who doesn't. I just wanted to make sure."

Skelly continued small talk as they crossed Westchester Avenue.

When they entered Westchester Square, Skelly pointed out Square Pizza.

"There it is. I love their pizza."

Lilly couldn't believe it. Square Pizza was right next door to her father's Westchester Square Diner. She had noticed it last week but didn't think anything of it.

"Lilly, if you want, we can get a quick burger at the diner over here instead. It's under new ownership. I ate there yesterday. The new owners really fixed up the place. The previous owners really ran it to the ground."

"You're kidding. That's my father's diner. He owns it with my uncle Charlie."

"Wow, that's cool! But we better get pizza. How would it look if I took you to lunch to your father's restaurant?"

"I understand."

As they were walking past the diner, Maria, while sitting by the cash register, noticed Lilly and came out and called to her.

"Lilly!"

"Mom."

"Where are you going?" Maria asked as she looked at Skelly.

"Mom, I want you to meet a friend of mine. This is Tony. Tony Scorzelli. He goes by Skelly. We're going for pizza. Skelly, this is my mom, Maria."

"It's a pleasure to meet you, Mrs. Ioannis."

Skelly couldn't take his eyes off Maria. Her beauty was breathtaking.

"Nice to meet you too, Tony," said Maria as she extended a hand to shake.

"Anyway, Mom, we only get forty-five minutes for lunch. We need to get going."

"All right then. Please be careful, and make sure you get to your next class on time," Maria said as she again extended a hand to shake with Skelly. Maria then reached over to Lilly and gave her a kiss.

"Don't worry, Mrs. Ioannis. We won't be late," chimed in Skelly.

Inside, Michael asked Maria where she went.

"I saw Lilly outside with a young man, going for pizza."

"A young man? And you didn't stop her? What's the matter with you? I'm going next door to the pizza shop."

"Hold on. It's nothing like that. When I said 'young man,' I meant a high school student. Let's give her a little space. It's only pizza at lunchtime."

"All right. You scared me. The move was adjustment enough. I don't need boyfriends on top of it."

"Don't worry, darling. I'll communicate with her. You know we're close."

"I know. Anyway, I need to go back in the kitchen."

"All right," Maria said as she took her place behind the cash register.

* * *

Next door in the crowded pizza shop, Lilly sat in a booth with Skelly. Although it was only the third day of school, Lilly felt moving to the Bronx would work out all right for her, especially since meeting Skelly.

"Lilly, how's the pizza?" asked Skelly.

"This pizza's great. I've never tasted pizza this good."

"It's a New York City thing. New York City has the best pizza in the world. It has something to do with the water. I know pizza owners in the Bronx who live on Long Island and Westchester County who tried to duplicate their pizza recipes to no avail. It's all about the New York City water."

"I didn't know that."

"Now you do." Skelly smiled. "By the way, your mom seems real nice. I like the way she showed concern. I can see you come from a caring family by the closeness you have with your brother."

"Yes, thank you for noticing."

"Your mom, if you don't mind me saying, is a beautiful woman."

"I know. I hear it all the time. She doesn't like it when I tell people, but she's actually a former Miss Connecticut."

"It's starting to make sense."

"What's starting to make sense?"

"Where you get *your* beauty from."

Lilly knew she was pretty. Back in Connecticut, the boys were always interested in her, especially the older boys, but they knew they had to behave themselves because Nikos was her brother, and as much as she knew she was pretty, it didn't stop her from blushing.

That evening during dinner, Maria, Lilly, and Nikos talked about the adjustment on Bronx living. Michael ate dinner at home half the time. Restaurant life took up most of his time, although he had an excellent working arrangement with his brother, Charlie. They split the openings and closings. One week, Charlie opened and was home for dinner, and the next week, Michael opened and was home for dinner.

Sundays, the diner was closed.

The Ioannises insisted the entire family went to church on Sundays.

"Lilly," said Maria, "tell me about Tony."

"Who's Tony?" Nikos jumped in.

"Lilly's new friend," said Maria. "They went to the pizza shop next to the diner today for lunch."

"Yes, Lilly. Tell us about this Tony person," said Nikos.

"Nikos, you know him. It's Skelly. His real name is Tony Scorzelli. You met him this morning."

"Yeah, I remember him. He seemed all right. But to tell you the truth, I'm not too sure."

"What do you mean?" asked Maria.

"Yeah, Nikos," said Lilly. "What do you mean? You met him this morning. He actually protected that Irving guy this morning, like you did the first day of school."

"What? What happened the first day of school?" asked Maria.

"Never mind the first day of school," Nikos said, looking at his mother.

"Don't tell me never mind. What happened, and who and why did you protect someone?"

"Mom, never mind, I said. I want to hear about Lilly's lunch date with Skelly."

"It wasn't a date," said Lilly. "It was just pizza."

"Whatever," said Nikos. "Right now, I'm not sure if I trust him or not."

"You always do this to me, Nikos. I'm tired of it. Can't you leave me alone to make my own decisions?"

"Yes, I can. But only when I feel your decisions are the right ones."

"Okay, you two. What's going on? Nikos, is there something going on with Tony I need to know about?" asked Maria.

"No, Mom! There's nothing going on!" snapped Lilly.

"Don't raise your voice at me, young lady," Maria snapped back but with a lot more authority.

"I'm sorry, Mom. But all I did was go to lunch with Skelly, and now Nikos isn't sure? Come on, Mom. It was only pizza."

"Nikos," said Maria, "please explain yourself. You seem to not like Lilly's new friend Tony. Can you give me a reason? Do you know something about him your sister and I should know about?"

"To tell you the truth, Mom, I'm not sure yet. All I'm saying is I want Lilly to be careful. This is a new place. We don't know anyone. At first, I liked Skelly. Don't get me wrong. First impressions are important. But sometimes first impressions aren't enough. Especially with family."

"Your brother's right," said Maria. "Please be careful. All right, Lilly?"

"Careful of what?" Lilly cried. "Careful of pizza?"

"Listen, Lilly," said Nikos, "no one's saying you can't have pizza with Skelly. All I'm saying is to be careful." Nikos stood and walked over to his sister and gave her a hug. "Lilly, I'm sorry if I upset you. It's just that I heard something today about Skelly, and I need to be sure. That's all."

Lilly looked up at Nikos with glassy eyes. She knew Nikos had her best interest in mind. She knew he wanted to protect her, not dominate her.

"I understand, Nikos. Again, it was only pizza. I don't know if I'm going to see him again. We haven't made any plans. Thank you for caring. Moving to the Bronx would have been so much more difficult without having my brother around."

"All right, you two," said Maria with glassy eyes, "let's finish up dinner, and do your homework."

"All right, Mom," Nikos and Lilly said at the same time.

* * *

That same evening, Skelly, Carmine, Fat Sal, Vito, and Capo met at the handball court of P.S. 14. Skelly leaned against the handball court, thinking of where to start.

The others waited for Skelly to speak. As tough as they all were, Skelly was not only the leader but also the toughest.

Not only the Lehman High School students but also many in the neighborhood knew Skelly as a rough and tough guy.

There were many students who lived in the neighborhood who went to other prestigious high schools in the Bronx who knew about Skelly.

Bronx High School of Science was not only the best high school in the Bronx but also one of the most recognized high schools in the country. You needed to be near genius to get into the school. All the students had the reputation of being nerds.

Sometimes, just for fun, Skelly would wait at the Westchester Square train station for the Bronx High School of Science students to get off the train. As they approached, he would insult them by calling them nerds, bookworms, and losers. Many times, he would humiliate a guy if he was walking with his girlfriend. He would stand in front of him and not let him pass as his girlfriend watched. When the guy would try to walk around him, Skelly would throw him to the ground. Then he would approach his girlfriend and make passes at her. Sometimes he would even grope the girl just to embarrass and humiliate the boyfriend.

"Listen up, guys," said Skelly. "I've been watching and asking around about Nikos. It's only the first week of school, and everyone seems to be taking a liking to him. That's not good."

"Why would anyone want to take a liking to such an asshole?" asked Carmine.

"Shut up," snapped Skelly. "Are you stupid or something? Take a look at what's happening. We run Lehman. We go around doing anything we want. We pick on anyone we want. If a girl has a nice ass, we grab it. And no one was able to stop us.

"Look at what's happening now. You told him to get out of his seat, and he practically told you to go fuck yourself. Then he deliberately bumps into you, and you guys didn't do shit. Then to add insult to injury, he beats the shit out of all three of you assholes in front of the entire cafeteria. Next thing you know, Irving will be taking *your* lunch money."

"Shut up, Skelly," said Carmine. "You know that'll never happen."

The 6'-0" 190-pound Skelly walked up to Carmine and looked down at him.

"You didn't just tell me to shut up, did you? Because that's what it sounded like," Skelly said as he grabbed Carmine by his shirt and held him up against the handball court as the others looked on.

"Skelly, he didn't mean it," said Fat Sal.

"Yeah, Skelly, he didn't mean it," Capo said.

"Come on, Skelly," chimed in Vito. "He didn't mean it."

Skelly held Carmine there a few more seconds before letting him go.

"Okay, guys. This is what's going down tomorrow."

For the next fifteen minutes, Skelly described in detail what they were going to do. After going over their plan several times, they all fist-pounded one another and went home.

The next morning at school, Lilly kept looking around for Skelly. In the meantime, Skelly went out of his way to avoid Lilly and Nikos. He didn't want to see either one of them. He needed to concentrate on his plan.

At the same time, he also kept his distance from Carmine, Fat Sal, Capo, and Vito. He didn't want to be seen anywhere near them either, not if he wanted to conquer Lilly. Lilly was his ticket to Nikos. He knew he needed to get to Nikos from alternate angles.

* * *

During lunch period, Skelly carefully left Lehman and walked toward Westchester Square. As he crossed over Westchester Avenue, he walked toward the Westchester Square Diner. He stood in front of the diner, looking on an angle for Maria. He didn't want Maria to see him. The minute Maria turned her back from the door, he snuck inside.

A moment later, Jackie, the waitress, approached Skelly and took his order of a cheeseburger and Coke. Skelly was careful to keep a soft-spoken voice, along with keeping his manners up to par. He wanted to make a good impression on anyone and everyone.

"Here you go, young man," said Jackie. "Can I get you anything else?"

"No, thank you. That'll be all."

Jackie wrote out the check and left it with him.

As Skelly finished his lunch, he sent a text, and within seconds, Carmine, Fat Sal, Capo, and Vito walked into the diner.

"Good afternoon, beautiful," Carmine said to Maria.

"Beautiful, she is," added Fat Sal as Capo and Vito laughed.

Maria ignored their comments. She was used to comments like that but never from high school kids. Nonetheless, she was cautious.

"How many?" she asked. "The four of you?"

"No," said Carmine. "There will be five of us. Four of us and one of you. A beautiful lady like you shouldn't be working. A beautiful lady like you should be sitting with us."

"Sorry, guys. I'm going to have to ask you to leave."

"We're not going anywhere. You're going to sit with us and take our order. And don't worry, gorgeous." Carmine winked. "We'll give you a good tip." He grabbed his crotch.

"Get out," Maria said, raising her voice.

"Excuse me, Mrs. Ioannis. Is there a problem?" asked Skelly as he approached the cash register.

Maria looked at Skelly, trying to figure who he was.

"Stay out of this, Skelly," said Carmine.

Maria then recognized the name Skelly.

"It's all right, Tony," said Maria. "They were just leaving."

"We're not going anywhere, lady," said Carmine.

Skelly's plan was working perfectly. He was going to impress Maria just like he had impressed Lilly when he stood up for Irving.

"Carmine," said Skelly, "why don't you guys leave?"

"Who's going to make us? You?"

"If need be, yes. But for now, I'm asking."

"Well, we're saying no."

"It's all right, Tony. I'm calling the police."

"Mrs. Ioannis, don't bother. You don't know these guys. By the time the police get here, these guys will make a lot of trouble and be gone. Please let me take care of it."

Skelly didn't give Maria a chance to answer. He bumped aside Fat Sal and stood in front of Carmine as he looked down at him. Skelly then put his hand on Carmine's chest and pushed him toward the door.

The plan was working perfectly. Capo grabbed Skelly and pushed him aside. They all knew there would be lots of shoving and even punches thrown, but they didn't expect the unexpected.

"What the fuck's going on?"

They all turned and saw Nikos.

They didn't know what to do.

They were in shock.

"Mom, what's going on?"

"Nothing, Nikos. Everything's fine."

"It doesn't look fine."

"Mind your own business, asshole," said Carmine.

From behind the counter, Jackie yelled, "Nikos, they were being extremely disrespectful to your mother! When she asked them to leave, they refused. This young man here"—she motioned toward Skelly—"was trying to convince them to leave, but they refused."

"Which one was being disrespectful?" asked Nikos.

"All of them, especially that one." Jackie pointed to Carmine.

"I guess you'll never learn," Nikos said to Carmine as he looked everyone over. He wasn't sure if he could take all four of them, but it looked like he would get some help from Skelly, but he didn't care. He never had and never would back down from a fight.

By now, Michael had come out of the kitchen to see what the commotion was.

Even at fifty years old, Michael was no slouch. He stood 6'-1" and 190 pounds. Growing up in the ghetto of Hartford, Connecticut, he had his share of fights. He taught Nikos to never back down as *he* never backed down.

"What's going on out here?" Michael asked.

"Why don't you go back into the kitchen, old man? That's what's going on," said Vito.

Nikos grabbed Vito by the collar and threw him across the diner. Fat Sal and Capo grabbed Nikos and together pushed him up against the door. Michael grabbed Fat Sal and threw him across the diner floor and watched him bump into Vito as he was getting up. Carmine and Capo jumped on top of Michael, and Nikos immediately went to his father's aid. It was out of control. Skelly couldn't believe it. His plan was out the window, but a new and better plan was taking place.

Skelly immediately started swinging punches at Carmine. He wasn't hitting him very hard as no one noticed. Within a minute, Carmine, Fat Sal, Capo, and Vito were thrown out onto the sidewalk. The perfect plan was even better. Skelly impressed not only Maria but also Nikos and Michael.

Now there could not be a reason for any of the Ioannises to doubt him.

After the smoke cleared, Nikos shook hands with Skelly and gave him a shoulder hug. Skelly was only too happy to accept Nikos's hug. Michael also shook hands with Skelly, as did Maria.

"Skelly," said Nikos, "come, sit down. Let us buy you lunch."

"Thanks, Nikos. I can't. I have to get back to school. Besides, I already ate."

"Give me your check," said Michael. "The least we can do is not let you pay."

Skelly covered all his bases.

"It's all right, sir," said Skelly. "I already left the money on the counter. There's no need to buy me lunch. Those guys deserved everything they got. I know them from school. They're nothing but a bunch of bullies. I don't understand what makes them tick. Anyway, I need to get going. I have a calculus class."

Skelly then shook hands with Nikos and Michael again. Then he shook Maria's hand but not before slightly bowing his head in the utmost respectful way. Then he walked out the door.

"Nikos," said Michael, "do you know this young man?"

"Kind of. I met him in school yesterday."

"Michael," said Maria, "that's the young man who took Lilly for pizza yesterday."

"I see," said Michael. "Anyway, Nikos, please show the same enthusiasm that Skelly showed, going back to class on time."

"All right, Dad."

"Nikos."

"Yes, Dad?"

"Thanks for your help. I'm sure Skelly and I wouldn't have been able to handle those four guys without you."

"Dad, I still have my money on you. Besides, being a Ioannis is being at the right place at the right time."

"Maria," said Michael, "if any of those guys ever come back here, have Jackie call the police and immediately come into the kitchen to get me."

Glastonbury, Connecticut . . .

"Come on, Gary," said Richie. "Let's go. The guys are waiting."

"Hold your horses. I have to take a leak."

"Just hurry up. And don't spend an hour fixing your hair."

"Are you jealous?"

"Just hurry the fuck up."

"I'll be right out."

Five minutes later, Gary came out of the bathroom with his full head of dark hair all gelled.

"I'm ready to go," said Gary.

"Oh, come on, Gary."

"What?"

"Look at yourself. You really put the G in guinea."

"At least I have hair." Gary laughed.

"Fuck you and your hair." Richie laughed back.

"Mom, I'll see you later," said Gary.

"Where you going?"

"Probably to the park, but we're not sure."

"Yeah, to the park to hang out like bums. Just don't get into any trouble. And be home early. Remember, you have to be at work at midnight."

"I know, Mom."

"Richie."

"Yes, Mrs. Cellucci?"

"I spoke to your mother today. We made a deal. If you guys get into any more trouble, we're going to let you guys hang out to dry."

"I know, Mrs. Cellucci. My mom told me."

*   *   *

In the car, while Richie drove, Gary was wondering how he was going to tell his mother he had gotten fired. He knew she would be upset. She wanted so much more for her son than he was showing since he had dropped out of high school this past June. Both his parents wanted Gary to go to college, but school wasn't his thing. At this point in his life, all he wanted to do was hang out with his friends.

"Gary, when are you telling your mother you got fired?" asked Richie.

"I don't know. I'm afraid to. She's going to get really pissed."

"You have to tell her."

"Yeah, I know. I just don't want to hear any of her lectures. Next thing you know, she's going to start crying. I hate when she cries. It makes me feel like shit. I need to move out."

"You're the only person I know who can get fired from a night watchman's job."

"You think it's easy working nights? All I did was stare into a television monitor. You try looking into a monitor from midnight till eight in the morning without falling asleep. I can't believe they fired me for falling asleep. It's not like I was guarding Fort Knox. It was a recycling plant. I was guarding shredded paper. Who wants to steal shredded paper? Anyway, Richie, where we going tonight?"

"I spoke to Vinny before. He said he was picking up a case of beer, and then he was going to swing by and pick up Lenny and meet us at Diamond Lake."

"Cool. Let's stop by the deli first. I want to get some chips and shit."

"Good idea. I hope you got money. I ain't got shit."

"You never have money."

When Richie and Gary reached Diamond Lake, Vinny and Lenny were already drinking.

"What took you guys so long?" asked Vinny.

"I had to wait for Gary to get his hair done," said Richie.

"Gary, what the fuck?" said Lenny. "Don't you think it's time for your hair to get an oil change?"

"Fuck you." Gary laughed. "Just give me a beer."

"Sure, Gary," said Lenny as he tossed Gary and Richie each a beer. "Richie, pass the chips over, and don't let Gary touch them. There's enough grease on the chips. I don't need any more from Gary's hair."

"Very funny, asshole," said Gary.

Although the shortest, Lenny Colucci was the toughest one of the group. He stood at only 5'-8" and weighed 215 pounds but had the balls and strength of a bull. He never took any crap from anyone. All through high school, the football coach had begged Lenny to play football. Lenny never bothered. He didn't like taking orders. Since he graduated in June, he refused to look for a job. He didn't have time to work. He spent most of his time at the gym, from 9:00 a.m. till noon. Then he'd go back again from 2:00 p.m. to 5:00 p.m. It drove his parents crazy.

Vinny Stasi stood 6'-2" and weighed 195 pounds. At this time in his life, he was on his best behavior. Since his father had died five years ago, his mother hadn't been able to control him. He was always getting into fights and starting trouble. He'd been arrested six times in the past year. The only reason he didn't have a police record was because his father was a cop who had died in the line of duty. The last time his mother had picked him up from the police station, she was told if Vinny got arrested again, they would throw the book at him. Vinny knew he had to leave Glastonbury.

Richie Cisterno was the son of an Italian drunk. He stood 5'-9" and weighed two hundred pounds. Since Richie's father had lost his job a year and a half ago, he took to drinking. Every night he would come home from the bar and beat Richie's mother. He was always accusing her of having an affair with the UPS man. Three months earlier, Richie couldn't take it anymore. He beat the shit out of his father. After that, things kept going downhill in the Cisterno house. He also needed to leave Glastonbury.

"Nikos, are you all right?" Lilly asked, with her eyes tearing up as school was letting out.

"I'm fine. Why do you ask?"

"I just heard about the fight at the diner."

"How did you hear about it?"

"Are you kidding? The whole school's talking about it. You, Skelly, and Daddy beat the shit out of Carmine and his friends."

"Yeah, do you believe those scumbags?"

"Did they actually put their hands on Daddy?"

"They sure did. Did you also hear they were disrespectful to Mommy?"

"No. What did they do to her?"

"Nothing physical. Just verbal."

"What did they say to her?"

"I'm not sure exactly. Mommy wouldn't tell me. But Jackie told me they were calling her beautiful and shit like that. They wanted her to wait on them. Then they told her they would give her a good tip as they grabbed their crotches."

"I don't believe those assholes."

"Well, you better believe it. Those guys are bad news. Thank God for Skelly."

"I heard. What was Skelly doing there?"

"Nothing, he was just having lunch. He got knocked around a little. Then I saw him throw some punches."

"Did he get hurt?"

"Nah, he's fine. He can fight. But you should have seen Daddy. He's still got it. He really kicked some ass."

"Daddy's not the only one who's still got it."

"Don't worry. I'll never lose it."

"I'm not talking about you."

"Who are you talking about? Skelly?"

"No, brain-dead." Lilly laughed. "I'm talking about Mommy. She's still got it."

"Come on, Lilly. That's our mother you're talking about. Ewww."

"Like it or not, big brother, Mommy's still hot."

"Skelly," said Carmine at P.S. 14's schoolyard that same night, "this thing blew up in our faces."

"What the hell are you talking about? Everything worked out perfect."

"Yeah, for you maybe," jumped in Vito. "You didn't get your ass kicked. We got our asses kicked. No one punched *you*. *You* did all the punching."

"Oh, come on, you little bitches. It wasn't that bad. You guys threw a few punches at me too, and you know it."

"Skelly," said Fat Sal, "you're wrong. We got our asses kicked. We should have aborted."

"Aborted? What are we, in the fuckin' army?"

"No, we're not in the fuckin' army!" yelled Capo. "But we're supposed to be friends."

"We are friends, dickhead. How would I have known Nikos would show up? And when he did, what did you expect me to do?"

"We expected you to help us!" yelled Carmine. "That's what we expected you to do. Yes, help us."

"All right, just listen," Skelly said, lowering his voice. "We need to get control of ourselves. Just look at what's happened in the last few days. Nikos comes to our school and humiliates you on the first day in homeroom class. Then he beats the living shit out of all three of you assholes in the cafeteria." This time, Skelly started raising his voice. "And let's not forget our little punching bag, Irving Feldman. We can't even fuck with him anymore. Imagine that. Huh? Imagine that. Little Irving Feldman will be off limits. All the shakedowns we've done will be history. This fuckin' Nikos will take over if we let him."

"So what are we going to do?" asked Carmine.

"I'll tell you what we're going to do. We're going to continue playing the game. I'm sure by now, Lilly found out what happened at the diner. We're going to keep it up. I'm going to befriend Nikos, which I'm sure I already have. I know his father likes me. Shit, I'm pretty sure his hot mother even likes me too. Just trust me. The Ioannises are going down."

19

The next day at school, Lilly was eating lunch with a few other girls when Skelly walked into the cafeteria. Skelly knew Lilly was in there. Instead of approaching her, he sat at an empty table alone. He knew he was already a hero in her eyes.

Like a lion with a beautiful mane, he sat alone as Lilly, the lioness, watched him.

"Skelly," said Lilly as she approached his table.

Hook, line, and sinker, thought Skelly.

"Oh, hi, Lilly. How are you today?"

"I'm fine. Where've you been?"

"I'm not sure what you mean."

"I've been looking for you. I heard what happened at the diner. Are you all right? Are you hurt?"

"Do I look hurt?" Skelly smiled.

"No, you don't. I want to thank you for helping my family yesterday."

"It was nothing. I can't believe those guys. How anyone can be so disrespectful to someone like your mother is beyond me. Besides, it's Nikos *I* should be thanking. If it wasn't for him, who knows what those guys would have done to me? Your brother can really fight."

"Anyway, Skelly, thank you for helping them. I really appreciate it."

"You're welcome."

"So, Skelly, what were you doing at the diner?" Lilly smiled, hoping Skelly would say, "I was looking for you."

"Eating." Skelly smiled. "Like I told you, the new owners really cleaned up the place. Remember?"

"I remember." Lilly smiled back.

"Lilly, have a seat."

"Thanks, Skelly. Do you usually eat alone?"

"For the most part, yes. I do have a few friends in school, but I usually keep a low profile," Skelly said as he watched Vito walk into the cafeteria. "See that guy over there?" Skelly motioned toward Vito.

"Yeah, what about him?"

"He's one of those morons from the diner. You should have seen Nikos throw him across the diner. And as he was getting up, your father threw some guy everyone refers to as Fat Sal like a bowling ball and knocked him down. I don't think your family needed me at all," Skelly said, trying to be impressively modest. "But what upset me the most were the sexual advances they were making toward your mother."

"I heard. Do you think they would have done anything to her?"

"I don't know. Maybe they were just acting likes jerks. But, Lilly, please do me a favor."

"Sure, Skelly. What is it?"

"Whenever possible, please stay away from those morons."

"Don't worry, I will."

"Good. Lilly, can I ask you something?"

"Sure, Skelly."

"Can I take you out to dinner tomorrow tonight?"

"I would love to. Where do you want to go?"

"There's a restaurant on East Tremont Avenue called Bruno's. It's been around for years. They have great Italian food."

"I know the place. It's across the street from the bus stop. I see it all the time."

"Great. How about I pick you up at seven?"

"Seven is fine. Anyway, Skelly, I have to get to gym class. I'll see you tomorrow at seven."

"Looking forward to it."

Lilly quickly gave Skelly her address and walked away blushing, as any schoolgirl would.

* * *

Skelly wanted to play it cool. Knowing Lilly was only fifteen years old and from a close-knit family, he had to win over her parents. Once he won over her parents, he knew Nikos wouldn't be a problem. He knew a few natural gifts he had were his good looks, sex appeal, and charm. He wanted to show up thirty minutes early with the hope of Lilly not being ready so he could spend some time with her family, especially Maria. If the mother liked him, the daughter would follow, along with the father. Besides, he, like most men, could stand there looking at Maria for hours.

* * *

Skelly rang the Ioannises' doorbell at 6:25 p.m. Maria answered the door, wearing a tight pair of designer jeans with a yellow knitted V-neck pullover shirt that clung to her. He was careful not to stare.

He was the master.

"Hello, Mrs. Ioannis."

"Hello, Tony. Please come in."

"Thank you, Mrs. Ioannis."

"Lilly told me you were coming by at seven. You're a little early. She's not ready yet."

"I hope it's not a problem."

"Don't be silly. Please come in and have a seat. Can I get you something to drink?"

"No, thank you, Mrs. Ioannis. I'm okay."

"Please let me give you something."

I wish you would give me something, thought Skelly.

"Have you ever tasted baklava?"

"I'm sorry, but no. I've never heard of baklava. What is it?"

"You never heard of baklava?" Skelly heard Nikos say as he walked into the room.

"No, I haven't. But I guess I'm going to try some," joked Skelly.

"What's going on, Skelly? Doing all right?" asked Nikos as he extended his hand to shake.

"I'm doing all right, Nikos. How about you?" replied Skelly as he stood and shook Nikos's hand while giving him a shoulder hug.

"Me? I'm doing great."

"Glad to hear it."

"Tony, please sit down," said Maria. "I'd like to speak to you about something."

"Sure, Mrs. Ioannis. Is there anything wrong?"

"No, Tony, nothing's wrong. I just want to talk to you for a couple of minutes before Lilly comes down."

"Of course, Mrs. Ioannis."

"Well, first, I want to thank you for your help at the diner."

"Please, Mrs. Ioannis. Stop right there. There's no thank you necessary."

"There is a thank you necessary. So please allow me to say thank you."

"I understand. You're welcome then."

"Thank you for accepting my thank you. Second. Lilly tells me you're taking her to Bruno's. Is that correct?"

"Yes, ma'am. I hope it's all right."

"It is all right. But I need to remind you that Lilly is only fifteen years old. She's never been on a date before. Ordinarily, her father and I wouldn't allow it unless we know the young man but also know the young man's family."

"Mrs. Ioannis, please, if I may interrupt you. I know what you're getting at. I have a twelve-year-old sister. I promise you, my intentions are honorable."

"I'm sure your intentions *are* honorable. If I had the slightest doubt about your intentions, we wouldn't be having this conversation. Try to understand. This is a new city for us. It's not easy letting our daughter get into a car at fifteen years old."

"Daughter and sister," Nikos added.

Nikos then approached Skelly and shook his hand again but this time with a grip of authority. Skelly squeezed back as he felt Nikos's manly grip.

At the same time, Lilly came down the stairs. Like her mother, she had on a pair of designer jeans and a tight shirt. Even at fifteen, it was apparent she was developing into a beauty like her mother. It didn't go unnoticed, especially by Maria.

Before anyone spoke, Maria took charge.

"Lilly," said Maria, "can I see you in the kitchen a moment?"

"Now, Mom?"

"Yes, please. Now."

"All right."

"Excuse us for a moment," Maria said to Skelly and Nikos as Skelly was trying not to stare at Lilly.

In the kitchen, Maria asked, "Young lady, what do you think you're doing?"

"What?" Lilly asked, confused.

"Don't ask me what. That shirt you're wearing. Where did it come from?"

"I bought it today. Why? Don't you like it?"

"Where did you buy it from? The children's department? Or did you go to the paint store and have someone paint it on you? Go upstairs and change."

"No! I'm not changing!" Lilly snapped.

"Don't raise your voice at me, young lady. You go upstairs right now and change that shirt of yours, or you're not going anywhere."

"Come on, Mom," Lilly said, lowering her voice, knowing she wasn't going to win this argument. "Skelly already saw me in this shirt. How am I going to just go up and change?"

"Listen, Lilly," Maria said, also lowering her voice in a motherly tone. "I know he saw the shirt. He's a guy." She smiled. "Why don't you do this? Go into the living room. I'm going to bring in some soda for everyone. All you have to do is accidently spill some on yourself. Then you'll go upstairs and change."

Lilly started walking toward the living room.

"Hold on a second. Help me with the drinks."

A minute later, Lilly was carrying a tray of soda into the living room, while Maria carried the baklava.

The four of them sat, chatting a while. Maria pulled no punches. She asked Skelly about his family. Skelly explained that his father was a pharmaceutical salesman and was on the road constantly.

"It must be difficult for your mother, with your father on the road a lot."

"It is difficult, but we manage. I help out as much as I can."

"I'm sure you do."

"Anyway, Lilly, before I fill up on your mother's delicious baklava, maybe we should get going."

Maria looked at Lilly as Lilly accidently spilled her soda on herself.

"Oh no!" said Lilly. "How clumsy of me. Skelly, give me a minute to change."

"Sure, Lilly, take your time."

Within minutes, Lilly was back downstairs, wearing something much more appropriate.

"Tony," Maria said with authority, "please have Lilly home by ten."

"Yes, Mrs. Ioannis."

Maria then shook hands with Skelly, telling him it was nice seeing him again, as did Nikos. As Maria gave Lilly a hug, she whispered in her ear, "Be careful. If there's a problem, call me immediately."

"Okay, Mom," said Lilly as she hugged her mother and whispered, "Your shirt is just as tight as mine was. The only difference is you're wearing a V-neck and showing a lot of cleavage." Then Lilly quickly turned and walked out the door with Skelly.

That same evening . . .

"Irving, what are you doing?"

"Nothing, Mom. I'm just doing my homework."

"It's a Friday night. I'm worried about you. All you ever do is schoolwork."

"I'm all right, Mom. You know I want to get into a good college. I want to bring up my SAT scores."

"I know, son. But your scores are near perfect. Irving, unlock your door, please. I want to talk to you."

"What is it, Mom?"

"Will you open the door, please?"

"Coming, Mom."

Irving's mother entered her son's room, hoping not to see all his books out. She was really hoping he was a typical teenager looking at porn and masturbating, but as she entered his room, she noticed his textbooks were scattered on his desk, along with his notebooks and SAT practice tests.

"Irving, is everything all right?"

"Yes, Mom. Why do you keep asking?"

"You're spending too much time in your room. That's why I keep asking."

"You know I want to get into a good collage. I need to get good scores."

"Irving, your scores are fine, and you know it."

"Mom, what do you want from me?"

"I want you to be a typical teenager. That's what I want from you. I want you to go out. I want you to have friends."

"I'll make friends in college."

"That's a year away. Is there anyone that you *are* friends with?"

Irving's eyes started to water. He knew he had no friends. The only entertainment he had in school was the math team.

"Irving, I know it hasn't been easy since your father left us. But we need to move on. It's been over a year now."

"Don't bring up Daddy ever again," Irving snapped. "I hate him for what he did to you. I still can't believe he ran off with that whore."

"Irving, it's all right." She smiled. "I still have a man in my life."

"Thanks, Mom. But I'm not much of a man."

"Oh yes, you are. If it wasn't for you, I never would have survived your father leaving me. Now close your books. Let's go out to dinner."

Suddenly, Irving's cell phone rang. Irving didn't recognize the number.

"Hello?"

"Irving?"

"Yes, who is this?"

"It's Nikos."

"Oh, sorry, Nikos, I forgot to save your number in my phone."

"No big deal. How's it going?"

"It's going fine. How's it going with you?"

"Great. I'm just a little bored, that's all. What are you doing right now? Are you busy?"

"I'm just doing some studying. That's all."

"You hungry? My father bought me a car this afternoon. How about we go for a spin and get a slice of pizza or something?"

"Sounds good, Nikos. What time can you pick me up?"

"How about in fifteen minutes?"

"Great. I'll be waiting outside."

Irving then gave Nikos his address.

"What was that all about?" asked Irving's mother.

"Well, Mom, there's this new guy in school I kind of made friends with."

"That's great, Irving. Have a nice time."

"Thanks, Mom."

* * *

Irving was waiting outside, playing a game on his phone, when Nikos pulled up.

"Nice ride, Nikos."

"Thanks. Get in."

As Nikos pulled away from the curb, Irving asked, "Where we going?"

"How about we go to Square Pizza? I hear it's the best."

"It is."

"Great."

"Nikos, I didn't know your family owns the Westchester Square Diner."

"Yeah, my father and uncle bought it a month or so ago. How'd you know?"

"It's all over the school. By the way, I heard about the fight you had at the diner."

"Yeah, it was pretty messed up. Carmine and his friends are a real bunch of assholes."

"That, they are. But the scary thing is I heard Skelly actually helped you."

"He did."

"I still don't trust him."

"Well, from what you've told me, Skelly *was* friends with those assholes. But not the other day. He actually helped me and my father kick some ass."

"Wow, I wish I was there to see it."

"I wish you were there too. But to be honest with you, Irving, those guys scare me a little."

"I didn't think you were afraid of anyone."

"I didn't say 'afraid.' I said 'scare me a little.'"

"In what way?"

"I've known tough guys my whole life. All different types of tough guys. The short time I'm in the Bronx, for the most part, these tough guys ain't shit. In Hartford, Connecticut, there are tough guys. Real tough. My friends in Glastonbury and I had our share of fights. Lots of fights. But we always respected our elders. But these guys aren't your typical tough guys. Did you know they made sexual advances toward my mother?"

"No, I didn't. But it doesn't surprise me. It doesn't surprise me at all. You don't know it, but a little over a year ago, my father left us for some whore he worked with. Most everyone knows about it. A few months ago, I was walking into the supermarket with my mother. Next thing you know, Carmine, Fat Sal, and Skelly—yes, Skelly—were walking by, and when they saw us, they approached my mother and made sexual advances. Telling her she had nice tits and shit. Asking her since her husband left her, they would be more than happy to suck on her tits. And believe it or not, Skelly was doing most of the talking."

"Are you kidding?"

"I kid you not."

"What did you do?"

"Come on, Nikos. What do you think I did? I got my ass kicked. That's what I did. I didn't even get in one punch. When I approached Skelly to punch him, Carmine grabbed me from behind and threw me on the ground like a rag doll. There were three of them. Even if there was only one of them, there wasn't much I could have done."

"I'm sorry, Irving. I didn't know you then, but if I did and if I was there, it would have been two against three. But to tell you the truth, it's hard to believe Skelly was like that."

"Believe it or not, I still don't trust him, and neither should you."

"I promise I'll keep an eye on him. By the way, he's out with my sister tonight."

"What? Are you kidding me?"

"I'm not kidding. But like I said, I'm going to keep an eye on him."

* * *

At the pizza shop, Nikos and Irving got to know each other a little better. After about an hour or so, Nikos's cell phone rang. He looked at the caller ID and smiled.

"Holy shit, Lenny, how you doing?"

"I'm doing great, Nikos. How you doing?"

"I'm adjusting."

"Glad to hear it. Listen, we want to come by tomorrow. Is it all right?"

"Are you kidding? That'll be great. Who's we? All four of you?"

"Damn right, all four of us. We need to get the fuck out of here. Everyone's breaking our balls to get jobs and shit. We need a break."

"Make sure you guys pack a bag. Stay for a few days. We'll hang out."

"What about school? Don't you have school?"

"Of course, I have school. So what? Did school ever stop any of us from taking a day off?"

"No, it didn't." Lenny laughed.

"Great. Leave real early tomorrow. We got plenty of room at the house. I can't wait to see you guys."

"Same here. We'll be there before noon. Your mother's going to cook, isn't she?"

"You know it. See you guys tomorrow."

"What was that about?" asked Irving.

"That was my friend Lenny from Glastonbury. He's coming over tomorrow for a few days with three other friends of mine. I can't wait for you to meet them."

"Are these the tough guys you were talking about?"

"Yup, that's them. In Glastonbury, we were called the Five Glassmen. We were inseparable. You're going to love them."

"I can't wait to meet them. I'm not sure I'm their type, but nonetheless, I can't wait to meet them."

"Don't worry about being their type. Any friend of mine is a friend of theirs. Anyway, Irving, I need to get going. I promised my father I would open the diner tomorrow. I need to get some sleep."

* * *

As Nikos pulled in front of Irving's house, Nikos thanked him again for telling him about Skelly.

"It's all right, Nikos. No need to thank me. You're a nice guy. And your sister seems like a good person too. I just don't want to see your family getting hurt because Skelly seems to be on the same path as his father."

"What do you mean by 'the same path as his father'?"

"His father's all messed up."

"What do you mean 'his father's all messed up'?"

"His father's in jail for all kinds of shit."

"His father's in jail?"

"Yes, in jail. He's doing hard time."

"Skelly told me and my mother his father's on the road a lot because he's a pharmaceutical salesman."

"Pharmaceutical salesman? I guess he was half right."

"What do you mean by 'half right'?"

"He's a drug dealer. I guess that's pharmaceutical. I told you he's messed up. He lied to you."

"Thanks, Irving."

"Okay, I'll see you tomorrow."

After Irving exited the car, Nikos drove home as fast as he could. As Nikos was driving, his cell phone rang. He looked at the caller ID and answered. "Mom, is everything all right?" Nikos asked, concerned.

"No, Nikos. How did you know something might be wrong?"

"I had a hunch."

"Your hunch was right."

"What happened?"

"Where are you?"

"Mom, what happened?" Nikos asked a little louder.

"Never mind what happened. Where are you?" snapped Maria.

"I'm five minutes away."

"If you say five minutes, I want you to slow down and take ten. Just drive safe."

"Mom?"

"Yes, son?"

"Is Lilly all right?"

Silence.

"Mom! Mom! Answer me! Answer me now! Is Lilly all right?"

"Just get home safe, son," Maria said, holding back tears.

21

Nikos pulled into the driveway, slammed on the brakes, and ran into the house. Lilly was on the couch crying as Maria was holding her while trying to be strong by holding back her own tears.

Michael was in the kitchen, pacing back and forth, screaming at the top of his lungs, "That motherfucker! When I get my hands on him, he's going to be sorry he was ever born!"

Nikos thought it would be better to talk to his father. By now, he speculated what had happened. He knew his mother would be the rational one, but Nikos didn't want to be rational.

Nikos was exactly like his father, hot-tempered and always thinking violence would solve everything.

"Dad, what happened?"

"I don't believe this fuckin' guy! He never took Lilly to the restaurant! They drove around in the car, and then he took her to some parking lot and tried all kinds of shit on her! Wait till I get my hands on him!"

"Dad, don't worry. I'll take care of it."

"No, son, you stay out of it. *I'll* take care of it. I'll fix his ass."

Nikos entered the living room and asked Lilly what had happened. He wanted to hear it from her. Maria wanted Nikos to back off.

"Nikos, I want you to calm down. Just look at your father. I don't need another one like him. Besides, you two wanting to do what you think is right will have you both ending up in jail. And going to jail is not what's best for this family."

"Lilly, did he . . ."

"Nikos!" snapped Maria. "No. He didn't rape her. But he did forcibly put his hands where they didn't belong and tried to tear at her clothes. He wouldn't let her out of the car. He kept grabbing at her. Finally, Lilly opened the door and started screaming as Skelly drove away. Some other couple in this lover's lane called Ferry Point Park took her in their car and drove her home. I want to call the police, but Lilly's too embarrassed."

"I agree with Lilly. No police. They'll only give him a slap on the wrist."

"I hate to agree with you, but you're right. But I cannot have you or your father breaking the law. Because the next thing you know, you two will be in jail, while that piece of shit will be walking the streets."

Nikos hugged his mother and sister and whispered in their ears, "Don't worry, no one's going to jail. But Skelly needs to learn not to mess with an Ioannis. Now I need to go out for a while. I'll be back a little later."

"Nikos, where are you going?" asked Maria. "Come back here!"

Nikos ignored his mother and continued walking.

"Michael!" yelled Maria. "Stop him! Please stop him!"

Michael ran toward Nikos, but it was too late. Nikos was already pulling out of the driveway.

* * *

Who can be calling me at this time of night? Irving thought as he heard his phone ring.

"Nikos, is everything all right?"

"No, Irving. I need your help."

"Sure. I'll borrow my mother's car."

"No, I need *you*. I don't need your mother's car. I need *your* help."

"What happened?"

"You were right. You were right all along. That piece of shit was all over my sister. I need to find him. Do you know where he lives?"

"No, I don't."

"I need to find him."

"Calm down, Nikos. Tell me what happened."

"I'll explain when I get to your house. I need your help finding him."

"All right. I'll be waiting outside."

"Thanks."

"Irving, where are you going?" asked his mother. "It's eleven o'clock."

"I'm not sure. My friend needs me. He's having family trouble."

"What kind of family trouble? Are you sure that's all?"

In actuality, Irving wasn't lying. Nikos was having some sort of family trouble, just not the kind of family trouble Irving's mother thought.

"All right then. Please be careful."

"Don't worry, Mom. I will."

Outside, Nikos came to a screeching stop.

"Nikos, calm down. You're driving like a maniac. Tell me what happened."

Nikos explained to Irving everything he knew.

"You were right all along. That piece of shit played me. He played my whole family."

"All right. What are you looking to do?"

"When I find him, you'll see. Now come on, you have to know someone who knows where he lives."

"Yeah right. I'm Mr. Popularity. I know so many people. I have a million friends," Irving said sarcastically.

"Irving, you're the only friend I have in the Bronx. I need you to think."

Irving was shocked. *I can't remember the last time anyone referred to me as his friend,* he thought. He liked the way it sounded. He liked Nikos. He looked at Nikos as a stand-up guy.

"Nikos, I don't know where Skelly lives. But I do know where he and his friends sometimes hang out."

"Where?"

"I'm not sure if he's there. But if he is, he won't be alone."

"Like I care."

"I'm telling you, Nikos. We can't kick all their asses."

"We? There is no we. I'm not involving you. Now where do they hang out?"

"Fourteen."

"Fourteen? What's 14?"

"P.S. 14. The schoolyard of P.S. 14."

"Show me how to get there."

Irving directed Nikos to the schoolyard.

* * *

"There they are. Down there by the handball court."

"There's about five or six of them."

"Yeah, that's them. The whole gang. Carmine, Fat Sal, Capo, Vito, and their leader, Skelly."

"Shit, that's five of them. I never fought five guys before. My record is four . . ."

"Well, you're not going to break your record. You're going to tie it."

"What are you talking about?"

"You told me earlier that if you were with me the day those assholes insulted my mother, it would have been two against three. Well, I'm here with you. It's going to be five against two."

"No, Irving. You'll get hurt."

"You have any idea how many times those guys kicked my ass?"

"Irving, there's a difference between getting pushed around and getting the shit kicked out of you."

"Oh, really? There is no difference. Besides, it's about time I stood up for myself. Let's do this."

"You sure you're up to it?"

"Don't chicken out on me, Nikos," joked Irving. "Let's go."

"All right. This is what I need you to do. From what I've seen so far, Skelly's the toughest. I would like for you to lure him away somehow. I'm pretty sure I can handle the other four. After I kick their asses, I'll pull Skelly off you. Once I get Skelly down, I'll let you kick him a few times for 'ole times sake. But after that, his ass is mine."

"Let's do it."

Nikos parked down the street. He didn't want the car noticed as he parked. The shutting of his headlights would bring attention to himself.

After Nikos parked the car, they walked back to the entrance of the schoolyard. The handball court was straight ahead, at the far end. They planned it all out. As they slowly entered the schoolyard, they went left and started walking back along the fence toward the handball court.

"So far, so good," whispered Nikos.

They continued walking back down toward the handball court. The handball court was not only blocking their view but also blocking Skelly and his friends' view. Not one of them was able to see Nikos and Irving.

"Irving," Nikos whispered as they both were unseen, directly behind the handball court, "do your thing."

"Just watch me."

Irving walked from behind the handball court in front of all five of them.

"Irving," said Fat Sal. "Is that you, you little Jew?"

"No, I'm a figment of your imagination, asshole."

"You little prick. You got some pair of balls showing up here, let alone talking to me like that. What the fuck are you doing here?"

"Nothing. I'm just passing through."

"Does your hot mother with the big tits know you're out this late?" Skelly laughed.

"Yes, she does. But, Skelly, why don't you leave me alone? I need to get home. My dick is still dripping from the blowjob your mother just gave me."

"What did you say, you little fuckin' Jew?" Skelly said as he ran toward Irving.

"You heard me." Irving laughed as he started running away.

Irving had several steps on Skelly. As quick as Irving was, Skelly had longer legs and was in excellent shape. After thirty seconds, Skelly grabbed Irving by the back of his collar and threw him on the ground.

At the same time, Skelly's four friends started walking toward them to watch Irving get his ass kicked.

Nikos saw his opening. The first person he grabbed from behind was Fat Sal. Nikos grabbed him by the back of his hair and pulled him to the ground.

"Help!" yelled Fat Sal.

Everyone heard him.

Nikos knew it wasn't going to be easy. He immediately kicked Fat Sal in the stomach as he tried to get up. Then he quickly stepped on his head twice.

One down.

Capo, Vito, and Carmine turned toward Nikos and surrounded him.

It was a stalemate.

Each one of them was waiting for someone to make the first move. Suddenly, Skelly showed up, holding Irving by his hair.

"Skelly, let him go," warned Nikos. "This is between you and me. Let him go and call off your dogs. Your fat friend here needs your help. He's hurt real bad. Let your three healthy asshole friends help him before they end up just like him. Then you and I will go behind the handball court and settle this. Just you and me."

"Listen up, you Greek fuck. You're not in any position to speak."

"I said let him go."

"Let him go? This little Jew with the mother with big tits tried to set us up, and you want me to let him go? Fuck you and your whole family. By the way, I loved putting my hands all over your sister's tits. I can't wait till the next time. And the time after that, I'm going after your hot mother."

Irving saw that Nikos was getting to his boiling point.

"Hey, Skelly," said Irving, "your mother sucks a good dick." He threw a useless punch at Skelly's face.

Skelly threw Irving onto the ground like an empty pack of cigarettes. Now the four of them surrounded Nikos.

"Man, your sister's tits felt good. I can't wait to grab your mother's," said Skelly.

Simultaneously, all four attacked Nikos. Nikos threw punches. One at a time, Nikos could have handled them. But with all four, with eight punches versus his two, Nikos couldn't keep up. They were too strong. Besides, as angry as Nikos was, Skelly and his friends were just as angry.

Carmine took Nikos's first punch. *Crack*. Carmine's nose started to bleed as it broke. When Nikos went to hit Carmine again, it was all over for him. Vito threw two quick punches as Skelly kicked Nikos in the back. Nikos was dazed. As he attempted to shake off the cobwebs, Skelly hit him three more times. Nikos fell to one knee.

As Skelly was about to kick Nikos in the face, Irving jumped onto Skelly's back. Skelly flipped Irving onto Nikos as he was trying to stand. They both ended flat on their backs.

It was all over. Except for Fat Sal, who was still on the ground, they all went to town on Nikos and Irving. They kept kicking and kicking them.

After a few minutes, Skelly grabbed Nikos by the hair and looked him in the eye. Nikos was almost unconscious. Skelly was only a blur.

"Listen, motherfucker. If you know what's good for you, I suggest you go back to where you came from. If you decide to stick around, I want you to pay me $100 a week protection money. I know you can afford it. Your family owns a diner. And when you pay me, you're going to do it in the cafeteria in front of everyone. Do you hear me, motherfucker?"

"Fuck you," Nikos said before he fell unconscious.

"Nikos, are you all right?" asked Irving, with blood dripping from his face.

"I think so. What about you? You look a little banged up yourself."

"Yeah, well, maybe it's because I am a little banged up. I can't believe those guys. They really suck. They had you down. They didn't have to keep beating on you."

"Yes, they did, Irving. They had to. Because if they didn't, I would have never stopped."

"I hear you. Anyway, let's get you home. Can you stand?"

"I'm not sure. Here, help me. I'm pretty sure I can if you help me."

Nikos wobbled to his feet.

"I'm all right. Let me walk around a little. I need to shake out the cobwebs."

Nikos and Irving sat in the schoolyard, leaning against the handball court wall for thirty minutes. They didn't know what to do.

Finally, Irving asked, "Nikos, are you going to give Skelly $100 a week?"

"Are you crazy?"

"You heard him. You saw what they did to us. I know Skelly. He won't let up. He doesn't care. He and his friends will beat the shit out of us every day."

"Irving, take a good look at me. Then when you get home, take a good look in the mirror."

"Why?"

"Because it's the last time we'll ever look like this. Now let's go. I need to drop you off and get to bed. I'm opening the diner tomorrow."

* * *

During the ride home, Nikos's cell phone rang.

"Mom."

"Nikos, where are you?"

"I'm on my way home. Don't worry, I'm all right. How's Lilly?"

"Lilly's fine. But we have a problem."

"Now what?"

"The diner. The alarm went off. Someone broke the window. Your father's on the way there now. Can you check on him? He's already accusing Skelly. I'm worried about him."

"Sure, Mom. I'll be there in five minutes."

"Thanks, son. And please be careful."

"Don't worry, Mom, I will."

"What was that all about?" asked Irving.

"Someone broke the window at the diner. You think it's a coincidence?"

"Coincidence, my ass."

"That's exactly what I think."

As Nikos pulled up in front of the diner, there were already two police cars as a third approached. In the short time that Michael and Charlie owned the diner, they had made friends with most of the cops in the neighborhood.

The minute Nikos pulled up to the diner, Michael approached him.

"Nikos, what happened to you?"

"Nothing, Dad. What happened here?"

"Never mind *what happened here.* What the hell happened to you?"

"What's it look like? Anyway, Dad, I want you to meet my friend Irving. Irving, this is my dad."

"Nice to meet you, Mr. Ioannis."

"Same here, Irving."

Michael looked at Irving and couldn't figure anything out. Irving looked in worse shape than Nikos. Nikos always had big tough-looking friends. Irving was a nerd.

"Who did this to you?"

"I had a run-in with Skelly and four of his friends. Irving actually helped me."

"Why did you go after him? I don't want you doing stuff like that."

"Come on, Dad. You didn't think I would let Skelly get away with what he did to Lilly, did you?"

"No, I didn't. But I still don't want you getting involved with this. I'll handle it. Do you hear me? I said I'll handle it."

"Yes, Dad."

"Look what happened already. You not only got *your* ass kicked. You got Irving's ass kicked too."

"Dad, there were five of them. But don't worry. By tomorrow afternoon, the Five Glassmen will be back together."

"What are you talking about?"

"I didn't tell you?"

"Tell me what?"

"The guys are coming over tomorrow."

"Oh no. We're not doing this. Not this way. I can't believe you called them. What are you looking to do, start a war? I can't believe you called them."

"Dad, I didn't call them. They called me."

"Bullshit. I don't believe you."

"It's true, Mr. Ioannis," interrupted Irving. "Earlier this evening, we were having pizza when Nikos's friend Lenny called. The plan of his friends coming tomorrow was made before all this happened."

Michael didn't answer Irving. He just looked at him.

"Nikos, go home. I'll handle this. I don't want the cops asking you any questions. As far as all this goes, it's only a window. We must remember. It's Lilly's best interest we're going to keep in mind. Do you hear me?"

"Yes, Dad."

"Nikos. Do you hear me?" Michael repeated with a lot more authority.

"I said yes, Dad."

"All right then. Go home and get some sleep. I still need you to open tomorrow morning."

"All right, Dad."

During the drive back to Irving's house, Nikos thanked him again for his attempt to help him.

"No, Nikos, it's me who should be thanking you. I don't know how it happened, but you gave me the confidence to fight back. I'm not going to give them the $5 every week anymore. I don't care if they kick my ass every day. There're not getting it anymore."

"That's the spirit. All right, here's your house. I'll see you tomorrow. Why don't you come by the house tomorrow for dinner? When my mother finds out the Five Glassmen will be together again, she's going to cook a dinner and a half."

"Sounds good, Nikos. Thanks."

"Great. See you tomorrow."

* * *

When Irving approached his front door, something didn't look kosher. The doorknob looked broken. When he entered the house, he couldn't believe his eyes. The house was ransacked. The furniture was turned over. All the little knickknacks were all over the floor. There was broken glass everywhere.

"Mom!" Irving yelled in panic.

"Irving! I'm upstairs! Help me! Please help me!"

Irving ran upstairs two steps at a time. He followed the cries of his mother into her bedroom.

He couldn't believe it.

His mother was hogtied and naked.

"Irving, please help me."

Irving untied his mother and quickly covered her with a blanket.

"Mom, what happened?"

"These five guys broke into the house and ripped off my nightgown and tied me up."

"Did they . . ."

"No. They barely touched me. They did threaten to do many things to me but didn't. But they warned me if you didn't change your friends and if I didn't raise your allowance, they would come back and make what they did to me tonight feel like a day at the spa. Irving, I think I recognized a couple of those guys. What's going on? Why did they do this to me? Who are these friends they're talking about?"

"Mom, are you sure you're all right? Are you sure they didn't hurt you?"

"I'm fine. They didn't hurt me. Irving, are you in any kind of trouble? And what did they mean by raising your allowance? Do you owe them money? Are you on drugs?"

"No, Mom. I'm not on drugs."

"Thank God. We need to call the police."

"No, Mom. No police. I'll handle it."

"Handle it? *You?* How are *you* going to handle it? There were five of them."

"Mom, please trust me."

Irving's mother wrapped the blanket around herself and ran to the phone. The line was dead. They had ripped the phone out of the wall. Then they both noticed her smashed cell phone.

"Irving, give me your phone."

"Get dressed, Mom," Irving said as he took his phone out of his pocket and called Nikos.

"Irving, is everything all right?"

"No, Nikos, not at all."

"What happened?"

"I need you. I need you to come to my house."

"I'll be there in five minutes."

Nikos made a U-turn and passed a red light on the way to Irving's house. Irving was standing at the window as Nikos approached his house. Irving motioned Nikos to come inside.

"Holy shit. What happened?" asked Nikos.

"What do you think?"

"I don't believe those guys."

"What guys?" asked Irving's mother as she came down the stairs, crying and confused.

"Mom. This is my friend Nikos."

"Nice to meet you, Nikos."

"Likewise, Mrs. Feldman."

"What's going on?" asked Mrs. Feldman. "What did you do to cause this?"

Nikos knew he was responsible for all this. If he hadn't involved Irving, they wouldn't be in the room talking.

"Please, Mrs. Feldman. Sit down. I'll explain everything."

"Nikos, where would you like for me to sit? On my upside-down couch? Or on all the broken glass on the floor?" asked Mrs. Feldman, all choked up.

"I'm sorry, Mrs. Feldman."

For the next fifteen minutes, the three of them sat in the kitchen, talking. Nikos explained how his first day of school had gone. He also explained how Irving had always been disrespected.

He explained in detail what had happened to Lilly and how he and his family were set up by Skelly and his friends. Then he talked about tonight and about how guilty he felt that all this had happened because Irving helped him.

"I'm calling the police," said Mrs. Feldman.

"Please, Mrs. Feldman. Don't call the police."

"Don't call the police? Do you know what they did to me tonight?" Mrs. Feldman cried.

"No, I don't."

"They ripped off my nightgown and tied me up! That's what they did to me! And no, they didn't rape me. But the fear they gave me almost made me wish they did. They made all types of threats. Irving, you give them $5 a week for protection? What protection? They pick on you every day and humiliate you in public! You call that protection? Why didn't you tell me? I would have gone to the principal!"

"Please, Mrs. Feldman. Please leave the police and the school out of this. I know guys like these. They won't back down. They'll try to somehow convince everyone that you lured them into your house. You don't want to go through that embarrassment."

At that moment, Mrs. Feldman broke down. "The things they said to me were inhuman. These people aren't human!" she cried. "I don't know what to do. Nothing's working. Damn your father, Irving. Damn him. If he was home, none of this would have happened."

"It's all right, Mom. Please give us a chance."

"A chance for what? What are you going to do? Kill them? You want to end up in jail?"

"Mrs. Feldman, please. Give me a chance. I can fix this. I really can," said Nikos.

"Fix it?" snapped Mrs. Feldman. "Fix it? You're the one who broke it! If it wasn't for you, none of this would have happened!"

"Mom, I'm so sorry they did this to you. I really am. But please try to understand. For the first time ever, I'm not afraid to stand up for myself. I actually threw a few punches. I've never stood up for myself before tonight. I trust Nikos."

"You trust Nikos? You don't even know Nikos. How can you trust him? Look at the results. He may be playing you just like Skelly played *him*."

"Irving," Nikos said while standing, "I'm leaving now. Again, I'm sorry I got you involved. Mrs. Feldman, I apologize for all this. I promise you. I promise both of you. I'll fix it. I'll fix all of it. I'll also make do to pay for all this. Good night. Irving, call me tomorrow."

"Will do, Nikos. We have business we need to finish."

"Again, Mrs. Feldman, I apologize for everything."

"Nikos, Irving's all I have in the world. Do you hear me? He's all I have. Don't let anything happen to him. Because if anything does," she said with fire in her eyes, "I'm going to hold you personally responsible."

"You have my word, Mrs. Feldman. I won't let anything happen to him," Nikos said as he walked out the door.

23

The next morning . . .

As Nikos opened the diner at 5:30 a.m., he was cautious. He kept looking over his shoulder. Jackie showed up at 5:45 a.m. to help get things started for the 6:00 a.m. opening.

"Nikos, what happened to the window?" asked Jackie.

"I don't know. It looks like someone threw a brick threw it. My father was here last night. I don't have any details. All I know is later this afternoon, the window guy is coming to replace it."

"Oh my God, Nikos, what happened to your face?"

"Nothing. A book fell off the shelf and hit me in the eye."

* * *

At 11:00 a.m., Irving came into the diner and sat in a booth. Jackie took his order of bacon and eggs.

Five minutes later, Nikos sat with him.

"How's your mother doing?" asked Nikos.

"Not good. But you know what, Nikos? She'll be fine."

"I'm sure she will."

"But, Nikos, I'm too involved in this already. I hope you're going to see this through."

"Irving, you have my word. I'll never forget the way you tried to warn me—"

Just then, Nikos's cell phone rang.

"Lenny."

"Nikos, we're getting off at the Randall Avenue exit. Are you home?"

"No, not yet. I'm leaving the diner in five minutes. My parents are home. They're expecting you guys."

"Great. I hope your mother cooked. We're starving."

"You know she did."

Come on, Irving, let's go. I want you to meet the other four Glassmen."

"I'm right behind you."

Meanwhile, at Skelly's house, Skelly was holding a meeting about last night.

"Listen up, guys. You're getting soft. I turn my back for a little while, and too much shit happens. We need to start doubling the pressure. Although we did a pretty good job on Nikos last night, he still embarrassed all of you. The nerve of him trying to get that little fuckin' Jew to set us up. We had that Jew eating out of our hands. And look at what he did. He tried to set us up. We need to make an example out of Nikos and Irving."

"Didn't Irving pay enough last night with what we did to his mother?" interrupted Fat Sal.

"Are you out of your fuckin' mind?" Skelly snapped back. "It's never enough. I want his ass kicked in school every day. Do you hear me? Every day. As far as Nikos goes, we need to continue to keep him in line. We need to keep the pressure on him. He's too big and strong for us to give him any latitude. I told him he's paying $100 a week. If he's one day late, we all need to get it from him. And as far as his sister goes, she's getting her ass grabbed every day. And their hot mother—let's harass her whenever we can. We can't do to her what we did to Irving's mother, not with her husband and Nikos living there. And last but not least, once a week, I want the diner's window broken. Mix up the days. Let's keep them guessing which day it's going to happen."

"I don't know, Skelly," said Fat Sal. "It might be a good idea to lay low for a while."

"The fuck did you say?"

"Come on, Skelly. You know. Look at what we did. We broke into someone's house and ripped the clothes off a woman and tied her up. We could go to jail for that. I'm just saying, maybe we should lay low for a while. That's all I'm saying."

"You fat chickenshit. We're not laying low. We're keeping up the pressure."

"I don't know if I want to be a part of this anymore."

"Come over here, you fat fuck," Skelly said as he approached Fat Sal.

"Calm down, Skelly," said Carmine. "We can't fight among ourselves. Maybe Fat Sal's right. We can all end up in jail for what we did to the Jew's mother."

"I don't give a shit. We're keeping the pressure on, and that's final."

No one spoke. Fat Sal was the only one to lower his head.

"Stand up and look at me, you fat fuck!" yelled Skelly.

Fat Sal stood with fear.

"You pussy. How dare you want to lay low!" Skelly yelled again as he grabbed him by the collar and put him up against the wall.

"I'm sorry, Skelly, I'm sorry. Please, Skelly, I'm sorry."

"Look at you, begging like a little bitch." Skelly then started punching Fat Sal in the stomach. After a few shots, Fat Sal fell to his knees. "Look at you. You look like you did last night after Nikos grabbed you. Two days in a row, you're getting your ass kicked. You're a disgrace."

"Skelly, what are you doing?" yelled Carmine. "Leave him alone! You need to calm down."

Skelly walked over to Carmine and kicked him as he sat. Carmine flew off his chair right on his ass.

"Another chickenshit!" yelled Skelly.

Carmine could only sit on the floor, looking up at everyone, embarrassed.

"Help these two assholes!" Skelly yelled to Capo and Vito.

Capo and Vito were out of their seats in an instant.

Nikos pulled up to his house a few minutes before noon. He smiled when he saw the Connecticut plates on Lenny's car. By the time Nikos parked the car, the guys were already outside to greet him.

"Holy shit, I miss you guys," said Nikos.

"We miss you too," said Vinny.

"Nikos, what the hell happened to you?" asked Lenny after noticing his bruises.

"It's a long story. Anyway, guys, I want you to meet a friend of mine. Guys, this is Irving. Irving, I want you to meet the rest of the Five Glassmen of Glastonbury."

"Nice to meet you, guys. I heard a lot about you."

"Irving, what the hell happened to you too?" asked Gary.

"The same long story Nikos has."

"Nikos," said Richie, "what's going on?"

"Yeah," said Lenny. "Talk to us."

"Let's sit on the porch," said Nikos. "Are you guys hungry?"

"No," said Vinny. "The minute we got here, your mother fed us."

"Great. Let's sit and talk."

Nikos started talking. He explained everything from the first day of school up to the point when he had found out what Skelly did to Lilly. As he was about to continue, Maria approached them with refreshments. As soon as Nikos saw her, he fell silent.

Maria sensed trouble and said, "Continue talking, guys. Don't mind me."

"Sure, Mrs. Ioannis," said Vinny as the rest of the Glassmen nodded, along with Irving.

"So, Nikos," said Richie, trying to show they were talking about school, "how are you adjusting to calculus?"

"Not bad," said Nikos.

"Guys, let's stop the bullshit," interrupted Maria. "Please, Nikos. Let it go. I don't need for your Connecticut friends to get arrested."

"Please, Mom, go back inside. We need to talk."

With tears in her eyes, Maria put the refreshments down and went back into the house.

"Holy shit," said Lenny. "They're not getting away with that shit . . ."

"Let me continue," said Nikos.

For the next few minutes, Nikos explained in detail the schoolyard incident. He then glanced over at Irving, and Irving just gave him a nod. Then Nikos continued with his story about what had happened to Irving's mother.

"Holy shit," said Gary. "Let's go. Let's get those scumbags."

"Hold on," said Nikos. "We need to plan this. Irving knows the neighborhood better than any of us. He knows where and when they hang out."

"All right," said Vinny. "But they're getting what's due to them."

The next day . . .

"Skelly, come in here," said Antonio Giovanni with authority. "Sit down. I understand there was a problem."

"No, sir, there wasn't a—"

"Did I ask you to speak?"

"I'm sorry, Mr. Giovanni."

Giovanni sat looking at Skelly. Meanwhile, Skelly sat patiently and nervously, waiting for Giovanni to continue. Giovanni liked Skelly. He knew Skelly would do anything he was instructed, but Giovanni never liked being interrupted.

For the past two years since Skelly's father was in jail, Skelly had been working for Giovanni, doing all sorts of things.

It didn't matter what Giovanni needed. Skelly did whatever Giovanni instructed.

At first, Skelly mostly ran errands and washed Giovanni's car.

But for the last six months, Skelly had been collecting protection money.

"So, Skelly," said Giovanni, "what's going on? The word on the street is your boys got their asses kicked at the Westchester Square Diner . . ."

"No, let me explain . . ."

Skelly fell silent when Giovanni looked at him as he was again interrupted. After several seconds, Giovanni asked Skelly to continue.

"Yes, sir. Thank you, sir. Well, you see, sir, I set it all up. I wanted to get a girl's mother to trust me with her daughter . . ."

"Stop right there and listen. I have friends. Many friends. Friends in high places. You are in low places. So you need to know your place. I don't care about your desire to impress a girl's mother. Do you hear me?"

"Yes, sir."

"Good."

Skelly wanted to explain the entire story to Giovanni but wouldn't dare interrupt him again.

"Now, Skelly, my friends in high places tell me your boys also got their asses kicked in school by some new big guy. I understand his father owns the Westchester Square Diner, which, by the way, hasn't yet joined my protection agency."

Silence.

"You may speak."

"Yes, sir. Thank you, sir. Well, you see . . ."

Skelly started to stutter.

"That's enough. I don't want to hear anymore. It sounds like you're getting ready to make excuses. And you know what I say about excuses. Excuses are like assholes. Everyone's got one, and they all stink. Now get out of here. Go do your job. There are too many people behind in their payments and too many people not signed up. Go. Get the fuck out of here. I don't want to hear another word come out of your mouth. And always remember. Excuses are like assholes. Everyone's got one, and they all stink."

* * *

"Moose. Come in here."

Anthony Caramooso was Giovanni's personal bodyguard. Everyone knew him as Moose. Moose was forty years old, stood at 6'-5" and weighed 275 pounds. He didn't have a body builder's body but was stronger than anyone who had ever challenged him. When he was in his early twenties, he served ten years for manslaughter. The manslaughter conviction was a gift. Everyone knew it should have been murder in the first degree. Giovanni's lawyer cut a financial deal with the district attorney to get the charges reduced. Moose had been indebted to Giovanni ever since.

"Yes, Mr. Giovanni. What can I do for you?"

"Keep an eye on Skelly. I'm afraid he's getting either soft or incompetent."

"Sure thing. I'll ask around too."

"You do that."

"Nikos, where are you guys going tonight?" asked Maria.

"I don't know, Mom. I figure maybe we'll go get something to eat. Maybe pizza or something."

"I went shopping this morning. I bought some steaks. Maybe you can barbecue them for your friends."

"No, thanks, Mom. We want to go out."

"Nikos," Maria said firmly, "I want you and your friends to stay home tonight. Do you hear me? Stay home."

"Come on, Mom. What do you think we're going to do? We're getting some pizza or something. I've been home nearly every night since we moved here. I miss hanging out with my friends."

"So hang out in the basement."

"Don't worry, Mrs. Ioannis," said Vinny. "Nothing's going to happen. We've matured a lot. We know we need to behave ourselves. We know we can't get into any trouble with the law. We already have first and second offenses. I promise you. We'll be home early."

Maria didn't say anything. She just turned and went inside.

They all followed Nikos to his car.

"Listen up, guys," said Nikos. "Let's split up. Irving said we can hang at his house. Irving, you go with Lenny in case he gets lost. The rest of you guys, ride with me."

In Nikos's car, Vinny asked, "Nikos, what's the deal with Irving? He doesn't look like a typical Glassman."

"Irving's cool. He's not tough. As a matter of fact, he gets his ass kicked a lot. Correction. He's *gotten* his ass kicked a lot. But not anymore. He's now one of us. He's not afraid of anything. He's got a pair of brass balls. He just has trouble backing it up. I'm telling you. He took a beating right beside me and never gave up."

"That's good to hear," said Richie. "We need people with balls."

"Oooh yeah," chimed in Gary.

At the same time, Nikos's cell phone rang.

"Yeah, Irving?"

"You're not going to believe it."

"Believe what?"

"It's Fat Sal. He's walking along Waterbury Avenue."

"Holy shit. Did he see you?"

"No."

"Good. Now tell me where Waterbury Avenue is."

"Irving, give me the phone," said Lenny.

"Sure."

"Nikos, it's Lenny."

"Lenny, stay with him. We're a block away."

"No, Nikos. Stay away. I got this. I'll have Irving drop me off on the corner. That fat fuck will only see me. Let me have a little fun kicking his fat ass. I won't say a word. He doesn't know who I am."

"Doesn't know who you are *yet*." Nikos laughed.

"That's right, Nikos. *Yet*.

"Irving, you got a driver's license?" asked Lenny.

"Yeah."

"Good. This is what I'm going to do. I'm going to drive past Fat Sal and make a right at the corner. Then I'm going to drive halfway up the block and get out. You'll get into the driver's seat and wait for me. Then I'm walking back to Fat Sal and do my thing."

"Okay."

Lenny quickly sped past Fat Sal without him noticing. After he turned, he quickly stopped and exited the car. Irving quickly got behind the driver's seat as Lenny hurried to the corner and turned left as he now faced Fat Sal from twenty feet away.

As Fat Sal and Lenny approached each other, Lenny spoke first. "Hey, you fat fuck. Where you going?

Fat Sal looked at the unfamiliar muscular person who had just disrespected him.

This was Fat Sal's neighborhood. He didn't care how big and strong Lenny looked.

"Who the fuck do you think you're talking to like that? Do you know who I am?"

"How about I show you who the fuck *I* am, you fat fuck?" He grabbed Fat Sal by the collar and threw him up against a parked car.

Fat Sal gave a yell as his back went up against the passenger-side mirror.

"You motherfucker!" yelled Fat Sal. "Do you know who you're fuckin' with?"

"Yes, I do. A fat fuck," said Lenny as he took a step toward Fat Sal. Fat Sal threw a punch and missed.

Lenny again grabbed Fat Sal by his shirt and put him up against the car. This time, he didn't toy with him by waiting for a reaction. Lenny went to town on Fat Sal. He punched him six times in the face and then kneed him in the stomach. When Fat Sal fell to the ground, Lenny kicked him in the ribs several times.

Suddenly, one of the neighbors came out of the house and started yelling at Lenny.

"Hey, leave him alone!"

"Mind your own business and go back inside," Lenny said calmly as he stared at him.

"Leave him alone before I call the police."

Ignoring him, Lenny turned and walked to the corner, turned right, and entered his car as Irving drove away—but not before kicking Fat Sal two more times in the ribs.

Nikos looked at his phone as it rang.

"Lenny."

"Nikos. One down."

"What did you do?"

"It's what I didn't do." Lenny laughed.

"Anyone see you?"

"Yeah, some man came out of the house yelling."

"Did he get a look at you?"

"Yes, he did. But I don't care."

"You never do. I'll see you at Irving's in a few minutes."

* * *

"Irving, what's going on?" Mrs. Feldman asked as she saw Irving drive up in Lenny's car.

"Nothing, Mom. A few of my friends are coming over."

"Whose car is that, and why are you driving it?"

"Mom, this is my friend Lenny. It's his car."

"Hello, Mrs. Feldman," said Lenny as he extended his hand to shake. "It's a pleasure to meet you, ma'am."

"Likewise, Lenny," she replied while admiring Lenny's muscular body. "Irving, why are you driving Lenny's car? Lenny, do you live in Connecticut?" Mrs. Feldman looked at the license plate.

Before Lenny had a chance to answer, Nikos pulled up. Mrs. Feldman watched Nikos exit the car along with Vinny, Richie, and Gary.

"Good afternoon, Mrs. Feldman," said Nikos. "How are you today?"

"I'm fine, thank you, Nikos."

"Glad to hear it, Mrs. Feldman. I'd like to introduce you to a few of my friends."

After all the introductions, while feeling and looking totally confused, Mrs. Feldman took Irving aside.

"Irving, what's going on? Who are these people?"

"Mom, they're friends of mine."

"Friends of *yours*? They're not *your* friends. They're *Nikos's* friends. And I'm not sure if Nikos is even a friend. What we have here looks like a gang of hoodlums and thugs. Irving, are you looking for revenge?"

"Mom, we're going in the basement to hang out. You've been worrying about me not having friends, haven't you? Well, now I have friends."

28

George Coniglio ran down the steps to help Fat Sal. Fat Sal was barely able to move. Coniglio knew Fat Sal from the neighborhood. He knew he and his friends were troublemakers. Coniglio, along with his wife, Mary, had always kept their distance, but today, although Coniglio knew Fat Sal got what he deserved, he felt he now could be a friend of someone the neighborhood feared.

"Here, let me help you up," said Coniglio. "Do you want me to call the police?"

"No. No police. Just help me up."

Coniglio had difficultly lifting Fat Sal. When he had finally gotten him to his feet, he decided to help him into the main level of the house. He knew Fat Sal wouldn't make it up the steps.

"Salvatore, is there anyone you want me to call?"

"Yes."

Fat Sal took out his cell phone and called Skelly.

Skelly looked at the phone as it rang.

"What?" answered Skelly arrogantly.

Fat Sal had difficulty speaking, so he handed the phone to Coniglio.

"Who is this?" asked Coniglio.

"Never mind who this is. Who the fuck are you?"

Coniglio started to stutter. He didn't know who was on the other end of the phone but knew he was trouble.

"My name is George Coniglio. I live in Salvatore's neighborhood. Someone beat him up. He beat him up real bad. He can barely speak. He handed me the phone."

"Motherfucker!" Skelly yelled in anger. "Where are you guys?"

Coniglio gave Skelly his Waterbury Avenue address.

"I'll be there in ten minutes."

Coniglio waited by the door for Skelly. When Skelly approached the house, Coniglio greeted him with an extended hand to shake. Coniglio had no idea whom Fat Sal had called, but when he saw Skelly, he instantly recognized him as one of the troublemakers in the neighborhood. *What did I get myself into?* thought Coniglio.

"Where is he?" Skelly asked arrogantly.

"He's inside. My wife is—"

Skelly didn't let Coniglio finish. He walked into the house uninvited as Coniglio stood there with his hand still extended.

Inside, Skelly saw Mary Coniglio wiping Fat Sal's bruises.

"What the fuck happened?" asked Skelly.

"He got jumped," said Mary.

"I'm not talking to you, bitch."

"Hey, don't talk to my wife like that!" yelled Coniglio. "We helped your friend. If it wasn't for us, he would still be out there on the ground. I chased the guy away. He might still be out there getting his ass kicked if it wasn't for us."

Skelly turned toward Coniglio. Coniglio saw fire in Skelly's eyes. Very few people had ever spoken to Skelly like that, and fewer had ever gotten away with it.

Skelly grabbed Coniglio by the throat as Mary pleaded with him to let him go.

"Skelly!" yelled Fat Sal. "Leave him alone. He tried to help me. He chased the guy away."

"How can you let Nikos do this to you?" yelled Skelly. "You look like shit. You're an embarrassment."

"It wasn't Nikos."

"What?" yelled Skelly as he threw Coniglio onto the couch as Mary ran to her husband, crying. "It wasn't Nikos? Then who was it?"

"I don't know. I've never seen him before."

"What kind of car did he have?"

"He was on foot."

"You," Skelly said to Coniglio. "Did you get a good look at him?"

"Get out of my house!" yelled Mary. "How dare you! We tried to help your friend, and you treat us like this! How dare you!"

Skelly started pacing. He knew he needed to control himself. He knew the Coniglios were right. He felt he was losing control after his meeting with Giovanni.

"All right," said Skelly. "You're right. You did try to help my friend. Tell me what happened."

Coniglio and Fat Sal explained what had happened. Skelly knew no one in the neighborhood who fit Lenny's description. Nothing made sense.

"Okay, we'll find this guy," said Skelly. "And when we do, he'll regret he ever did this to you. In the meantime, let's get the fuck outta here. I'll drive you home. I'll be waiting for you in the car."

Skelly walked out the door without acknowledging the Coniglios, not an apology or even a thank you.

In Irving's basement, the guys sat looking at one another for several minutes before Vinny spoke.

"Lenny, tell us what happened."

"It was beautiful. At first, the fat fuck tried to intimidate me by asking me if I knew who he was. After that, I basically threw him up against a parked car and beat the living shit out of him."

"Nice," said Gary.

"How bad did you kick his ass?" asked Richie.

"Pretty bad, but he'll live."

"Irving," said Vinny, "this guy, Fat Sal—of the five guys you and Nikos fought, as far as toughness goes, where does he rank?"

"He's the least tough," interrupted Nikos.

"Oh, come on." Lenny laughed. "The least tough? You didn't put me up against the toughest? I had to take care of your fat light work? Who ever heard of fat light work?"

Everyone laughed at Lenny's *fat light work* joke.

"What's so funny?" Mrs. Feldman asked as she entered the basement with soft drinks. "I hope you're all thirsty. I have some refreshments."

"Thank you, Mrs. Feldman," said Nikos respectfully. "That's very kind of you."

"All right, guys," replied Mrs. Feldman. "Let's cut the bullshit."

Everyone looked up in silence.

"First of all, please call me Sylvia. Second, I demand to know what's going on. And don't bullshit me."

"Mom, nothing's going on. We're here to hang out. Haven't you always said it's good to stay out of the streets?"

"Cut the shit, Irving. All right? Let's just cut the shit."

"What do you want to know, Mrs. Feldman?" asked Nikos respectfully.

"Sylvia," replied Sylvia.

"I'm sorry, *Sylvia.* What exactly do you want to know?"

"What are you guys planning?"

"We're not sure right now. But we do need to do something."

"Nikos, please listen to me. Irving's going away to college in less than a year. Once he graduates, I'm selling the house and moving to Florida. That's what *we're* going to do. Please don't throw a monkey wrench in our plans."

"Sylvia," said Vinny, "please try to understand. The five of us have known one another since grade school. The beating that Nikos took cannot go unretaliated. And the beating Irving took helping Nikos makes him one of us now."

There was silence in the room for several seconds.

"Sylvia," said Gary softly, "we know what they did to you. That was worse than what they did to Nikos and Irving combined."

This time, the silence was longer as tears dripped down Sylvia's cheeks. Sylvia looked at Irving as his eyes watered as he lowered his head in embarrassment.

"Sylvia," Nikos said breaking the silence, "do you know what we were called in Glastonbury?

A gang of thugs, thought Sylvia.

"They called us the Five Glassmen of Glastonbury. Do you know why?"

"No. But I'm sure you're going to tell me."

"They called us the Five Glassmen because we have the strength and determination of five horses, but everyone was afraid to call us horses. That's why. But not anymore. It's a new town, and I'm changing the name to the Six Bronxmen. Irving is now one of us."

30

"Nikos, wake up," said Maria.

"What time is it?" Nikos asked, half asleep.

"It's eight o'clock."

"Eight o'clock? It's Sunday."

"That's right. It's Sunday. Let's go. We're leaving for church in an hour."

"I'm not going to church. My friends are here."

"They're welcome to come with us. But for now, get up. I don't want to hear another word out of you."

Still half asleep, Nikos rolled over and went back to sleep.

Five minutes later, Michael came into his room.

"Nikos, come on. Let's go. Get up."

"Daaad. My friends are over."

"I know. They're already awake, and your mother's making them breakfast. Let's go, I said."

"Mrs. Ioannis, you make the best pancakes ever," said Richie.

"Thank you, Richie. And don't worry, Vinny. I know you don't like pancakes. Your french toast is coming right up."

"Thanks, Mrs. Ioannis."

"Guys, I think it's about time you start calling me Maria."

"Okay, Maria," they all said together.

"Great. Now how long are you guys staying?"

"Well, Maria," said Gary. "Last night, we did a lot of talking—"

"I'm sure you did," Maria interrupted. "And that's what scares me. I've known you guys since you were in grade school. So don't think you can fool me. Whatever you guys are planning stops. It stops now. Do you hear me? It stops now."

"No, no, no, Maria," said Lenny. "I know what you're thinking. It's nothing like that. May I explain?"

"Please do." *I cannot wait to hear your line of shit,* thought Maria.

"Well, Maria," continued Lenny, "as you know, there isn't any future for us in Glastonbury."

The way you guys act, there isn't any future for you anywhere, thought Maria.

"It's a small town. We're young and ambitious. Although Hartford is only twenty minutes from Glastonbury, New York is where the opportunities are. We all decided we want to relocate to New York. And if it's all right with you, we would like to stay here until we find a house to rent. We won't be here very long. We plan on leaving after breakfast. Then we'd like to come back and look for jobs. We have enough money for one month's rent and one month's security. We were even looking online for civil service jobs. We already signed up for the New York City sanitation test."

Maria looked at everyone in silence. They all stared at her. They knew they couldn't fool her, but in actuality, they did want to start new lives in the Bronx.

"Guys," said Maria, "do me a favor. Stick around a few extra hours. I want you to come to church with us."

"But, Maria," said Gary, "we're not Greek."

"Has that ever stopped you from eating my Greek cooking?"

They all laughed.

* * *

As they were about to leave for church, Nikos's cell phone rang.

"Irving, what's going on?"

"Nothing much. You guys want to come over for breakfast?"

"Nah, we already ate. Besides, we're all getting ready for church."

"All right then. Maybe I'll catch up with you guys later."

"Irving, wait a minute."

"What?"

"Why don't you meet us at church?"

"Are you kidding? I'm Jewish."

"So was Jesus."

"I never thought of it that way. All right. I'll meet you there."

"Good. Do you know where the Greek church is?"

"Who doesn't? I go to the Greek festival every year."

"Good. We'll wait for you in the parking lot."

"You got it."

* * *

Inside the church, the Six Bronxmen took up an entire pew. In the Orthodox Church, the liturgy (mass) was much longer than other traditional masses. Of course, Nikos was used to the long services. The other Five Bronxmen were bored and fidgety.

After church services, most attended coffee hour. It was a time when the entire congregation got together to socialize.

Unknown to Nikos, Michael had paid the presiding priest, Father Lou, a visit during the week. Michael told Father Lou about his family moving to the Bronx from Glastonbury, Connecticut. The Ioannises had always had an excellent relationship with Father John at their parish in Hartford. As it turned out, Father Lou was good friends with Father John. On two occasions, while Father Lou had liturgical business in Connecticut, he served in Hartford and had met the Ioannises.

"It's nice to see you, Michael," said Father Lou. "I hope church services were to your liking."

"It was wonderful, Father. It's always good to come to church and have my spiritual batteries charged."

"Good. I'm glad to hear it. So I thought about your concerns with Nikos. He's here today, isn't he?"

"Of course, he is. As you know, there comes a point in our lives when we no longer have complete control over our children. But so far, Nikos cooperates with the church part."

"I'm glad to hear that. Without a doubt, it's a reflection on you and Maria."

"Thank you, Father."

Michael spent the next few minutes explaining the fight at the diner and what had happened to Lilly. He expressed his worries about Nikos wanting to retaliate. Then Michael informed Father Lou about Nikos's Connecticut friends and about them wanting to move to the Bronx.

"I don't understand. What's wrong with them wanting to move to the Bronx?"

Michael explained in detail the Five Glassmen. None of them had jobs or futures, not even Nikos. After Michael explained as much as he could, he watched Father Lou think for a few seconds.

"I'm glad they're all here. Please bring them to me."

Father Lou and Michael walked together into the community hall. He noticed them right away. They did look as tough as Michael had described. Irving was the only one who didn't look much like a physical threat.

"Nikos," said Michael, "come here, please. Say hello to Father Lou."

Nikos immediately approached Father Lou and kissed his hand, as was tradition in the Orthodox Church.

"Nikos, how are you today?"

"I'm fine, Father."

"It's always nice to see a young man in church on Sunday. My congregation has been thinning out with your age group."

"Thank you, Father," Nikos said with the utmost respect. "It's great to be here."

"I see you've brought a few friends. I'd like to meet them."

"Sure, Father. I'll introduce you."

Nikos went to where his friends were gobbling down coffee and bagels.

"Guys, the priest wants to see us."

"Why?" asked Vinny.

"I have no idea. That's the way priests are. They always have to see someone."

The Six Bronxmen followed Father Lou into his office. They were amazed by the decor. Most priests in the Orthodox Church decorated their offices with religious items. Father Lou did have the traditional items, like icons of Jesus and the Virgin Mary. He also had a picture on the wall of his wife and son. The rest of the office was decorated with guitars.

* * *

In his previous life, before becoming a priest, Father Lou was in a rock band. He traveled the country in a broken-down van with four other guys, playing in any bar or club that would hire them. In his old high school in Brooklyn, he was 5'-8" and weighed 225 pounds of solid muscle, and captain of the wrestling team. His nickname was Bruno Sammartino.

One evening, while playing his guitar, out of nowhere, he saw the image of God calling his name. After that, he cut his shoulder-length hair and went to the Holy Cross Seminary. After graduation, he was ordained and assigned to the Zoodohos Peghe Greek Orthodox church in the Bronx.

* * *

"Sit down, guys," said Father Lou. Father Lou sized everyone up and needed to take charge. He knew Nikos was probably the leader, so he needed to ask the leader to go out into the hall to get one more chair. *I need to show the leader who the real leader is,* thought Father Lou.

Once Nikos returned with the chair, the Six Bronxmen sat looking at Father Lou. Father Lou continued sizing everyone up and started the introductions. He knew Nikos was the only Greek among the six, although none of that mattered to him. When Irving introduced himself as Irving Feldman, there were some giggles.

Father Lou smiled and asked, "Guys, you ever read the Bible?"

Silence.

"Come on, guys. Really. Have you ever read the Bible?"

There were a few mumbles and smiles.

"Well, guys, Galatians 3:28. 'Greek or Jew, man or woman, slave or free, we're all one in Christ.' Got it?"

Silence.

"Got it?" Father Lou asked a little louder.

They all mumbled yes.

"Irving?"

"Yes, Father?"

"Got it?"

"Got it, Father." Irving smiled.

They sat in Father Lou's office for an hour. Father Lou was careful not to do all the talking. He wanted to listen. The more he listened, the more he got to know them. Once he got to know them, then he was able to minister to them.

He listened to them talk about their futures. He knew they weren't college material not only by the way they spoke but by the way they presented themselves. Irving was the only one who showed academic potential.

"Well, guys," Father Lou said as he stood, "it's getting late. I have a few hospital visits to make. It was a pleasure meeting all of you. When you get settled into the house you plan on renting, please give me a call. I would love to come by and do a house blessing. As a matter of fact, tomorrow morning I'm doing a blessing at the Ioannises' diner. Then I'm blessing their home on Wednesday."

Father Lou shook hands and kissed each one of them on both cheeks, as was traditional in the Orthodox faith. He wished them luck and watched them leave his office.

Two weeks later, Nikos's friends from Glastonbury rented a house on Quincy Avenue just four blocks from Nikos. For the first two weeks, they sat around doing virtually nothing. Virtually nothing meant drinking beer and eating. Lenny was the only one who kept physically active. Every morning he would wake up and go for a run. Since his mother cut him off completely, he wasn't able to join a gym. That didn't matter to him. He brought along some barbells.

By now, Nikos was playing hooky every day.

Maria was crying herself to sleep every night.

"Nikos," she would cry to him, "please. You have to go to school. You can't wake up every morning and go to Quincy Avenue and waste your life away with those guys. They're all alone without any parental guidance. They can get away with it. You can't. Do you hear me? I said you can't."

"Come on, Mom. Leave me alone. I don't like school. School sucks."

"Watch your language when you talk to me."

"Oh, come on, Mom, you curse all the time."

"When do I curse?"

Nikos only looked at Maria and smiled.

"Just get ready and go to school."

"All right."

"Don't 'all right' me. Let's go. Get up now. Your father bought you a car for school. Not for gallivanting."

Nikos dragged himself out of bed and showered. Maria, as always, made breakfast for Nikos and Lilly. When Nikos went downstairs to breakfast, Lilly had already put her dish into the dishwasher.

"Ready, Nikos?" asked Lilly.

"No. I just got downstairs. I didn't even eat yet."

"We need to leave now. I don't want to be late."

"Hold your horses. I'm having breakfast first."

"Mommm!"

"What is it, Lilly?"

"I need to get to school. I'm having a test today."

"So go. What's stopping you?"

"It's Nikos."

"How's Nikos stopping you?"

"He wants to have breakfast before driving me to school."

Maria glanced at the clock above the sink.

"Nikos, what are you doing?" asked Maria.

"Nothing, Mom. I'm eating first. Can't I eat breakfast first? Is it against the law to eat breakfast before school?"

"Mommm!" cried Lilly. "I have a math test first period. I can't be late."

"Nikos. Get up. Do you hear me? I said get up."

Nikos ignored Maria and went for a piece of toast.

"I said get up!" Maria screamed this time. "Get your ass out of that chair before I knock you out of it."

"Hey, Mom, watch your language."

"Get up! Get your ass out of that chair right now and take your sister to school!" Maria screamed even louder.

Maria had a breaking point, and Nikos knew he had crossed the line.

Maria then grabbed Nikos by his ear and pulled him out of the chair. As Nikos stood towering over Maria, she smacked him in the face and told him to take the bus to school.

"*I'm* driving your sister to school with your car. Give me the keys."

Silence.

"Give me the keys, I said!"

With tears in his eyes, Nikos handed his mother the keys. The tears weren't from his mother taking the keys. The tears were because he knew he had hurt his mother and sister.

"I'm sorry, Mom."

"Don't 'I'm sorry, Mom' me. Grow up."

Nikos then watched Maria storm out of the house as Lilly followed her.

Nikos sat back down and ate his breakfast. *This is beautiful. No one home to break my balls,* he thought. When he had finished, he decided to go hang out with his friends.

He walked the four blocks to Quincy Avenue. Deep down, he wished he lived in the house with his friends. As he approached the house, he decided to use the key they had given him.

When he walked into the house, he didn't see anyone.

"Hey, is anyone home?"

No answer.

"Hey, guys, where are you?"

"Nikos, is that you?" asked Vinny.

"Yeah, it's me. Don't tell me you guys are still sleeping."

"What time is it?" asked Gary as he walked into the kitchen in his underwear, scratching his balls.

"It's eight thirty," said Nikos.

"Come on, guys, shut the fuck up!" yelled Richie. "Some people are trying to sleep."

Within five minutes, they were sitting around the living room when Lenny entered the house from his morning run, plopped himself down next to Gary, and leaned against him.

"Come on!" yelled Gary. "Get off me. You're all sweaty."

They all laughed as Lenny got down and did fifty pushups.

"Guys," said Nikos, "I'm in deep shit with my parents."

"What happened?" asked Richie.

"Well, as you know, I haven't been going to school lately, and my parents are really pissed about that. I feel bad, but let's face it. I'm not going to college or anything like that."

"Neither are any of us." Vinny laughed. "By the way, none of us have jobs. What are we going to do?"

"I have no idea," said Richie.

"Nikos," said Gary, "what about the diner? Would your father hire us?"

"I don't think so. My mom's already pissed that I'm spending all my school hours with you guys. Besides, it's a small diner. He'd have to fire all the Mexicans. And believe me when I tell you, you don't want to work for Mexican pay."

"I know I don't," said Lenny.

33

The next morning, Skelly needed to take charge. He desperately needed to show Giovanni he could be depended upon. Ordinarily, whenever he approached a new merchant for protection money, he would take along a few of the guys for intimidation, but not this time. This time, he was doing it alone. He not only wanted to be respected but also wanted to be feared, and this time, it was personal—strictly personal.

On East Tremont Avenue, a new Chinese laundromat had opened three weeks ago. Skelly wanted to give them ample time to get adjusted to the neighborhood. That afternoon, Skelly entered the Chinese laundromat and introduced himself. Mrs. Wong approached Skelly and asked if she could help him as she respectfully bowed slightly.

"How's business?" Skelly asked arrogantly.

"Oh, beezness vedy kood. You need loan-gree?"

"No, I don't need no fuckin' *loan-gree.* I need your money. Open the register. Give me $200."

"I no understand. You hav loan-gree?"

"No, you fuckin' gook!" Skelly screamed as he pushed Mrs. Wong aside, stepped behind the counter, and punched her in the face. "Open the register! Don't make me ask you again! Open the fuckin' register! Now!"

Mr. Wong ran to the counter and started tending to his wife, who was near unconscious as her nose was clearly broken and bleeding profusely.

"Get out my store," Mr. Wong said. "Why you do dis? I call pole-lease. You vedy bad man. Why you do dis? Get out my store."

"'Get out my store'? It's 'get out *of* my store,' you fuckin' gook. And it's not 'vedy' bad, you asshole. The word is 'very' bad. Not 'vedy' bad. And the word is 'laundry,' not 'loan-gree.' Why don't you people learn to speak English?"

"I said get out my store. I call pole-lease."

Mr. Wong proceeded to stand to dial 911 when Skelly kicked him in the stomach and watched him land on top of his wife. Then Skelly went to the cash register and tried to open it. Unable to open it, he threw it at the floor and watched it open. Although Skelly's intention was to establish a payment of $200 a week, he decided today to set an example and took all the money and left.

Ten minutes later, by coincidence, Maria walked into the Chinese laundromat to drop off some articles of clothing. The minute she entered the store and saw the store ransacked and the Wongs sitting on the floor, she quickly ran to their aid. She sat them both in chairs and called 911. Within five minutes, two patrol cars appeared from the 45th Precinct. Maria explained how she had entered the store and discovered the Wongs sitting on the floor.

After the ambulance left, Maria spent fifteen minutes answering questions with the police.

* * *

That evening at dinner, Maria explained to Nikos and Lilly what had happened at the Chinese laundromat.

"Mom," said Lilly, "that's pretty messed up. I'm beginning to wonder if it was a good idea moving to the Bronx. Too many bad things are happening."

"I know, Lilly. I'm beginning to think the same. But please, whatever you do, do not repeat this in front of your father. He feels bad enough uprooting us from Glastonbury."

"Listen, Mom," said Nikos, "it was pretty fucked up that we had to move. But you know me. I'm a survivor. I'll make it work. It's already working for me."

"First of all, Nikos, you watch your mouth in this house—"

"Oh, come on, Mom," Nikos interrupted. "That's the way I talk. I can't help it."

"Don't 'oh, come on, Mom' me, young man. If I ever hear that language in this house again, I'm going to wash your mouth out with soap. Do you hear me?"

Silence.

"I said, *do you hear me*?"

Nikos looked at his mother with an attitude. He knew he was wrong for cursing, but he didn't like the idea of anyone threatening to wash his mouth out with soap either.

"Mom," said Nikos, "that's the way I talk. Since you don't like it, I'm leaving."

"Oh no, you're not. You're not going anywhere. Do you hear me? You're not going anywhere. Now get upstairs right now and do your homework."

"Mom, I don't have any homework."

"Bullshit!" snapped Maria. "Don't tell me you don't have any homework. I'm going to your school tomorrow and talking to each and every one of your teachers. And if they tell me you have homework missing, you're in big trouble." Maria started to cry.

"Don't bother. I'm quitting school. It's not for me, and you know it."

"Oh no, you're not!" screamed Maria. "Tomorrow we are both going to school together to see the principal."

"Have fun, Mom. Knock yourself out. I'm not going," Nikos said as he stormed out of the house.

For the next several months, Richie, Lenny, Vinny, and Gary worked odd jobs while taking civil service tests as they became available. As the months continued, Nikos ended up quitting school and working at the diner full-time. Although Michael wasn't happy about Nikos quitting school, he was privately proud of Nikos as he learned the restaurant business.

One Sunday evening Nikos approached Michael as he watched television.

"Dad, can I have a word with you?"

"Sure, son. What's on your mind?" Michael said as he muted the television.

"Well, Dad, I've been doing some thinking."

"Thinking about what?"

"About our family's future."

"What's wrong with our family's future?" Michael asked, concerned.

"We're at a road block. Business is good, but I was thinking about expansion."

"Expansion?"

"Yes, expansion."

"Business is great. Why do we need to expand?"

"Just hear me out."

"I'm listening."

"Well, this is what I see. I agree with you that business is great. First, I think we should open on Sundays—"

"Open on Sundays?" interrupted Michael. "No way. Six days a week is more than enough. I can't handle seven days a week. And with your uncle Charlie's health failing and wanting to move to Florida, it'll be too much for me."

"Dad, listen to me. We can do it. We can do it together."

"Do what together? Work seven days a week together? I'm getting too old for that. Besides, I want something better than that for you."

"Are you going to hear me out or not?"

"Go ahead. I'm listening," said Michael reluctantly.

"Okay. Now, as we both agree, business is good. We pay $7,000 a month rent for six days a week. If we open on Sundays, I'm sure we can add another thousand to our weekly income. The rent will stay the same.

"Now we know Uncle Charlie wants to retire. I'll become your partner. With the extra thousand we would make on Sundays, that thousand, we can use to make payments to Uncle Charlie until he is bought out at whatever price you two mutually agree upon."

"Nikos, how do you know we could make $1,000 on Sunday? I think the place will be dead."

"No, it won't."

"How do you know it won't?"

"Dad, the pizza place next door does crazy business on Sunday. I was there today with my friends to get some pizza, and we waited forty-five minutes for our order."

"Really?"

"Yes, really. And you know what else?"

"What?"

"We couldn't even get a table. We took the pies to the diner to eat. And as we were eating, people saw us and banged on the door. They thought we were open."

"Nikos, what time was that?"

"Dad, it was three o'clock, the slowest time of the day in the restaurant business."

"Who's going to work on Sundays? You and me? We have church. I'm not giving up going to church on Sundays, and neither are you."

"Dad, listen to me."

"I'm listening. But I don't like what I'm hearing so far."

"Okay, I'll give it to you straight. Uncle Charlie isn't doing well. The diner is open from 6:00 a.m. to midnight. He's barely holding his own weight. You're going to have to buy him out, and for you to do that, you're going to have to work insane hours. Let's buy him out now. We'll give him a fair price. We'll give him a down payment and pay him notes for a certain number of years. We'll treat him fairly.

"Dad, we have to do it. The diner will fall apart if Uncle Charlie continues the way he is—if he doesn't die in the meantime."

"Did you come up with this idea by yourself?"

"Yes and no."

"That scares me."

"Look, Dad, Irving's a genius. He reads accounting and business books just for the fun of it. During tax season, he works part time for some local accountant. He even has two businesses he keeps books for. We talked about it. He pounded the calculator and feels it will be a home run. Besides, we have another idea."

"Now I'm really scared. But I'm still listening."

"Oh, now you're listening? The minute I mention Irving's name, you're still listening."

"Irving's a smart kid."

"Yes, he is. He's also Jewish. I think it's his Jewishness that's piquing your curiosity."

"Very funny. Now tell me about Irving and his calculator."

"Okay." Nikos laughed. "Now listen. But I need you to keep quiet and pay close attention."

"I will."

"Good. Now this is the plan. We open on Sundays. I'll handle it. You can go to church. I have plenty of time to go to church when I get old like you."

"Very funny. You want to go in the backyard and have me show you what an old man can do?" Michael smiled.

"Dad, that's not necessary. I saw what you can do a few months ago at the diner, and believe me when I tell you, I don't want to find out." Nikos smiled. "Now let me finish."

"Go ahead."

"We buy out Uncle Charlie. Now listen to this. Remember I told you we had to wait forty-five minutes for our pizza?"

"Yeah."

"That's because they suck. Their pizza is great, but their service sucks. And the only reason their service sucks is because their kitchen area is too small. They can't keep up. Now remember how you sometimes say you wish you can convert part of our large storeroom into seating?"

"Yeah."

"Well, I recently discovered the pizza shop's lease is up in a year. We'll talk to the landlord, Mr. Goldstein, and ask him not to renew their lease. We then make a deal with Mr. Goldstein to rent the pizza shop—"

"You want to double the space of the diner?"

"No, we keep it as a pizza shop and convert part of our back storeroom as part of the pizza shop kitchen to serve the customers quicker. Dad, we can do it."

"And how do you know Mr. Goldstein will do this?"

"Irving already spoke to him."

"Irving spoke to him? Why is Irving getting involved in our family's business? And why would Mr. Goldstein even speak to Irving?"

"Come on, Dad. You know, Jew to Jew, like Greek to Greek."

"You got to be kidding."

"Dad, I'm not kidding."

"Okay, make an appointment . . . Sorry, have Irving make an appointment with Mr. Goldstein. You know, Jew to Jew." Michael smiled.

The next day at school, as Lilly sat in the cafeteria, Skelly approached her and asked if she wanted company.

"Get the hell out of here, you piece of shit," she said.

"Oh, come on, beautiful. Let's blow this joint. There's a nice spot waiting for us at Ferry Point Park. You remember, just like last time. Maybe I'll grab some tit again. Hey, wait a minute, why don't we stop by your house and pick up your hot mother? She's got nicer tits than you. That would make it a really nice mother–daughter team."

"You're an asshole."

"Skelly, leave her alone."

"Who the—" Skelly said as he turned to see who it was.

"You gotta be kidding." Skelly looked down at Irving. "You little fuckin' Jew. I think these Greeks made you delirious."

"I said leave her alone."

Irving didn't know what hit him. All he remembered was flying through the air as Skelly punched him in the face, but Skelly wasn't satisfied. Quick as a cat, Skelly was on top of Irving, punching him. By the time security had pulled Skelly off, Irving was unconscious.

"I'm going to get you, bitch!" Skelly yelled at Lilly as security dragged him away.

* * *

Mrs. Feldman sat in the hospital room, looking at Irving as tears dripped down her cheeks. All she could think about was how her life had fallen apart since her husband left her. Although she knew it was coincidental, the way things had been going, she couldn't help blaming him. *I need to move,* she thought. *I need to move out of this neighborhood.*

As she sat next to his bed, Irving opened his eyes and saw his mother crying.

"Don't cry, Mom. I'm fine."

"Oh, Irving. I'm so sorry. It's my fault. We should have moved as soon as your father left us . . ."

"No, Mom," Irving whispered. "Nothing's your fault. What happened to me today had nothing to do with you or Daddy. I'm here because I not only stood up for myself but also stood up to help someone. That's why I'm here. So please, please stop blaming yourself."

Before Mrs. Feldman was able to answer, Maria and Michael walked into the room.

"Mrs. Feldman?" said Maria.

"Yes."

"Hi, I'm Maria Ioannis. This is my husband, Michael. We are Nikos's parents. How's Irving doing?"

"How's Irving doing? Just take a look at him. That's how Irving's doing," Mrs. Feldman snapped. "None of this would have happened if it wasn't for your son. Look at him. Just look at him. If it wasn't for Nikos and his friends, this never would have happened."

"I'm sorry you feel that way. We came because Irving is Nikos's friend."

"Maria? Did you say your name is Maria?"

"Yes."

"Well, Maria, there's an old saying. 'With friends like Nikos, we don't need enemies.'"

"Mrs. Feldman," said Michael, "please believe us when we tell you we're sorry about all this. We actually feel guilty because Irving was trying to help our daughter, Lilly. Is there anything we can do? Do you need help with the hospital bills?"

"We don't need your help. Can't you see you've done enough?"

"Irving, are you all right?" Nikos asked as he entered the room, with Richie, Vinny, Gary, and Lenny following behind. "Tell us exactly what happened."

"Nikos," said Maria, "keep quiet. As a matter of fact, I think you should leave. Take your friends and leave now. Irving needs his rest."

"Please, Maria," said Lenny. "Irving's our friend. We want to see how he's doing."

"Take a look. He's doing great," Mrs. Feldman said sarcastically.

"Mrs. Feldman—" said Nikos.

"Enough of that 'Mrs. Feldman' stuff. I told you months ago. Call me Silvia."

"Okay, Silvia," said Nikos. "I'll give it to you straight. This fuckin' Skelly—"

"Nikos!" screamed Michael. "You watch your language! Do you hear me?"

"Yes, Dad, I'm sorry. But this guy Skelly had no right doing this to Irving. And believe me when I tell you he's not getting away with it—"

"Stop talking like that," interrupted Maria. "Do you hear me? Stop talking like that."

"Please, Mom, stay out of it. We're going to fix this."

"Fix this?" said Silvia. "Fix this? You've done enough fixing. I want you to leave."

"Mom, please . . ." Irving interrupted in a faint voice. "Please, Mom, calm down . . ."

"It's okay, Irving," said Nikos. "We're leaving. But believe me when I tell you; Skelly's not getting away with this."

Nikos turned and left the room as the other four Bronxmen followed.

Two months later . . .

At 12:30 a.m., at the Ioannises' house, Lilly was sound asleep as Maria waited for Michael as she always did the weeks he locked the diner. It was also something she always did whenever her children were out late. She could never get to sleep unless she knew her family was safe at home. The last several weeks, Nikos had basically moved into the Quincy Avenue house with the other Bronxmen.

At 12:45 a.m., Maria walked to the window to see if Michael was pulling into the driveway. She knew Michael was always home by 12:30 a.m.

Maybe he got busy the last few minutes before closing, she thought, but nonetheless, she started to worry. *Where could he be? I could set my watch by him the nights he closed. The few times he would be late, he always called.*

At 12:50 a.m., Maria called Michael's cell phone as it went straight to voicemail.

"Michael, give me a call," she said, leaving a message.

By 1:15 a.m., Maria was starting to panic. Her hands started sweating as her heart rate kicked up a notch.

Where could he be? Why isn't he answering his phone? she thought.

Then she took the phone and dialed again.

"Mom," said Nikos as he answered on the third ring, looking at the clock. "What happened? Is everything all right?"

"I don't know, Nikos. Daddy's not home yet, and I'm starting to worry."

"What time is it?" he asked as he looked at the clock and rubbed the sand from his eyes.

"It's 1:21. He's always home by 12:30. Nikos, I'm worried . . ."

"Mom, did you call him?"

"Of course, I called him."

"And he didn't answer?"

"Nikos, wake up. Why would I be calling you if he answered? His phone went straight to voicemail."

"Sorry, Mom, I'm still half asleep. I'll drive over to the diner now."

"No, Nikos. Not alone. Come pick me up first. I don't want you going there alone. I'm worried something might have happened to him."

"Okay, Mom. Give me ten minutes." Nikos also felt something was wrong. His father always called when he ran late. He called Maria back and told her when he was going alone.

"Hey, guys," said Nikos. "Wake up."

"What's going on?" asked Lenny.

"It's my father. My mother thinks something might have happened to him. We need to go to the diner."

"Then what are we waiting for?" said Vinny.

Lenny drove with Nikos, riding shotgun, while Vinny, Gary, and Richie sat in the back. Lenny dropped off Nikos and Richie in front of the diner.

"We'll drive around back," said Lenny.

Nikos quickly ran to unlock the front door as Lenny took off and made a right onto Fink Avenue and another quick right onto Blondell Avenue. As he parked the car, Nikos was exiting the back door onto Blondell Avenue, with Richie one step behind.

"Dad!" screamed Nikos. "Dad! Dad! Oh my God, Dad!"

Michael lay dead in a puddle of blood, barely recognizable with his face smashed in.

"Dad, Dad, oh my God, Dad," Nikos repeated over and over.

Vinny and Lenny were the only ones strong enough to pull Nikos off his father's bloody body. Richie called 911 as Gary ran into the diner, grabbed a few tablecloths, quickly returned, and covered Michael's bloody body. Within minutes, the place was surrounded by police cars.

Nikos was in shock as paramedics were tending to him. Gary was speaking to the officer in charge, explaining to him the timeline of the events, from the time Maria called Nikos to their arrival at the diner.

By 2:30 a.m., Nikos glanced at his phone and noticed fifteen missed calls from his mother as well as several missed calls from the other four Bronxmen.

A block away, Irving stood behind a police barricade, unable to get anywhere near the other Bronxmen. After Maria didn't hear from any of the five Bronxmen, she had reached out to Irving. Irving pleaded with the officer for several minutes, unable to convince the officer that he was friends with the diner owners. Finally, they let him through.

"Vinny," said Irving as he approached, looking at the covered body, "what happened?"

"It's Michael. Someone killed him."

"Holy shit."

"Irving, how did you find out?"

"Maria called me. She told me Michael didn't come home and none of you guys were answering your phones."

Vinny looked at his phone and saw many missed calls from Maria and Irving.

"Shit, with all the commotion, I didn't hear the phone ring."

"Do they know who did it?"

"I doubt it. It just happened. Irving, this is your neighborhood. Does this shit happen a lot around here?"

"No, not really. I've never seen this happen before."

"Irving, you don't think Skelly could have anything to do with this, do you?"

"I doubt it. Don't get me wrong, Skelly's a real piece of shit, but I doubt if he's capable of murder. Then again, nothing would surprise me about him."

"Hey, guys," said Gary, "the cops want us to give a statement."

"A statement?" said Richie. "We don't know anything."

"I know," said Gary. "But come on, guys, there was a murder, and we were the first ones here. They're going to ask if we've seen anything and shit. That's all they want. Anyway, where's Nikos?"

"Holy shit," said Vinny. "He's in the ambulance."

When the five Bronxmen looked toward the ambulance, they saw Nikos inside with an oxygen mask as paramedics were taking his blood pressure.

Vinny led the way to the ambulance as two police officers stopped them and ask them to come to the side. The two officers kept the five Bronxmen for thirty-five minutes. After that, they sat with Nikos for fifteen minutes. Finally, Irving spoke.

"Nikos, my phone hasn't stopped ringing. Your mother keeps calling. You need to get to her before she finds out from someone else."

"How's she going to find out? Who's going to tell her?" snapped Richie.

"Calm down, Richie," said Lenny. "Irving's just thinking out loud."

"I'm not *thinking* out loud," snapped Irving. *"I'm thinking.* Look around. Look at all the people taking pictures. There are reporters out already. Maria's not sleeping. She's pacing the house. Who knows? She may even have the TV on to help distract her worrying."

"Irving's right," said Nikos. "I need to get home. I have to tell my mother and Lilly before they find out from someone else."

"We'll come with you," said Lenny. "You shouldn't do this alone."

"Thanks, guys. But just drive me home. Let me tell my mother and sister alone. Trust me, it'll be better this way."

"I agree," said Vinny as the others nodded.

A few hours earlier . . .

At 12:15 a.m., as Michael was locking the diner and exiting the back door onto Blondell Avenue, where his car was parked, he was approached by Skelly.

"What are you doing here?" Michael asked arrogantly. "You better get the fuck outta here if you know what's good for you."

"Listen up, old man. I'm going to say this one time and one time only. Every week I want $500 from you. I'll show up every Friday morning at 10:00 a.m., and Nikos, not you but Nikos, will hand me the money. And the Fridays I can't make it at 10:00 a.m., I'll show up in the afternoon. And when I show up in the afternoon, that piece-of-ass wife of yours with the nice tits will hand me the money, and she *will* thank me for the honor of paying me."

"How about I pay you right now with a good old-fashioned ass kicking, you piece of shit?"

"Let's see what you got, old man."

Michael immediately took a swing at Skelly, which knocked him to the ground, but Michael didn't let up. As quick as a cat, he was on top of Skelly, punching him, but Skelly was much younger. As he lay on his back, he wrapped his arms around Michael tight and held him so he couldn't punch anymore. But as Skelly held him tight, Michael was able to put his hands on Skelly's face, and with his thumbs, he started to dig into Skelly's eyes. Skelly screamed as he feared his eyes would pop out.

Suddenly, Michael felt a blow to the back of his head and started bleeding profusely. Skelly then rolled Michael over onto his back and saw a small puddle of blood under his head. When Skelly looked up, he saw Moose standing over Michael with a baseball bat.

"Get up, Skelly," said Moose.

Skelly shook the cobwebs out and slowly stood. By the time Skelly was standing, Moose was going to town on Michael. Within a minute, Michael's face was totally caved in as he lay there, dead.

"Skelly," said Moose, "get outta here. Go. Get the fuck outta here, and don't look back."

Moose watched Skelly as he disappeared into the darkness. When Skelly was out of sight, Moose continued pounding Michael's head until he couldn't pound anymore. Then Moose emptied Michael's pockets of all the evening receipts, along with his wallet. He wanted to make it look like a robbery.

Then Moose walked away as Michael's head was totally unrecognizable.

Present moment . . .

The moment Nikos entered the house, Maria took one look at him and started crying hysterically. She knew it. It was written all over his face. She knew Michael was dead.

"Oh my God!" she screamed over and over.

"Mom," said Nikos, "he's dead. Daddy's dead. Someone killed him. He's dead, Mom."

Lilly heard the commotion and came down the stairs, half asleep. Maria didn't want to wake her as she paced the past few hours. She felt it wasn't necessary to worry her too, but when Maria told her that her father was murdered, she screamed and hyperventilated at the same time.

The three sat in the living room, crying for thirty minutes, when homicide detectives rang the bell.

Nikos slowly walked to the door and let them in. After several minutes of consoling the Ioannises, Detectives Levas and Johnson got down to business.

"Mrs. Ioannis," started Detective Levas, "I need you to think. Is there anyone you think may have wanted to hurt Mr. Ioannis?"

"I do," interrupted Nikos.

"Who?" asked Detective Johnson.

"There's this group of assholes—"

"Nikos!" snapped Maria. "Be respectful to the police."

"Sorry, Mom. Sorry, Officer."

"Don't worry about it," said Detective Johnson. "We know you're upset. But please continue. Tell me more about these people who might have done this."

Nikos spent thirty minutes explaining to the two detectives everything from the first day of school to Skelly friending him, what he did to Lilly, the fight at P.S. 14, and finally putting Irving into the hospital.

"Does this guy Skelly have a full name?" asked Detective Johnson.

"His name is Anthony Scorzelli," interrupted Lilly. "He's a real piece of shit—"

"Lilly, please," interrupted Maria. "Please, no cursing . . ."

"Scorzelli, huh?" said Detective Levas. "We know Scorzelli. The kid's bad news. He's definitely a chip off the ol' block. He should be in jail like his father. But to tell you the truth, I'm not sure if he's a murderer. We definitely will pay him a visit tomorrow."

"Tomorrow?" said Maria. "Can't you pay him a visit tonight?"

"Mrs. Ioannis," said Detective Johnson, "please try to understand. We need to have our questions in order. Okay? Do not worry. I promise I'll personally see to it—"

Just as the detectives were speaking, the doorbell rang.

"Who could that be?" asked Lilly.

"Stay right where you are," said Detective Levas as he walked to the door. Within seconds, Detective Levas opened the door with his suit jacket open, ready if necessary to pull out his gun. "Can I help you?" asked Levas.

"Father Lou! Oh, Father Lou," cried Maria as she ran to the door.

"Maria, I'm so sorry. I was at the hospital for an emergency, and a doctor had informed me about a Greek Orthodox body coming in. When I asked the name, I couldn't believe it. I'm so sorry. When I heard the name, I drove right over. I'm so sorry."

Maria broke down again, hugging Father Lou as she cried in his arms along with Lilly. Nikos could only sit on the couch and try to hold back his tears. He didn't want to break down in front of Father Lou. He wanted to be strong. He needed to be strong.

After several minutes, Father Lou approached Nikos and hugged him. At that point, Nikos wanted to continue fighting back tears as he stood.

"Nikos," said Father Lou, "it's okay to cry. Let it out."

"Sorry, Father. But I have to leave."

"Leave? Leave where? You're going to leave your mother and sister? No, you're not. Not tonight. They need you."

Nikos stood there for a few seconds and broke down as he approached Maria and Lilly.

"Mom," he said, "I'm so sorry for thinking of leaving. I'm so sorry. I'm so ashamed for even thinking of doing such a thing. Can you ever forgive me?"

"Detectives," said Father Lou, "are you done here?"

"Yes, we are, Father, for now," said Detective Levas. "We're leaving unless you need us for something."

"I'll walk you out to your car."

Outside, Father Lou spent fifteen minutes asking the detectives about their next step in the investigation. The detectives basically told Father Lou the same thing they had told the Ioannises about getting a game plan together, starting with Skelly later that morning.

"Okay," said Father Lou as they exchanged business cards. "I know you guys will get to the bottom of this. Have a good night, and God be with you."

After they all shook hands, Father Lou went back inside, where he sat with the Ioannises for another hour.

"I'll see you later on today," he said as he stood.

"Thank you, Father," said Maria. "And thank you for coming right over. Thank you so much."

"Try to get some sleep. I'll be here in the afternoon, and we'll go together to make the necessary arrangements. Nikos, can I see you outside a minute?"

"Sure, Father. Mom, I'll be right outside. And don't worry, I'm not leaving."

"I know, Nikos. I know."

Outside, Father Lou lit a cigar and sat on the porch as he stared at Nikos and started to speak. "Nikos, I know what you're thinking."

"Do you?" Nikos asked arrogantly. "Do you really?"

"Yes, I do. But I'm telling you now. Let the police handle this. Do you hear me?"

Nikos stood in silence.

"I said*; do you hear me*?"

"Yes, Father, I hear you."

"Good, because if you're thinking of taking matters into your own hands, you will completely bury your mother."

Nikos knew he needed to tell Father Lou exactly what he wanted to hear, but at the same time, he knew Father Lou was right. He had to let the police handle it. He knew New York City had the best police force in the world, and they would use their unlimited resources to get the people responsible for his father's death.

"Good night, Father. I hear you loud and clear."

"Good night, Nikos. I'll see you this afternoon. Try to get some sleep."

"Thank you, Father."

* * *

Unknown to the Ioannises, Detectives Levas and Johnson went immediately to the Scorzelli home to question Skelly. By now, it was 5:30 a.m., and the house was quiet, as were all the houses on Pennyfield Avenue. It took several minutes of doorbell ringing before Fran Scorzelli answered. Fran answered the door at the wee hours, afraid of what might have happened to her husband in prison. She always suspected this would happen.

"Mrs. Scorzelli?" asked Detective Levas.

She closed her robe tightly, concerned about the two strangers at her door at that particular hour.

"What can I do for you?" she asked.

"I'm Detective Levas, and this is Detective Johnson." Both detectives held up their badges.

"What is this about? Is it my husband?"

"We would like to speak to your son, Anthony."

"What did Anthony do this time?"

"Nothing. Absolutely nothing. All we want to do is talk to him."

"Well, he's not home."

"Are you sure? It's five thirty in the morning. Where could he be? It is a school night, isn't it?"

"Yes, it is a school night. But a school night has never stopped him from staying out all night before. Why should tonight be any different?"

"Are you sure he's not home?" asked Levas. "Can you check his bedroom, please?"

"Detectives, you rang my bell at five thirty in the morning. My husband is in jail. Don't you think I went into my son's bedroom to get him to answer the door?"

"I'm sorry," said Levas. "When Anthony does come home, please have him give me a call." He handed her his card. "It's very important."

"Can you at least tell me what it's about?"

"We don't know yet."

39

Early that afternoon, the five Bronxmen visited Nikos. Nikos had mixed emotions. On one hand, he was happy to see his friends and have their support. On the other hand, he felt he needed to be alone with his family, but after a few minutes, Nikos realized the Bronxmen were his family too. He needed them, and he also knew he could count on them. Even Irving—although he hadn't known him long, he knew he could count on him by the beatings he had taken for him at the schoolyard and for standing up to Skelly, which ended up putting him in the hospital.

* * *

That afternoon, Father Lou accompanied Maria and Nikos to Pafedes Funeral Home on East Tremont Avenue. Both Maria and Nikos felt Lilly shouldn't go. Besides, Lilly didn't want to go. It would be too upsetting for her. The five Bronxmen stayed with her.

Although Michael's casket would be closed, Maria brought with her his blue suit, white shirt, and blue-and-black-striped necktie along with shoes and proper undergarments. She also picked out a modest casket.

"When will my husband be arriving?" Maria asked as she choked up.

"Mr. Ioannis arrived an hour ago. He won't be available until tomorrow afternoon," said Mr. Pafedes, the funeral proprietor.

"I would like to see him, please."

"I'm sorry, Mrs. Ioannis. He's not ready for viewing."

"It's okay. I would still like to see him."

"I'm sorry, Mrs. Ioannis. He's not ready."

"He's my husband, and I demand you show him to me . . ."

"Mom," interrupted Nikos. "Believe me when I tell you, you don't want to see him the way he is."

"Don't tell me what I want and don't want to see. He's my husband. Do you hear me? He's my husband, and I demand to see him immediately."

Before Pafedes could open his mouth, Father Lou intervened.

"Maria," Father Lou said in a soft priestly tone, "Michael would not want you to see him looking the way he is. Please give Mr. Pafedes a little time to prepare him for viewing. When Michael is ready, Mr. Pafedes will give you a private viewing. But not now. Please trust me. I know what Michael would want."

"Please, Father, with all due respect, please don't tell me what Michael would or would not want. I'm not leaving until I see my husband."

Father Lou looked at Pafedes helplessly, looking for any way Maria would be able to get a glimpse of her husband. But Pafedes shook his head as an *absolutely not*.

"Mrs. Ioannis," interrupted Pafedes, "tomorrow afternoon I promise you can view your husband in private. But not today."

"I'm not leaving until I see my husband. I know I won't recognize him. I know that. But I don't care. He's my husband, and I'm not leaving until I see him."

Pafedes noticed Father Lou's stare as he gave him a nod.

"Okay, Mrs. Ioannis. I'm going to take you to see him. But please understand. He will be unrecognizable."

"Mr. Pafedes, my son told me what he saw. I know what to expect. We're both going together."

"May I come with you?" asked Father Lou.

"Only if you can lead us in prayer," Maria said with a faint smile.

"Of course."

Father Lou and Nikos both took Maria by the hand as they followed Pafedes into the cold room, where Michael lay under a blanket. When Pafedes pulled the blanket from Michael's face, she stared at him and smiled as tears rolled down her cheeks.

"I recognize him. It's my Michael."

Then she bent down and kissed his caved-in face. Maria knew she now had to remain strong, not only strong for Lilly but even stronger to keep Nikos under control. She knew he would want to take matters into his own hands, and with his Connecticut friends now living in the Bronx, she needed to focus on her living children.

Michael is in a better place, she thought.

* * *

Back at the Ioannises' house, Father Lou walked Maria and Nikos inside. He not only wanted to make sure they were all right for the evening but also wanted to see Lilly. He knew Lilly was a real *daddy's little girl.* He also needed to see what kind of frame of mind the Bronxmen were in.

As he entered the house, Lilly ran to Maria and hugged her tight. Maria let Lilly cry in her arms for a full minute and then broke the bond as she started to speak.

The guys all hugged Nikos one at a time and assured him they were there for anything and everything he or his family may need.

"Lilly, my dear Lilly, it's going to be all right," said Maria.

"Mom, how could it ever be all right? Daddy's dead. He's dead. It'll never be all right."

"Lilly, we need to get through these next two days. After the funeral, we will group together with Nikos and survive. After we get through these next few days, we will somehow get on with our lives. Not so much for me, but for you and Nikos. You both have your entire lives to live. I promise you, we'll get through this. We're Ioannises. And Ioannises are tough."

* * *

Meanwhile, Father Lou was in the basement, talking with all Six Bronxmen. He had made them promise to continue with their lives and not to take matters into their own hands.

"Don't worry, Father Lou," said Vinny. "We came here to make new lives for ourselves and be with our friend. We're going to continue looking for jobs and establish ourselves as New Yorkers. That is our sole intention."

Before Father Lou had a chance to respond, Irving spoke.

"Father Lou, this sort of thing doesn't happen around here much. It had to be a robbery and nothing like what you may think happened."

"And what do you think I think happened? Huh, Irving? Please educate me on what I think."

"I'm sorry, Father, I didn't mean it like that."

"Like what Irving? Huh, Irving? Like what? Let me tell you guys something. What's going on here stops now. Do you hear me? It stops now. Don't look at me like that, Lenny. I see the adrenaline rushing through your body. Don't even think about it. None of you better think about it. Let the police handle it. Now, Nikos, walk me out to my car. I want to talk to you in private."

Once outside, Father Lou, although knowing Nikos was hurting, needed to let him know he meant everything he had said in the basement.

"Father, I appreciate everything you're doing for me and my family. Believe me, I really do appreciate it. But I'm sure you're needed back at the church. We'll see you at the wake tomorrow."

Before Father Lou had a chance to speak, Nikos gave him a hug, kissed him on each cheek, and then turned and went back into the house.

The next day . . .

The Ioannises arrived at Pafedes Funeral Home at 1:30 p.m., thirty minutes before the official 2:00 p.m. viewing. When the Ioannises entered the funeral home, Father Lou was already inside. As always, they kissed Father Lou's hand and kissed him on his cheeks. Lilly was, without a doubt, the most visibly upset, although Maria and Nikos were a notch behind.

The other Bronxmen waited outside until the official 2:00 p.m. viewing. They wanted to give the family time alone for the initial shock.

Mr. Pafedes led the Ioannises and Father Lou into the viewing room and continued to the closed casket. The second Lilly saw the casket, she instantly started to cry as Maria and Nikos held her.

"Mrs. Ioannis," Pafedes whispered to Maria, "I can open the coffin for the family's private viewing before your friends and family get here. We did a good job with him."

"Yes, please. Let's get it over with before anyone shows up."

"Take your time. Do not worry about anyone showing up. Official viewing will not start until *you* are ready."

"Thank you, Mr. Pafedes. You're very kind."

Pafedes nodded as he approached the casket.

"Before you open the casket, do you want privacy? Would you like for me to leave?" asked Father Lou.

"Of course not," said Maria as Nikos remained silent and Lilly started to cry again.

Pafedes slowly opened the coffin. The second Lilly saw her father, she started to shake uncontrollably.

"Daddy! Daddy!" she cried. "Oh my God, Daddy!" She vomited on the lower unopened part of the casket.

Maria and Nikos could only hold back their own tears. Mr. Pafedes quickly ran to get someone to clean up the mess.

By 2:15 p.m., the casket was closed, and viewers were allowed to enter. Maria was surprised to see many friends from their old neighborhood in Glastonbury attend. As it turned out, the Bronxmen had contacted their families back home, and the word spread.

Outside, besides police officers, the press was taking pictures and talking to anyone who would talk to them. At one point, Richie and Vinny confronted the reporters and told them to leave before they got their asses kicked. Of course, it was all recorded on film. When Vinny tried to take the camera from the reporter, the police had him up against the wall within seconds.

"Get off me!" yelled Vinny.

"Calm down, kid. I know it's a funeral, but you *will* go the jail unless you calm down."

"All right, all right, I'm calm. But come on. Like you said, it's a funeral. These reporters are heartless."

"Yes, they are, kid. Yes, they are. But there still is freedom of the press. So if you know what's good for you, shut your mouth and go inside."

Vinny knew he had no choice: shut up or go to jail.

* * *

That evening, the Ioannises' house was full of supporters. The Bronxmen were in the basement trying to figure out who could have done this. Skelly was nowhere to be found. His mother was worried that something might have happened to him. The police even questioned Carmine, Fat Sal, and Capo, but they had no idea where Skelly was.

* * *

At the funeral the next day, Lilly could barely move. She was numb all over. At the church, when everyone went up to the closed casket to pay their final respects, Father Lou asked everyone to wait in their cars for the funeral precession. When the church was empty, Father Lou brought up Maria, Nikos, and Lilly, along with Michael's brother, Charlie, and his family. Father Lou then had the pallbearers open the casket and had Charlie and his family say their final goodbyes first. Then Maria and her children kissed Michael's hands, turned, and walked away, crying.

At Saint Raymond's Cemetery, the service went as well as could be expected. Maria asked for a minute to be alone with Michael.

As she kneeled next to the casket, she whispered, "Damn you. Damn you for bringing us here and leaving us," and then turned and walked away. When she approached the limousine, she froze in her tracks, turned, ran back to the coffin, cried hysterically on the coffin, and repeated, "I'm sorry. I'm sorry. It wasn't your fault. I'm so sorry, Michael. Please forgive me."

Nikos ran next to Maria and cried next to her, not knowing what Maria was talking about as Lilly sat in the limousine, numb. Nikos eventually led Maria back to the limousine as she continued crying.

From the cemetery, everyone left to go to Gus's Diner for a fish luncheon, as was tradition in the Orthodox religion. At the luncheon, there was always small talk about the deceased in a celebratory way into the kingdom of heaven. It was a way of softening the blow of the family never seeing their loved one here on earth again.

* * *

That evening at home, Nikos didn't want to see any of the Bronxmen. As angry as he was, he didn't want to leave his mother and sister home alone. He knew his father would have wanted him to stay close to them. Besides, although they had just buried his father hours ago, Nikos was concerned about the family's future.

"Mom," said Nikos as Maria sat holding Lilly's hand, "we need to talk about the future of our family."

"Yes, we do, son. Yes, we do."

"Are we going to be able to still live here? Did Daddy have life insurance? Is the house paid for?"

"Nikos, we have life insurance. Your father always wanted to provide for his family in case of an untimely death. Your father bought life insurance the day after we found out I was pregnant with you."

"Is it enough for you to survive?"

"It's enough for all of us to survive. There's enough money to put both you and Lilly through college, pay off this house, and pay off our share of the diner. So stop worrying about the money. Unfortunately, your father was worth more dead than alive. So stop worrying and get back to school because that's what your father would have wanted for both of you."

For the next week, Nikos worked at the diner, covering Michael's shift at night, while his uncle Charlie worked during the day. At closing time, the five Bronxmen waited for Nikos. Meanwhile, Skelly was nowhere to be found. His mother had even filed a missing persons report with the police.

Although Maria knew about the $500,000 life insurance policy, she forgot about the double indemnity. To her surprise, she received a check for $1,000,000. The money was enough to pay off Michael's share of the diner, the house, and the funeral expenses and for state colleges for both her children, with money left over, but deep down, Maria knew Nikos wasn't even going to finish high school.

* * *

Three weeks after Michael's death, Skelly's body was found floating in the Westchester Square Creek with Michael's wallet in his pocket. The autopsy showed Skelly had died around the same time as Michael. The cause of death was drowning. It raised many questions as to why Skelly would drown after murdering Michael. Needless to say, the case remained open for further investigation.

* * *

Six months after Michael's death, the Ioannises started to find some sort of routine in their lives. Lilly was doing extremely well in school and continued making friends. Carmine, Fat Sal, and Capo kept their distance from Lilly, Nikos, and Irving, not because they were afraid of them but because never in a million years did they think Skelly would end up dead. They all wanted to keep a low profile.

* * *

Seven months after Michael's death, Nikos decided to talk to Maria about the family's future. So one evening, as Maria was cleaning the kitchen, Nikos approached her.

"Mom, need any help?" he asked.

"No, thank you. I have it under control. You've been working extremely hard at the diner. But I could use some company."

"Sure, Mom," Nikos said as he sat at the kitchen table. "But, Mom, there is something I've been meaning to talk to you about."

"Sure, Nikos. What is it?"

"Mom, come join me. Sit down."

"Uh oh. This seems serious. Are you all right?"

"I'm fine, Mom. But I need to talk to you about something."

"Sure, Nikos. What is it?" Maria said as she sat across from him.

"Before Daddy . . ." Nikos said as he choked up.

"Nikos," interrupted Maria, "it's okay to cry. You barely cried at Daddy's funeral. Let it out. You need to let it out."

Maria then stood, sat next to Nikos, held him tight, and whispered, "Go ahead, my son. Let it out."

Seconds later, Nikos cried in his mother's arms like a five-year-old. He cried for a full minute.

"Isn't that better, my son?"

"I'm sorry, Mom, but I need to be strong for you. I need to be strong for both you *and* Lilly."

"You are strong. Crying doesn't make you weak. That's a guy thing," Maria said with a faint smile.

"Okay, Mom, you did it. You made me cry. And believe me when I tell you, although I'm embarrassed, I'm also grateful because I actually feel better. Now please go sit where you were sitting. I need to look at you when I talk."

"Okay, my son," Maria said as she kissed him and stood. "Start talking."

"Mom, did Dad say anything to you about my plans of expansion?"

Maria sat looking at Nikos, thinking of how to respond. She knew exactly what Nikos was talking about.

"Yes, he did."

"What do you think about it?"

"Nikos, I really haven't thought about it lately. But when your father first mentioned it to me, I was totally against it—"

"Why, Mom?" Nikos interrupted.

"Because at the time, I was hoping you would finish high school and go on to college."

"And now?"

"Now? I would still love to see you finish high school and go to college. And that's what your father would have wanted for you too."

"Mom, Daddy's dead. Uncle Charlie will be dead soon too. If I left the diner, what would *you* do? Work it alone? I don't think so. You're going to need help."

Maria sat looking at Nikos, unable to answer him. How could she? She didn't have an answer. If it wasn't for Nikos, she didn't know what she would do.

"So, Mom, speak to me. What do you think?"

"Well, you know how I feel. But I must tell you. Your father not only loved the idea but was also one hundred times prouder of *you* than the idea. But I'm a little scared."

"Scared of what, Mom?"

"Nikos, what if it doesn't work? What would we do? First of all, we would need to buy out Uncle Charlie. That will cost $200,000. Then there's the renovation of the pizza shop to incorporate it into the storeroom of the diner. Your father said that would cost another $100,000. That wouldn't leave me with much, let alone be enough for Lilly's college. Besides, we're not even sure if Mr. Goldstein is even willing to not renew the pizza shop's lease."

"Mom, Irving and I sat with Mr. Goldstein today. He's okay with it. The only problem is he wants $25,000 in cash to do the deal. Mom, look at me. Look at me, I said."

Maria stared at Nikos a few seconds and said, "Nikos, if we do this, I can't do it without you. Do you hear me? I can't do it without you. Once it's done, it's done. There's no turning back. I can't do it alone. I not only need your full commitment. I also need your word you won't get into any trouble."

"Mom, I promise. Irving will do all the accounting stuff cheap, and what he can't do, he will get us a discount at the accounting firm he works at. My friends said they would work for me cheap."

"Hold it right there, Nikos. I don't want your friends working there."

"Mom, don't you trust them? I trust them with my life."

"Nikos, I also trust them with your life. But I don't trust their maturity, nor do I trust their responsibility. Besides, if we're going to take over the pizza place, we're going to need experienced pizza makers. Your newly acclaimed Bronxmen have no restaurant experience. As a matter of fact, they don't have any working experience at all. But I do trust them. So if you think it could be done, then let's do it. But I have two conditions."

"And your two conditions are?"

"One, you realize if it doesn't work, we will be completely wiped out. Do you hear me? Completely wiped out.

"Two, you become my equal partner."

"Done."

42

By the anniversary of Michael's death, the Ioannises owned Square Pizza next to the diner. They ran it as two completely different businesses. Uncle Charlie was bought out at $225,000, $25,000 more than his initial half of his share of the original purchase price. Mr. Goldstein gave the Ioannises a ten-year lease.

Nikos opened every morning and stayed until 8:00 p.m. Maria worked part time, generally between 11:00 a.m. and 2:00 p.m. She wanted to be home when Lilly got home from school. The other five Bronxmen took turns locking up the pizza shop and the diner. Besides, sometimes, during closing time, it got a little rough, and both places needed someone who could handle themselves. Although Irving wasn't afraid, he wasn't much of a physical threat. He just couldn't back it up. So he worked the cash register.

Within the next three years, Nikos's businesses grew tremendously.

Two years after that, Nikos purchased three buildings on the same block that were fully rented to a card store, a variety store, and an auto parts store. Each building also had two apartments upstairs.

Goldstein knew business was good for both the pizza place and the diner.

Knowing Square Pizza had been a tenant of Goldstein's for over twenty years, Nikos wanted to protect himself from a greedy landlord. After all, Goldstein showed no loyalty to Square Pizza by dropping them like a hot potato to get a better deal from Nikos. Nikos knew when his leases were up, Goldstein would practically make his restaurants pay a ransom. He needed to protect himself from him. He needed an ace up his sleeve, and that ace was being able to tell Goldstein to shove his buildings' leases up his ass and move into one of his own buildings.

Meanwhile, by now, Irving had a bachelor's degree in accounting and had his own accounting firm upstairs from the pizza shop. His accounting business was growing rapidly. It was Irving who had suggested expanding to Nikos. He explained to Nikos that the restaurants were making too much money without enough tax deductions.

Everything in the Ioannis family was going along great, except, of course, they would give it all up to have Michael back. Nikos knew the family needed to survive, and Michael's life insurance gave them the opportunity not only to survive but also to flourish.

By the eighth year, Goldstein approached Nikos about renewing his leases on the diner and pizza shop. Nikos agreed to meet him the following week in Irving's office.

* * *

One week later in Irving's office . . .

"Mr. Goldstein, please come in," said Irving.

"Come on, Irving, how many times have I told you? Call me Stu," Goldstein said, looking around at Irving's office.

Irving stood from behind his desk and walked to Goldstein and extended his hand. After both men shook hands, Irving motioned to Goldstein toward the conference room.

Irving's office was actually a three-bedroom apartment which he converted into office space for himself. It consisted of the smallest bedroom, which he kept for himself as an office, with a small adjoining office for a part-time secretary, along with a small staff for tax season. The original master bedroom was converted into a conference room. The living room was converted into a waiting area, with shelves of tax books that Irving had purchased online strictly for decoration. All he really needed were his tax programs, but the books made the office look professional.

"Of course, Stu. I'm sorry. How are you doing today, Stu?"

"I'm doing great. How about you? You doing all right?"

"I'm perfect now that tax season is over."

"Glad to hear it. Where are the Ioannises?"

"They're not here. Maria has a church meeting, and Nikos is either at the diner or at the pizza shop. That guy runs back and forth from those two places."

"I can imagine how busy he is. He's all over the place between his restaurants and his three buildings."

Irving smiled, knowing Goldstein thought he didn't know about him knowing about Nikos purchasing the three buildings on the same block.

"Well, to tell you the truth, Stu, the three buildings are on autopilot."

"I see. Anyway, I take it you're handling all of Nikos's business affairs."

"Not really. But it's safe to say most of them."

"But it looks like you're handling the leases for the diner and pizza shop."

"Yes, definitely."

"Good, so let's get down to business."

"Absolutely. Time is money."

"Yes, it is."

The sarcasm went back and forth a few more times as they both smiled, thinking they had the upper hand.

"All right," said Irving as they both sat. "I'm looking at it like this. Nikos has two years left on this leases. So starting to negotiate now is a little premature, but Nikos would love nothing better than to secure his restaurant's future. So when Nikos called and asked me what would be in his best interest, I told him I would try to secure a fair price starting now for the next ten years."

Goldstein smiled, knowing Nikos wanted to continue being his tenant.

"That sounds great on my end too," said Goldstein. "Now all we have to do is come to a mutual agreement."

"No, no, no. We already have a mutual agreement. We will just extend the leases for ten more years."

"With no price increase?" Goldstein smiled.

"Correct."

"You know I can't do that."

"I think you can."

"I said I can't do that."

"Oh well, we'll talk in two years when the leases expire."

Goldstein knew Nikos needed him but had the option of throwing out two of his tenants and reopening his restaurants in two of his three buildings on the same block, but Goldstein also knew the move would cost Nikos several hundreds of thousands of dollars.

"All right, we'll talk whenever. But keep in mind. I'm keeping all my options open."

"As you should, Stu. As you should. But if I may, can I give you another option?"

"There are no other options."

"Sure, there are."

"Such as?"

"You sell. Sell Nikos the buildings and do what our ancestors did and continue doing."

"And what did our ancestors do and still do?" Goldstein smiled.

"Live happily ever after in Boca."

"Boca?"

"Yeah, Boca Raton, Florida."

"So Nikos wants to buy my two buildings?"

"Maybe."

"Well, he can't afford them."

"Think of a price."

"I don't have to think. I know what they're worth, and I know what I would and would not accept. But since you've been thinking about this, why don't you humor me and make me an offer?"

"All right. Nikos is willing to pay you $1,000,000 for both buildings."

"Hold on a second. Let me think about this for a minute. Nikos pays me $15,000 a month for both places. You are willing to continue paying that same amount for the next twelve years. Let's check the numbers—$15,000 multiplied by twelve months is $180,000 a year. Now we multiple that by twelve years, and that comes to—"

"$2,160,000.00," interrupted Irving.

"Have a nice day, Irving."

"Hold on a second. Just hear me out. If Nikos moves in two years, you're going to lose a lot of money."

"How so?"

"Because when he moves, you're going to have two empty stores for several months before you start collecting rent—"

"Stop right there. You want the buildings? You're going to pay. Or I'll collect rent from someone else. I know I can get a lot more than what I'm getting now. So go tell your client to expect a letter from my attorney informing him when his leases expire, they will not be renewed."

Goldstein then turned and walked out the door.

43

Two months after negations had failed with Goldstein, as Nikos parked his car at the back door on Blondell Avenue like he always did, he was approached by Caramooso. Moose stood waiting at the back door for Nikos for only a few minutes. He knew Nikos's schedule.

As Nikos exited his car, he sized up the large man, ready for a physical altercation. One on one, Nikos had never lost a fight, but Moose looked like he could be a problem.

"Can I help you?" Nikos asked cautiously.

"Yeah. I want some breakfast."

Nikos looked at his watch and motioned toward it.

"We're not open for business till six. You're going to have to come back in half an hour. And when you do come back, please use the front door. This back entrance is for deliveries—"

"And opening and closing," interrupted Moose.

"Yes, and for opening and closing."

"Well, how about a quick cup a coffee?"

"I'll be happy to serve you coffee in thirty minutes when we open. Now if you would excuse me, I need to get inside."

Moose stood in front of the door, waiting to see Nikos's reaction.

"Is this how you wanna go?" asked Nikos as he took a step toward Moose. "We can go this way if you want. It's up to you."

"No, man, I don't wanna go there," Moose said, stepping aside. "Go inside. I'll go up front and wait for you to open."

Nikos cautiously watched Moose walk to Westchester Avenue and turn right. Then Nikos went back to his car, grabbed a baseball bat that he kept on the passenger seat, unlocked the back door, and stepped inside.

By 5:50 a.m., Jackie used her key and opened the front door.

"Good morning, Nikos," she said as she always did. "Doing all right this morning?"

Nikos didn't answer as he usually did with his usual "Fine, thank you. Yourself?" He answered a different way.

"Jackie," he said. "Get in here quick."

"Why? What happened?"

"Just get in here."

As Jackie walked into the diner, Nikos quickly walked to the door and locked it.

"Nikos, what's going on?"

"Nothing to worry yourself about. Did you see anyone out there when you came in?"

"No. Why?"

"There was some guy waiting for me out back when I pulled up at five thirty. It looked like he was testing me."

"Testing you for what?"

"Testing to see if I was afraid of him."

"What did he look like?"

"He was a big guy. Bigger than me. He looked like he was in his forties."

"Did you call the police?"

"No."

"Why not?"

"Because I didn't think it was necessary. That's why."

"Nikos," Jackie said, raising her voice, "did you forget what happened to your father—"

"Jackie!" snapped Nikos. "Not a second goes by every day that I don't think about my father and what happened to him . . ."

"I'm sorry, Nikos," Jackie said, starting to cry. "But you need to be cautious. What the hell was that guy doing outside waiting for you at five thirty in the morning?"

"I'm sorry I raised my voice at you, Jackie."

"It's okay. I didn't mean to bring your father into it."

"No, Jackie, I'm glad you brought my father into it. It shows you care. It shows you still think of him."

"Of course, I still think of him. Just because he wasn't my father doesn't mean I wasn't devastated."

"I know, Jackie. Again, I'm sorry."

"Forget it."

"Okay then. It's six o'clock. Let's open."

* * *

Moose never returned when Nikos opened, which left him puzzled. At 10:45 a.m., Maria entered the diner as she usually did. She said her brief hellos to Nikos and the rest of the staff, along with several customers. Then she took her place behind the register.

Nikos usually ran from the pizza shop to the diner during lunch but spent most of his time at the pizza shop. The Lehman High School students generally went there instead of the diner, and with only a forty-five-minute lunch period, the pizza shop needed him to help move things along. Besides, sometimes the kids got a little out of hand, and Nikos was needed there, although it never got bad enough for Nikos to get physical. His size alone kept everyone in check.

But on this day, Nikos didn't leave the diner. He was still thinking about the large man waiting for him that morning, and with his mother in the diner, he wouldn't dare leave.

"Nikos," said Maria, "how come you're not next door? I'm sure the pizza shop needs you now."

"Nah, they can handle it."

"Nikos, what's wrong? You're spending too much time next to me. Is something wrong, or are you afraid I'm going to skim from the register?" Maria smiled.

"No, Mom, nothing's wrong. I figure they can handle it alone."

"Nikos, what's wrong?" Maria asked again, this time with a more concerned voice.

"Nothing, Mom. I'm going next door now," Nikos said as he left.

* * *

When Maria left at 2:30 p.m., Nikos called the Bronxmen and asked if they could come by the diner for dinner and a meeting. That particular night, Vinny was working the pizza shop, and Richie was working the diner, with Irving at the cash register.

"What's going on?" asked Lenny as they all sat at the back of the pizza shop.

"Yeah, man," chimed in Gary. "I sensed something in your voice. Is everything all right?"

"Yes, guys, everything's fine. I think."

"What does 'I think' mean?" asked Richie.

"All right, guys. Listen up, and don't interrupt." Nikos spent the next few minutes explaining his incident that morning as he attempted to open. He left out no details as the five Bronxmen watched him.

"Nikos, any idea who this guy could be?" Irving asked.

"No idea."

"And you're saying this guy was bigger than you?"

"Yup."

"Okay then," said Lenny. "Tomorrow morning I'm opening the diner with you."

"That's not necessary," said Nikos. "I just wanted to let you guys know what happened."

"Nikos," said Irving, "I wish you took a picture of him."

"You know what, Irving? That would have been a good idea. I wish I'd thought of it."

"Don't worry," said Vinny. "When we lock the diner and pizza shop, we always leave through the back together. I think you need to open the diner through the front door from now on. Just park your car up front, and when Jackie comes in at six or wait till seven, move your car to the back. Or better yet, just leave your car up front and run out every two hours and feed the meter. Did you forget what happened to your father?"

Nikos was careful not to snap at Vinny like he had with Jackie earlier. He knew what Vinny meant.

"No way, guys," said Nikos. "No one is going to scare me into changing my routine."

For the next several months, everything went according to plan with what Nikos had discussed with Maria about the expansion of the Ioannises' businesses.

Nikos was now thirty years old and met with Irving daily, who was now a certified public accountant. Not only did Nikos trust Irving with the family's businesses money, but also, Irving managed the Ioannises' personal investments.

As far as the other Bronxmen were concerned, Irving formed a corporation called the Six Bronxmen. In the Six Bronxmen Corporation, Irving asked everyone to invest an equal amount of money monthly. During tax season, Richie and Gary worked part time in Irving's office, making copies and collating tax returns. They ran errands, going to local customers, picking up work, running to the post office, and anything else Irving needed. They were fast learners.

* * *

Nikos paid his friends well, maybe too well, but he didn't care because he was making money and his friends were extremely loyal to him.

Irving first started investing the Bronxmen's money in mutual funds. After the first year, they bought a small six-family building on Williamsbridge Road close to Nikos's restaurants. Vinny wanted to move in, but Irving suggested they continue renting the house on

Quincy Avenue. Within six months, Irving suggested they use some of the rent money from the six-family building to purchase the Quincy Avenue house. Things were moving along nicely.

Meanwhile, Lilly was engaged to a doctor she had met in nursing school. Lilly and Dr. Dennis Lichas were getting married within the next six months.

Maria, at sixty years old, was the most sought-after widow at the Zoodohos Peghe Greek Orthodox church. Being a former Miss Connecticut, she still possessed every bit of her beauty. She started dating five years after Michael's death but could never take any relationship past a third date. Although lonely, she would always bury herself in the restaurant work. She needed to work to keep busy. Besides, Nikos always kept her abreast in the businesses since she was his equal partner. Nikos had even encouraged her to meet with himself and Irving at least every quarter to keep her totally informed on the businesses.

Maria also kept busy at Zoodohos Peghe's women's charity ministry, called Philoptochos. Besides her children and the family businesses, the Orthodox church had kept her busy. For most Greeks and Cypriots, the church had always been the focal point in their lives.

One Sunday evening Lilly was out with her fiancé, Dennis. Nikos was sitting, chatting at the kitchen table with Maria about the probability of having to move the pizza shop and diner into their other buildings because it didn't look like he would reach an agreement with Goldstein. As they were chatting, Maria's cell phone rang next to her.

By the third ring, Nikos asked, "Mom, aren't you going to answer it?"

"No."

After a few seconds, it beeped, and Nikos saw it light up: "Missed Call — John Pappas."

"Mom, it's John Pappas. How come you didn't answer it?"

"Because I'm at a business meeting with my son. That's why."

"Come on, Mom, this isn't a business meeting. John has taken an interest in you. He's a really nice guy. You guys have been out a few times. Is there a problem?"

"Nikos, please stay out of this."

Nikos suddenly got defensive.

"Mom, did he hurt you in any way?"

"No, Nikos, he didn't hurt me. John is a gentleman, and you know it."

"So what's the problem?"

"Nikos," Maria said as she looked him in the eye, "if you think I'm going to discuss my love life or lack of it with you, you have another thing coming. John is a very nice man, and we are friends, and that is all there is to it. Understand?"

"Yes, Mom, I understand."

"Good."

"But, Mom—"

"'But, Mom' nothing. The subject is closed."

"Mom, Daddy's been dead for twelve years," Nikos said firmly. "Don't think I don't see what's going on—"

"Going on?" interrupted Maria. "Going on? What do you think is going on? There is nothing going on."

"That's my point—"

"Nikos, this conversation stops, and it stops now. Do you hear me? It stops now."

"No, Mom, it doesn't stop. We're going to talk about it."

"Talk about my love life? Huh, *my* love life?" she said, raising her voice. "What about yours? Huh? What about yours? You're thirty-one years old. Where's your girlfriend?"

"Mom, don't worry about me. Right now, I'm concentrating on the family business and trying to look out for you and Lilly."

"Bullshit."

"Mom." Nikos smiled. "Right now, I'm not interested in settling down. But if you really want to know, I'm getting more than I can handle."

"Thank you for too much information. I'm really not interested in how much you're getting."

Nikos sat staring at Maria for a few seconds as he watched tears dripping down her cheeks.

"Mom," he said in a soft loving tone, "what's wrong? Please tell me."

"There's nothing wrong," she said as she started to cry hysterically. "There's nothing wrong."

"Mom, talk to me. Please talk to me."

"Do you really want to know?"

"Yes, I do."

"Then I'm going to tell you. But you're not going to understand."

"Try me."

"I loved your father. I loved him more than life itself, along with you and Lilly. He is the only man I've ever loved and been with, and I miss him terribly . . ."

"I miss him too, Mom . . ." Nikos said as he started to cry.

"Let me finish. I loved him dearly. We had so many plans. Plans for you and Lilly and plans for ourselves. And what happened to those plans? They're out the window. I don't know if you know it or not, but I was very upset when I first learned we were moving to the Bronx . . ."

"Why, Mom?"

"Come on, Nikos. We had a lovely home in Glastonbury. We had four bedrooms, three bathrooms on three acres of land, and he moved me here. I never liked this house. But we needed to invest in the diner. Damn him. Damn him, Nikos, for bringing me here and leaving. We were supposed to be a team. Why did he have to leave me?"

Maria was now crying hysterically in Nikos's arms as he cried along with her. As they cried together, Maria's cell phone rang again as John Pappas's name lit up again.

"What the hell does he want? Why doesn't he leave me alone?"

"Mom, it's going to be all right. You know it wasn't Daddy's fault that he left. It wasn't his choice."

"I know, my son. I know. I know he was brutally murdered and his killer is still out there. I was hoping it was Skelly who killed him so I can somehow have some closure. But the police insisted it couldn't have been him."

"Mom, it wasn't him. The person who killed Daddy most probably killed Skelly because Skelly knew who killed Daddy."

"I know, Nikos. I've read the police report over and over, and I tend to believe it. But try to understand. Your father was not only a wonderful man. He was a wonderful husband—"

"And father," interrupted Nikos.

"Yes, and father. I know he didn't leave me by *leaving me*. I know it wasn't his choice. He died a painful death, and I wouldn't wish that on anyone, not even on the person who did that to him. How can I ever move on? How can I ever be happy with another man, knowing how your father died? If he left me for another woman, I might be able to move on. But even on a simple date, I feel guilty. I feel like I'm having an affair. Let alone allowing another man to touch me."

"Mom, you're not having an affair, and you know it. Daddy would want you to get on with your life. Mom, look at me. I said look at me," Nikos said, raising his voice slightly.

Embarrassed by mentioning a man touching her, Maria slowly looked Nikos in the eye.

"Mom, you are still young enough and pretty enough to not have to live the rest of your life alone. Mom, don't you think I struggle with Daddy's death? Don't you think a day doesn't go by with me feeling guilty that I didn't lock up that night? I'm constantly thinking to myself, 'If I locked up that night, Daddy would still be alive—'"

"You would be dead too, and Daddy would have killed himself with the guilt of moving us here," Maria interrupted.

"No, Mom, I might have been able to kick the guy's ass."

"You don't know that for sure."

"I guess we'll never know. But, Mom, Lilly's getting married soon. Let's concentrate on her wedding. And you give John a call back."

"I am so proud of you, Nikos. Since your father died, you have matured into the man that he was. You were thrown into the deep end of the pool and came out a lifeguard. I know he's looking down at you, as proud of you as I am."

Goldstein ended up selling the two buildings to Nikos. It did push Nikos's finances back somewhat but, at the same time, secured the Ioannises' future. Irving set up the Ioannises' corporation, with Maria and Lilly as equal partners, but Nikos was totally in charge. The Ioannises now owned the entire block. Nikos continued to pay rent, except this time, he paid his rent to a different corporation, a corporation he owned. Irving set it all up.

*   *   *

Lilly and Dennis's wedding finally came. It was at the luxurious Loizos on the sound, overlooking the Throgs Neck and Whitestone Bridges. Although it had been thirteen years since Michael's death, it was still an emotional day for everyone. Nikos, of course, walked Lilly up the aisle. Maria was as beautiful as the day she had been crowned Miss Connecticut. All the Bronxmen were there. They were all thirty-two years old and had steady girlfriends except for Nikos. Nikos had grown into a 6'-5" specimen of pure muscle and extremely handsome and would have had no problem getting a date—but not for Lilly's wedding. His date was his mother. He did not want to leave her side. No way was he going to let her feel alone.

As he walked Lilly up the aisle, he glanced over at Maria as she stood at the end of the first pew on the left-hand side, proudly watching them both. He watched his mother smile at him in a way of communicating to him to keep it all together for Lilly.

"Stay strong, my son, when you walk your sister up the aisle tomorrow," Maria had told him the night before. "You do not want to break down. It's your sister's day, and we want her to be happy. It's going to be hard enough for her to be walked up the aisle by someone other than her father, although she will be proud to have you do it."

When Nikos and Lilly reached the altar, he lifted her veil, kissed her on her cheeks, and shook hands with Dennis. Father Lou smiled at Nikos and then winked at him, insinuating, *Good job.*

The ceremony went well. Maria cried tears of joy when Father Lou had said, "Dennis, you may kiss your bride."

Maria took Nikos's arm and followed Lilly and Dennis down the aisle to line up for the congratulations.

As Nikos followed the newlyweds, from the corner of his eye, he thought he was dreaming. Suddenly, he thought he recognized the large man from more than ten years ago standing in the back of the church. The large man smiled and then turned and walked away. Nikos picked up the pace and almost ran into the back of the newlyweds.

When they reached the narthex, where the bride and groom, along with their parents, lined up to be congratulated, Nikos whispered to his mother, "Mom, I have to go to the bathroom. I'll be right back."

Before Maria could answer, Nikos quickly went into the church and motioned to the Bronxmen that he needed them. They all left their girlfriends, and as quick as cats, they followed Nikos out the side door.

"What's going on?" asked Vinny.

"Hey, guys," said Nikos, "remember about ten years ago, I told you about that big guy who waited for me at the diner at five thirty in the morning?"

"Yeah, I remember," said Gary.

"Well, I think I just saw him in the church."

"Are you sure?" asked Richie.

"I'm pretty sure it was him."

"Guys, look around," said Lenny. "You see anyone big around here?"

The Six Bronxmen scanned the area to no avail. No one saw anyone fitting that description.

Finally, Irving said, "Nikos, you better get back inside. We'll keep an eye out for anyone fitting that description."

"Thanks, guys," said Nikos. "Remember, the guy's about my size. You can't miss him."

"Don't worry, Nikos. Just go back with your family."

"Thanks."

When Nikos returned to the church, half the guests had already congratulated the newlyweds.

"Nikos," Maria whispered to him, "are you all right? Were you nervous? Does your stomach hurt? Is that why you had to go to the bathroom?"

"No, Mom. I'm fine."

"You went to go cry, didn't you? I'm so proud of you."

"Mom, I had to take a leak. That's all."

"Oh," Maria said, embarrassed.

* * *

At the reception hall, Maria had no idea about Nikos seeing the large man. The Bronxmen kept an eye out but never saw him.

The cocktail hour was all top-shelf liquor. The Ioannises' businesses had been thriving, as was the Bronxmen's diversified corporations. Irving had the wedding reception paid for by the restaurants' account to make the entire affair tax-deductible. When Nikos had first asked about the restaurant paying for the wedding, Irving explained that the diner and pizza shop were making too much money.

"Nikos," said Irving, "you need write-offs. If we can't find some expenses, then you're going to pay through the nose. This wedding is going down as customer appreciation."

The introductions were emotional. Of course, when Maria was introduced as the mother of the bride, she was escorted by Nikos. Although it was a joyous affair, there wasn't a dry eye in the house.

As expected, when the time came for the father–daughter dance, it was replaced with a brother–sister dance. Again, there wasn't a dry eye in the house.

* * *

That evening, Lilly and Dennis spent their honeymoon night at the five-star Andreadis Hotel in Manhattan. The next afternoon, they took a limousine to Kennedy International Airport and boarded a plane to Athens, Greece. From Greece, they boarded a cruise ship and toured the Greek islands, including Cyprus, the island where Michael's parents lived, but they had been unable to attend the wedding since their health was failing, being in their mid-nineties.

Lilly and Dennis spent five days with them in their small village of Vavla. For several hours during the day, Dennis and Lilly hired a stretch limousine and toured the beautiful island of Cyprus with Lilly's grandparents. They visited the ruins and monasteries that Cyprus was known for, including the world-famous Stavrovouni, the monastery that held claim to the actual cross Christ was crucified on.

Lilly made sure they returned to Vavla by no later than 3:00 p.m. so her grandparents could take their daily two-hour siesta. The first two evenings, they went to restaurants. The last two evenings, Lilly's grandparents insisted on cooking traditional village food.

"Dennis, my love," Lilly said on their last evening in Vavla, "thank you for adding Cyprus to our honeymoon. It meant the world to my grandparents."

"Look, Lilly, this is the island where your father's ancestors come from. When I first discovered your grandparents were unable to travel to America for our wedding, I knew we had to somehow come see them. After all, since Uncle Charlie died, their only two children are gone. All they have is their grandchildren."

"Dennis, I love you."

"And I love you too, my beautiful bride. But I also have a slight motive."

"A motive? What kind of motive?"

"If your father never moved to the Bronx, he would probably still be alive. But if that were the case, we might not have ever met. So the least I can do for him is to conceive his grandchild in the village where his parents are from."

That evening, they made love and again at 2:00 a.m. and then again at 11:00 a.m. before they headed to the airport.

46

Shortly after the wedding, life for the Ioannises was back to their routine. Nikos opened the diner in the morning, while Maria always showed up for lunch. With Lilly married, she usually worked through the dinner rush. The pizza shop was on autopilot. Every night one of the Bronxmen stuck around till closing. No way was anyone allowed to lock up alone since Michael's death.

Then it finally happened. One evening Nikos was on a date in the famous Arthur Avenue section of the Bronx, known for Italian restaurants, when he was suddenly startled. He couldn't believe his eyes. Sitting at an outside table with a much younger woman was the large man. Nikos recognized him immediately. There was no doubt about it. It was definitely him, but on this particular evening, he was out with Georgia. Georgia was a thirty-year-old woman Nikos had met at a church dance. He had known Georgia for a couple of years. They had started dating shortly after Lilly's wedding.

His instincts wanted for him to approach the large man.

It was one thing to show up at the diner at 5:30 a.m., but to show up at Lilly's wedding and actually come into the church—he wanted to just start pounding on him.

However, since he felt Georgia might be the one for him, he didn't want to scare her away with him fighting.

He took out his phone, which was on vibrate, and pretended it vibrated.

"Georgia, give me a second. This is the diner."

"Sure, Nikos. Take your time. I'll window-shop."

Georgia slowly walked down Arthur Avenue, looking at the many butcher shops and delicatessens as she checked out the hanging baby lambs, goats, and pigs, along with the various different Italian breads and sausages.

Meanwhile, Nikos sent a group text to the Bronxmen: "Hey, guys. I'm on Arthur Avenue with Georgia. You're not going to believe it, but that big guy that showed up at the church is sitting at a sidewalk café called Moretti's Italian Restaurant. I really don't want to approach him with Georgia with me. Is there any way one of you can get here? I don't want anyone to do anything, but I would love to have him followed."

Within seconds, Nikos received multiple responses. Everyone was either working or not around except for Gary. Gary had taken a job with the New York City Department of Sanitation and was not only off that evening but also at another restaurant on Arthur Avenue with his girlfriend, Lisa.

Gary texted Nikos. "Where are you?"

"I'm on Arthur Avenue."

"I know you are. I'm on Arthur Avenue too."

"Where?"

"I'm at Salvatore's."

Within a minute, after excusing himself from Lisa, Gary walked the block and a half and approached Nikos. Within a few seconds, Georgia approached them.

"Hey, Gary. Where's Lisa?" she asked.

"Oh, she's in Salvatore's. I just came out here to see if the cannolis were ready for takeout at the sweet shop. I'm going back to her. Hey, why don't you guys join us for dinner? She's at the bar waiting for me. Georgia, why don't you go keep her company until we get there? Nikos and I will check on the cannolis."

"Sure, that sounds great," she said as she kissed Nikos and walked to Salvatore's.

Nikos and Gary waited for Georgia to walk away, and finally, Gary spoke.

"Nikos, where is this guy?"

"That's him over there." Nikos motioned toward him. "The guy in the blue shirt. You see him?"

"Yeah, you ain't kidding. He *is* big. But he looks like an older guy. What do you want to do?"

"There isn't anything we can do. We got the girls here. I don't want to start anything with the girls around. I mean, if we were close to home, maybe. But not here. Not now. This is a real guinea neighborhood, and I don't know anyone around here, and he looks too much at home to not know anyone. Why don't you do this? Go play the tourist thing. Make believe you're taking pictures and take a few of him. Once I have the pictures, maybe I'll ask some of the guineas at the diner if they know him."

"Good idea—but easy with the guinea stuff." Gary laughed.

* * *

The Arthur Avenue section of the Bronx, although only four square blocks, had, for the past twenty years, been statistically the safest section in America. It consisted of only Italians who had always been looked upon and feared as mob controlled. There hadn't been a crime reported in those four square blocks in twenty years.

* * *

Nikos waited for Gary to take the pictures just in case there was a problem. After a minute or so, Gary and Nikos walked back to Salvatore's and met up with Georgia and Lisa as they waited at the bar.

"How about these two?" joked Nikos as they approached the girls.

"Yeah, they're pretty hot," joked Gary.

"Oh," Lisa said to Georgia. "Look at these two guys. They think they can come over here and call us hot and we'll just melt. But to tell you the truth, I like those other two guys who tried to pick us up ten minutes ago."

"I totally agree," said Georgia.

"Very funny, girls," said Nikos. "Anyway, let's get a table. I'm starving."

The rest of the evening went without incidence. When they all left Salvatore's, Moose was gone. They went to their cars and left for home.

* * *

Georgia was falling in love with Nikos, and Nikos knew it. He also knew he was falling in love with her. At this point in his life, he still wasn't ready to get his own place. If he moved out, Maria would have to live alone, and he wasn't ready to do that.

Meanwhile, Georgia was a nurse at Jacobi Hospital in the Bronx. She made good money and had her own apartment on Pelham Parkway, two blocks from the hospital. Although Nikos had had his share of women, he wanted to take it easy with Georgia. Like Nikos, the family of Georgia's father was from Cyprus. Her mother's family was from the same island as Maria's family, the island of Crete.

Nikos parked his car in front of Georgia's apartment building and, as always, walked her to her door.

"Why don't you come in?" she asked him after he kissed her good night.

"Sure."

They had only been out together six times, and Nikos had never been inside her apartment for more than a few minutes. The bit of kissing and light petting was limited to his car, but tonight Nikos sensed it was going to get better.

"Come in," she said as they stepped inside the apartment. "Have a seat." She motioned toward the living room.

"Sure."

"Would you like a glass of wine?"

"Nah, I'm not in the mood for wine. You have any beer?"

"Sure, I have beer. Any particular kind?"

"Not really, anything in a bottle. If it's in a can, I taste the metal."

Georgia opened two bottles of beer, brought them into the living room, and handed one to Nikos.

"Cheers," she said as they touched bottles.

"Hey, this beer's good," Nikos said as he looked at the label. "I've never heard of it."

"My father buys it. It's from Cyprus."

"Really? We never drank Cypriot beer in my house."

"You're kidding. What kind of Cypriot was your father—" Georgia caught herself. "I'm sorry, Nikos. I didn't mean to bring up your father. I'm really sorry. I'm sure your dad was a wonderful Cypriot—"

"Georgia," Nikos interrupted with a sympathetic smile, "it's all right. I know you didn't mean anything by it. Keep in mind, my father never drank. That's why."

"I'm so sorry I even brought him up."

"Why would you be sorry? He's always on my mind and in my heart."

"I understand. I shouldn't have asked what kind of Cypriot he was."

"Come on, you were joking."

"Thank you for understand and not being upset."

Georgia put her beer on the coffee table and locked her lips onto his.

They kissed for thirty seconds, and then Nikos broke away only to put *his* beer on the coffee table. He then reattached his lips onto hers while cupping her breast.

They continued for a few seconds when Georgia broke away and said, "Your hand went right to my tit." She smiled.

"Yes, it did."

With her eyes fixed on his, she said, "I have two of them, you know."

Nikos, with his eyes still fixed on hers, put his other hand on her other breast.

"Is that better?" he asked.

"A little bit. But I'm sure you can do better."

Nikos took the hint.

"I'll try." He reattached his lips onto hers as he, this time, put his hand under her shirt.

"You're getting there," she whispered while still attached to his lips.

Within minutes, they were both naked, with their hands and mouths exploring all parts of each other's bodies.

As Nikos penetrated Georgia, they both had their eyes open as he slowly glided himself into her, with their passionate eyes fixed on each other.

They lay naked together on Georgia's bed for two hours as they continued to explore each other's bodies.

At 1:00 a.m., Nikos penetrated her again as she moaned her pleasures in his ear.

When finished, he whispered, "I hate to leave you, but I have to get going."

"Please stay. Please stay the night."

"I can't. I have to open the diner tomorrow. I need to get home. I have to be there at 5:30. I don't have a change of clothes. I promise I'll stay next time. This is not a 'one and done.' Okay?" he whispered as he kissed her.

"I know I'm not a 'one and done.' And I do understand you have to work tomorrow. I worry about you not getting enough sleep. You're going to be all right, aren't you?"

"Don't worry about me. I'm indestructible."

47

For the next couple of days, Nikos was showing the picture of Moose to some of the people he knew. He was a little concerned when customers told him to stay away from him. They all said he was bad news.

By coincidence, Irving called Lenny because one of the tenants was late on their rent in the Williamsbridge Road building. Lenny was still the muscle when they needed him. So one afternoon Lenny rang the bell at apartment 5 and waited. When the woman answered the door, Lenny explained who he was and told her if she didn't pay, she must vacate the apartment by the end of the week.

"Who's at the door?" he heard from the back of the apartment.

"It's some guy threatening me with eviction because the rent is past due."

"I'll be right there."

"You're in trouble now. My brother's gonna to kick your ass."

"Are you threatening me?" asked Lenny.

"Yes, she is," Lenny heard as her brother approached.

When her brother approached the door, Lenny smiled.

"What are you smiling at?" asked her brother.

"You want some more?" asked Lenny.

"Some more what?"

"Some more beating, Fat Sal."

Fat Sal froze as he recognized Lenny.

Lenny knew he had to take control by handling things the only way he knew how.

"Hand over the money, motherfucker. Do you hear me? Hand it over now."

"Fuck you."

"I guess you want some more. Well, here it is." Lenny stepped into the apartment and started pounding on Fat Sal.

Over the years, Fat Sal had gotten heavier and more out of shape. Lenny, on the other hand, was in the best shape of his life. It was no contest as Fat Sal's sister screamed.

"Shut up, bitch!" yelled Lenny.

When she saw how easily her brother went down, she decided to shut up.

Then Lenny had an idea. For some reason or another, he took out his cell phone and showed Fat Sal the picture of Moose that Gary took.

"You know this guy?"

Although dazed, Fat Sal recognized Moose but didn't say anything.

"I asked you a question, you fat fuck. Do you know this guy?"

"Fuck you."

Lenny sensed Fat Sal knew him, but even after hitting him a few more times, Fat Sal remained silent. When Lenny felt he wouldn't get any information from him, he turned toward his sister and said, "You got two days. Do you hear me? Two days. And your ass better be out of here."

48

Giovanni looked at his cell phone as it rang, "Moose, what's going on? Where are you?"

"I'm home. I need to talk to you about something. Where are you?"

"I'm home. My wife is visiting her mother in Florida for a few weeks. I figure with her away, I can hang around here without getting my balls broken."

"Can I come by?"

"Sure, come on over."

Fifteen minutes later, Moose rang the bell at Giovanni's waterfront mansion in the exclusive section of the Bronx called Country Club.

Giovanni's maid, Roberta, answered the door and greeted Moose.

"Mr. Giovanni is on the patio, having breakfast. Please follow me."

"It's okay, Roberta. I know the way."

"As you wish, Mr. Moose."

Roberta knew the only person Giovanni trusted was Moose. Otherwise, Roberta never would have let him walk through the house alone. Moose was actually one of the few people who knew about Giovanni having a sexual relationship with his black maid. Although Giovanni has been unfaithful to his wife many times with many different women, Roberta was someone special to him. Mrs. Giovanni knew about it, but like most women who were married to mob figures, she looked the other way.

"Moose, have a seat. Can I get you some breakfast?"

"No, thanks, but I'll have some coffee."

"Sure. Hey, Roberta, bring Moose some coffee!" yelled Giovanni.

Within a minute, Roberta was pouring Moose his coffee and took Giovanni's empty breakfast dish into the kitchen.

"What's going on, Moose?"

"I'm not exactly sure, but I think there might to be a problem."

"What do you need?"

"Need?" Moose smiled. "I don't need anything. I just want to inform you of what's going on."

"Go ahead."

"Well, you remember Michael Ioannis, don't you?"

"Of course."

"Well, as you know, his son has been building a real-estate empire."

"I know. But we discussed leaving his family alone. But I'm beginning to think it was a mistake."

"I know. But I've seen his widow around from time to time, and she's looking good. As you know, she's a former Miss Connecticut."

"Are you interested in her?" Giovanni interrupted.

"Yes and no. I'm thinking of doing something with her whether she wants to or not, if you get my drift."

"I get your drift."

"I've also seen her son, Nikos, around. As you know, years ago, I showed up at the diner early one morning and confronted him. I'm not sure I know why, but I don't like him. I feel he could be a problem if he discovered I killed his father. And you know how I feel about problems. You either fix them or eliminate them. And I always feel the only way to fix a problem is to eliminate it. So I showed up at his sister's wedding during the church ceremony just to fuck with—"

"What do you want to do?" interrupted Giovanni.

"I'm not sure. But listen to this. A couple of weeks ago, I was on Arthur Avenue, and someone must have taken a picture of me because—now listen to this. You remember Skelly's friend Fat Sal, don't you?"

"Of course, I remember him."

"Well, remember years ago, someone beat the shit out of him?"

"Ahhh . . . yeah. If I remember correctly, someone kicked his ass real bad on Waterbury Avenue. Why do you ask?"

"Well, the other day, he was visiting his sister on Williamsbridge Road when the guy who kicked his ass years ago on Waterbury Avenue knocked on the door, threatening his sister with eviction unless she paid her past-due rent. Meanwhile, Fat Sal was in the living room and overheard the commotion and went to investigate. The guy ended up kicking Fat Sal's ass again right there in front of his sister. Then he took out his cell phone and showed Fat Sal a picture of me sitting at a sidewalk café on Arthur Avenue with a lady friend of mine and asked him if he knew me."

"Moose, I don't like this. I don't like this at all. Is Fat Sal sure the guy who kicked his ass the other day is the same guy who kicked his ass years ago?"

"Without a doubt. The guy actually asked Fat Sal if he wanted *some more* before he beat the shit out of him again."

"Do you think there's any connection between Nikos and this guy who kicked Fat Sal's ass?"

"I'm not sure. But tomorrow I'm bringing Fat Sal to the diner and setting this straight. We'll be there when Nikos opens, and I'll get to the bottom of this. I don't care who I have to confront to find out who asked Fat Sal if he knew me. Can you believe someone actually had the balls to take a picture of me and is asking God-knows-how-many people if they know me? Believe me, Mr. Giovanni, they're going to find out who I am."

"Moose, not only do you have my complete support, but also, any resources I have are yours."

"Thank you, Mr. Giovanni. I'll let you know tomorrow how it goes."

"Good luck, Moose, and be careful."

Moose just smiled with confidence.

"Roberta!" yelled Giovanni.

"Yes, sir?" Roberta asked as she stepped onto the patio.

"Please see Moose out."

"Yes, sir."

Two minutes later, Roberta returned to the patio, stripped down to her bra and panties. As always, she had on an old-school milky-white cross-your-heart bra that shone against her beautiful black body and drove Giovanni crazy.

* * *

The next morning, at five thirty, as Nikos pulled up to the back entrance of the diner, Fat Sal was standing under the light, as clear as day. Nikos immediately recognized him. He knew Lenny had kicked his ass a few days ago and Irving had already started the eviction proceedings.

I guess he connected us, thought Nikos.

Nikos knew he had to take control. He slammed his car into park, exited the car, and ran ten feet to Fat Sal. Unknown to him, Moose was waiting behind the dumpster. Moose knew Nikos would approach Fat Sal—but not so quickly.

Nikos was quite fast for a man his size and got to Fat Sal within seconds. Nikos punched Fat Sal twice, which sent him against the diner's back door. As Fat Sal was about to fall forward, Nikos kneed him in the stomach and grabbed him and threw him toward the dumpster, where Moose was running toward them. Moose lost his chance to ambush Nikos; he was slightly stunned as he actually ran into Fat Sal but was still able to keep his balance as Fat Sal fell to the ground. Although Moose was in his fifties, he was still strong as an ox.

Nikos recognized Moose within seconds. *This is where my father was murdered, but not me, not today,* he thought.

Nikos charged at Moose, and they both went flying. He knew Fat Sal would be out of the picture by the way he had fallen to the ground. He needed to concentrate on Moose. So when Nikos landed on top of Moose, Nikos pounded on him. He didn't let up. As strong as Moose was, Nikos was years younger, but although Nikos was younger, Moose was still able to wrap his arms around Nikos and roll him over. Still, Nikos was a step ahead of Moose as he used his momentum and rolled over again and landed on top of Moose again, but this time, when he landed on top of Moose, he used an old wrestling move he had learned in gym class in Glastonbury and immediately spread his legs so he couldn't be rolled over again.

I'm not dying here like my father did, he thought again.

Within seconds, Moose was bleeding profusely. Nikos didn't stop pounding on Moose. He was afraid of dying. For some reason, he thought Moose was there to kill him exactly the way he had killed his father, but the difference was Nikos wasn't a killer. When Moose was lying there, unable to defend himself, Nikos got up and pounded on Fat Sal again.

"You piece of shit!" he yelled at Fat Sal. "You tried to set me up! I should kill you both!" He kicked Fat Sal one more time.

Within minutes, after Nikos had called 911, there were five police cars at the back entrance of the diner. Immediately after calling 911, Nikos sent a group text to the Bronxmen, asking their availability to work the diner in the morning.

As the ambulances took Moose and Fat Sal to the hospital, Nikos opened the diner and sat with the police as they took his statement.

The officers in charge decided not to press charges against Nikos because of the circumstances. They knew Nikos was there only to open the diner and the other two had to be there for the purpose of assaulting him.

Richie and Vinny ended up working at the diner through breakfast with Jackie. It took the two of them to do Nikos's job, but they both had to leave by 2:00 p.m. because they were rookies at the New York City Fire Department and were both working the four-to-midnight shift. Nikos didn't want to go to the hospital. He cleaned himself up and gave basic instructions to Richie and Vinny.

"Guys," said Nikos, "just do the best you can. Jose will be in at eight. When my mother shows up at eleven, don't tell her anything."

"Come on, Nikos," said Richie. "She's going to ask where you are. What should we tell her?"

"Just tell her you don't know."

"Nikos," said Vinny, "we can't lie to her. She'll know something's up. Besides, where *are* you going?"

"I'm going next door to Irving's and taking a nap. Those two knocked the shit out of me."

"We're all getting old, my friend," said Richie.

"Speak for yourself," said Vinny. "But, Nikos, getting back to your mother, what should we tell her when she gets here?"

"You won't have to lie to her. Just tell her I'm upstairs at Irving's, talking business. Hopefully, she'll believe you, and everything will be okay."

"So we still have to lie," said Richie.

"It won't be a lie. Irving will come in at nine, and I will discuss business with him for five minutes, and that'll be that."

* * *

Maria showed up at 10:30 a.m., confused when she saw Richie and Vinny behind the counter.

"Where's Nikos?" Maria asked Jackie.

Jackie pretended not to hear her. She quickly went into the kitchen to get an order. As she passed Richie, she whispered, "You better see Maria. She's asking questions."

"Hey, Vinny," said Maria. "What's going on? I come in here and see you and Richie, I asked Jackie where Nikos is, and she runs into the kitchen. What happened?"

"Nothing, Maria. Me and Richie came in for breakfast, and Nikos asked if we could cover for him because he needed to see Irving about some accounting stuff."

Vinny looked at Maria and read her mind. He knew she sensed something but couldn't put her finger on it.

"Nikos is next door in Irving's office?"

"Yes."

"Okay, thanks." Maria immediately left the diner, went next door, and climbed the stairs up from the pizza shop. She was met by Irving's receptionist, Bess, who was now Irving's girlfriend.

"Good morning, Mrs. Ioannis. How are you today?"

"I'm fine, Bess, but please call me Maria."

"Yes, Maria. You told me that last time. I'm sorry."

"It's okay, I know in your line of work, you need to be professional. But you and Irving are like family."

"Thank you, Mrs.—whoops, Maria."

Maria could only smile at Bess's mistake.

"Anyway, Bess, where's Nikos?"

"Oh, he's in the conference room, lying down. He's not feeling well."

Maria glanced toward Irving's empty office.

"Where's Irving?"

"Irving's not in yet. He's meeting with clients most of the day. I don't expect him in until after three. Is there anything I can help you with, or did you come up to check on Nikos?"

"A little bit of both."

Vinny, you lying piece of shit. Meeting with Irving. Meeting with Irving about accounting stuff, my ass, she thought.

"Never mind. I'll just check on Nikos."

"Sure, Maria. You've been to the conference room before. You know the way."

"Yes, Bess, thank you."

When Maria entered the conference room and saw Nikos sleeping in a chair, she couldn't believe the bruises on his face. The second she saw him, she started to cry as any mother would.

"Nikos, what happened?" she said as she continued crying.

Nikos was startled as he heard his mother's loud voice. For a split second, he thought he was being attacked again.

"Mom, you scared the shit outta me. You can't do that."

"Never mind what I can and can't do. You look like hell. Who beat you up?"

"Mom, there's an old saying. 'You should see the other guy.' But in this case—'You should see the other two guys.'"

"Two guys? Nikos, what happened?"

Nikos spent the next several minutes explaining to Maria what happened when he had shown up to open the diner that morning.

"Mom, they were waiting for me. I don't know why, but they waited and had a plan that backfired on them. But, Mom, I don't know why they did it. It wasn't a robbery. They wanted to hurt me," he said as he started to cry, but he wasn't crying because someone wanted to hurt him. He had had his share of fights. He was crying because he was thinking about the time years ago when Moose had stood at the same door, waiting for him exactly like Fat Sal had that morning. He was thinking he could have gotten killed at the exact spot his father had gotten killed—and possibly by the same person—but couldn't prove it.

"Nikos, who did this to you?"

"Mom, I don't know who they were. But I kicked their asses so bad, they couldn't get away. They ended up going to the hospital in handcuffs. I was supposed to go to the police station to press charges, but I fell asleep."

"Did they hit you in the head?"

"They hit me everywhere."

"Nikos, you could have gotten killed the same way your father did, possibly by the same people. This doesn't look like a coincidence. And don't you know when you hit your head, you should never fall asleep? You could have gone into a permanent coma."

"I know," whispered Nikos. "I know."

"How come *you* didn't go to the hospital and only the bad guys did?"

"I didn't think I needed to."

"Well, you're going, and you're going now. Bess!" yelled Maria, "Please call 911 immediately. Nikos is going to the hospital."

Within minutes, the police and ambulance arrived. The police knew about the morning incident. Maria asked the police to check which hospital Moose and Fat Sal were taken to.

"The men who were arrested this morning were taken to Jacobi Hospital—"

"Take my son to a different hospital," interrupted Maria. "He won't be safe there."

"Ma'am, your son will be safe there. The two men are under arrest and are handcuffed to their beds and have uniformed police officers with them. Jacobi is not only safe but also the best hospital in the Bronx."

"Mom," said Nikos, "let me go to Jacobi. Georgia works there, and I'm sure she can rush me in to see a doctor. Otherwise, I could be in another emergency room, waiting all night."

The next day, Moose was still handcuffed to his hospital bed with a uniformed police officer sitting next to him. The day before, Moose had called Giovanni and told him he was in the hospital but under arrest. He couldn't speak in private because the police were standing next to him.

"Moose, are you telling me you were admitted into the hospital?"

"Yes, Mr. Giovanni. I'm in the hospital, along with Fat Sal. I'm guessing he's under arrest too. At this time, that's all I can say. I cannot speak in private. I'm handcuffed to my bed with a cop next to me. I need a lawyer."

"I'll have Cohen there as soon as possible. Just don't talk to anyone."

"Don't worry, Mr. Giovanni. I know the drill."

* * *

"Is everything all right with Moose?" asked Roberta as she poured Giovanni a glass of wine in her uniform of bra and panties.

"Not really. I'm going to have to cancel our outing tomorrow. Moose is in trouble."

"Is there anything I can do?"

"Of course, there is. Now come over here and do it."

* * *

The next morning, Moose and Fat Sal were brought into court by private ambulance and taken into the courthouse in wheelchairs by private nurses. Although they didn't need to be in wheelchairs, Cohen felt it necessary to show the judge that they were falsely accused and actually victims of Nikos. Giovanni posted bail for both as his lawyer, Cohen, took care of the bail.

Afterward, the ambulances and nurses took Moose and Fat Sal to Giovanni's mansion, and Cohen took all their information.

"Just tell me exactly what happened, and I'll tweak the story," said Cohen.

Giovanni was shocked to hear Nikos had done so much damage to Moose. Fat Sal, he could understand, but to do that much damage to his personal bodyguard was a shock to him.

"Moose, how strong was this guy?"

"One on one, I could have taken him out. But he threw Fat Sal against me as I ran toward him, and this fat fuck was like a bowling ball."

"Why you blaming me?" snapped Fat Sal.

All Giovanni had to do was look at Fat Sal, and he shut his mouth and instantly apologized to them both.

"I'm sorry. It must be the morphine that's making me say stupid things."

Moose gave Fat Sal a slap in the face that sent him flying across the room.

"I said I was sorry. You didn't have to hit me."

Moose kicked Fat Sal in the stomach as he lay on the floor. Moose had never gotten his ass kicked in his life, not even when he had done his stretch of ten years in prison. He needed an excuse, and Fat Sal was it.

"Okay, guys," said Cohen. "That's enough. We have major problems here—"

"What kind of problems?" interrupted Giovanni.

"This is going to be impossible to defend—"

"Why?" interrupted Giovanni again.

"Please, Mr. Giovanni, let me finish." Before Giovanna could open his mouth, Cohen continued. "You two guys were on the diner's property. No one is going to believe you two were there at five thirty in the morning, minding your own business, and Nikos jumped you both. No one's going to believe that."

"But—" interrupted Giovanni.

"But nothing," snapped Cohen. "Yeah, I could say these guys were out for a morning stroll and Nikos jumped them for no reason at all, but who's going to believe it?"

"Then what do you suggest?" asked Giovanni.

"I suggest you find a way to get Nikos to drop the charges. That's your best bet. Otherwise, these two guys don't have a leg to stand. Sal, do you have a criminal record?"

"No, sir, I don't."

"Nothing? Nothing at all?"

"No, sir."

"Well, *you're* not going to jail. But Moose, I'm afraid, is a convicted felon. And once the district attorney opens his file, he's going to question why he's still not in jail—"

"He can't do that," interrupted Moose.

"Don't tell me what he can or cannot do. The district attorney can do anything he wants. They're going to throw the book at you, Moose, unless you can get the charges dropped. So, Mr. Giovanni, I need for you to take out your magic wand and get Nikos to drop the charges."

Nikos took three days off before returning to work. Georgia visited Nikos every day for several hours. Maria was happy to see Nikos finally having a steady girlfriend. She was afraid he would remain a playboy bachelor his entire life.

The Bronxmen took turns visiting and covering the diner.

Three weeks later, at two o'clock, as the lunch crowd was subsiding and everyone at the diner was finally able to take a breather before the dinner crowd started moving in, Maria was seated at a booth, going over some paperwork, when an elderly gentleman stood next to her and asked,

"Mrs. Ioannis?"

Maria looked at the stranger and replied, "Yes, sir. How can I help you?"

"May I sit?"

The gentleman looked innocent enough. Maria was used to people coming into the diner looking for a charity donation. Financially, the Ioannises were doing better than okay. They always knew one day, when they would be judged, God would ask them, "With all the treasures I've given you, how much of them did you share not with your family but with thy neighbor?"

So when business started growing, she asked Irving to create the Michael Ioannis Memorial Foundation.

Although Maria didn't recognize the gentleman, she would give his request to Irving, who was the controller of the family business and the foundation.

"I'm a little busy," she said. "But I can give you a minute. Please have a seat."

"Thank you, Mrs. Ioannis."

"Okay, what can I do for you, sir?"

"I need a favor," the man said, looking a little scary this time.

"Sir, I'm a little busy. What is it you're looking for?"

"I want you to convince Nikos to drop all charges against the two men he is falsely accusing."

"Excuse me, sir, but I think you should leave."

"I think you should think about it."

"I want you to leave before I call the police."

The gentleman stood and politely bowed his head and extended his hand to shake.

"I said get out of here before I call the police," Maria said as she pointed to the door, refusing to shake his hand.

The gentleman smiled and asked her again to have Nikos drop the charges, but this time, it sounded more like a warning instead of a suggestion. Then he turned and exited the diner.

As Maria sat with tears dripping down her cheeks, Irving walked into the diner with paperwork for Maria to sign for the Michael Ioannis Memorial Foundation.

"Maria, is everything all right?" Irving asked. "What's the matter?"

"Irving, where's Nikos?"

"He's out with the guys, looking at a foreclosure. Why? What happened?"

"Can we talk in your office?"

"Sure, let's go."

When they approached Irving's office, Bess greeted Maria courteously and professionally. Maria barely heard her.

"Come on, Maria, let's go into the conference room. Bess, anyone needs me, tell them I'm not in."

"Okay, Irving."

As Maria stepped into the conference room, Irving closed the door behind them. "Maria, please sit."

"Thank you, Irv . . ." Maria couldn't finish the sentence. She burst out hysterically crying.

"Maria, what's wrong?"

"Irving. A man came into the diner. A well-dressed man. He was well-mannered and everything."

"Maria," Irving said, confused, "what happened? Who was this man?"

"A man . . . He asked me . . . He . . . He asked me to tell Nikos to drop the charges on the men who . . . jumped him. He was nice but scary. He wants Nikos to drop the charges . . . Irving, I can't take it . . . I can't take it anymore . . . Damn him . . . Damn him for bringing us here and leaving us . . . Oh, Irving . . . I can't take it. I'm so afraid . . ."

Irving stood and sat next to Maria and held her.

"Maria, let it out. Just let it out. Cry. It's okay to cry. Just let it out."

Maria cried in Irving's arms for what felt like an eternity for both of them. Irving just held her until she was finished.

* * *

That evening, Maria explained the incident at the diner to Nikos. Nikos was furious. He couldn't believe Moose and Fat Sal would involve his mother.

"Mom, who was he? What did he look like? If you saw him again, would you recognize him?"

"Nikos, the scary thing is he looked and acted like a gentleman at first. But then he was creepy . . ."

"Did he threaten you in any way?" Nikos interrupted.

"No, Nikos. It was a suggestion. But when I asked him to leave, his suggestion sounded creepier and threatening."

"You didn't answer my question. What did he look like, and would you be able to recognize him if you saw him again?"

"He was a well-dressed man, about sixty, with white hair, about your father's height . . ." Maria then started to cry hysterically. "Nikos, I'm so afraid. I'm so afraid of what could happen."

"Mom," Nikos snapped as he interrupted her, "there is nothing to be afraid of. Do you hear me? Nothing—"

"Nothing?" Maria snapped, interrupting as she cried. "Did you say nothing—"

"Yes, I did," Nikos snapped back, not letting his mother finish her sentence.

"Well, let me tell you what nothing would mean to me. Nothing would mean you not ending up in the hospital like you did. That's nothing number one. Do you want to know what nothing number two is? Huh? Nothing number two? Do you want to know what nothing number two is?"

Nikos's eyes started to water. He knew what was coming.

"Well, I'm going to tell you whether you want to hear it or not."

"Don't say it, Mom. Please don't say it," whispered Nikos as he started to cry.

"Nothing number two is your father would still be alive! That's what nothing number two is, Nikos!" Maria was now hysterically crying. "Who's next, Nikos? You again? Me? Your sister? Huh? Can you answer me? Who's next? I want you to drop the charges. Tell them you can't remember if it was them or not. I want to sell everything and move out of this hellhole your father brought us to.

"Damn him! Damn him for bringing us here for this!" Maria was crying so hard, she started to hyperventilate. As she was trying to catch her breath, she wrapped her arms around Nikos and continued yelling but this time changing her tune. "I'm sorry, Michael. I'm so sorry. I know it wasn't your fault. Please, Michael, please forgive me."

"Mom, it's all right. It's okay to let out steam. You need to do it from time to time."

"Nikos, I'm not a good person. I'm not a good person, and you know it."

"Shhh, Mom. Shhh. You're a wonderful person."

"Nikos, your father died a painful death, and here I am, saying, 'Damn him.' What kind of person would damn her husband for being murdered in cold blood?"

"Mom, you miss him. You miss him, and you know it. If Daddy could get in touch with you, he would tell you to get on with your life, and you know it. Daddy loved you and was devoted to you, and you know it. He would not want you to be miserable. Please, Mom. Please try."

Meanwhile, Irving was taking the Bronxmen Corporation to new heights. They mortgaged the Williams Bridge Road building and bought two more six-family homes and were negotiating for a McDonald's in New Jersey. The Bronxmen were getting rich thanks to Irving's brilliance in investing. Although the restaurant business had started out as the core, Nikos, along with Irving's brains, had turned the restaurants into only a small part of his small fortune. Irving was careful not to put all of Nikos's money into the Bronxmen Corporation. Nikos wanted his family's money separate. It was working out fine.

As the months progressed, Lilly gave birth to a beautiful baby girl and named her Anastasia. She and Dennis bought a large English Tudor home along Pelham Parkway, just four blocks from Jacobi Hospital, where they both worked.

Lilly wanted to continue working, so she looked into day care at the hospital where she worked. When Maria discovered Lilly wanted to put her precious grandchild in day care, she decided to try her hand at interfering.

"Lilly," Maria said, "I know as a mother and mother-in-law, there is a line I shouldn't cross. But I'm sorry. I'm crossing it."

"What's the matter, Mom?"

"I do not want you putting Anastasia in day care. I'll babysit."

"Mom, I can't have you do that. You already raised your kids. It's not fair to you."

"Are you kidding? It's my pleasure. I feel like I'm born again. Please. It'll be my pleasure."

"But, Mom, what about the diner?"

"Don't worry about the diner. I'll still work the diner a few days a week. The babysitting will not be work for me. Please let me. I don't want strangers raising my granddaughter."

"Mom, I would love nothing better for Anastasia than to have you be part of her life, raising her. Thank you."

* * *

The well-dressed gentleman never returned to speak to Maria, although she constantly kept an eye out for him. Nikos also never dropped the charges. Giovanni, meanwhile, had Cohen postpone the hearings, but sooner or later, Moose knew he would have his day in court.

Meanwhile, the Bronxmen Corporation now included six buildings and two McDonald's restaurants in New Jersey. They were all millionaires.

* * *

Maria's life was starting to become fulfilled. Between the diner and Anastasia, she was constantly busy. Lilly worked three days a week, nursing, while alternating on weekdays and on weeknights. The family businesses were under control with Nikos. Nikos was now engaged to Georgia and planning their wedding.

Maria was finally getting over the guilt of moving on with her life and was now keeping steady company with John Pappas. Usually, once a week, John would go over to Maria's for dinner, where they would enjoy each other's company. John was an attorney and also a widower. The two of them had much in common. One of the rules Maria had was never to bring another man into the bedroom she had shared with Michael. It just wasn't happening.

Saturday nights, they would go out to dinner and always end up at John's house. Five years after John's wife had died, his children married and were out of the house, so he decided to sell the house and buy something smaller. Although he loved his wife, he felt it would be best to start a new life in a different house. John respected Maria's wishes about entering her bedroom, and Maria had even discussed selling her house when Nikos got married, but meanwhile, Maria was enjoying the intimacy with John. Like most women, the thought of being with another man after her husband's death had never crossed her mind. Life was finally good for Maria.

* * *

Everything was falling into place with the Ioannises and the Bronxmen until Maria went to her mailbox. When she came home from babysitting, she brought in the mail as she always did and put it on her dining room table. She continued her routine by turning on the news to see what was happening in the world. As she sat at her table, she started going through the mail. Everything was routine except for a larger-than-normal envelope. It was addressed to Maria Ioannis without a return address.

When she opened it, she started to scream, "Oh my God! Oh my God!" as she shook. She instantly called 911 and then Nikos.

Within minutes, the police were there. Nikos showed up a few minutes later.

When Nikos entered the house, he saw Maria sitting on the couch, crying as the two uniformed police officers were examining the contents of the envelope.

"Mom," said Nikos as he ran to her, "what happened? What did you get in the mail?"

"Nikos," said one of the police officers, "come over here a second. We need to show you the contents of the envelope."

Nikos knew most of the cops in the neighborhood from the diner and pizza shop.

"Sure, Patrick." Nikos approached the dining room table as Patrick showed him the contents.

"Oh my God," Nikos said as he sank onto the dining room chair. "Do you know who sent this stuff?"

"No, we don't," said Patrick. "But we'll do whatever it takes to find out. Nikos, can we take this this stuff with us?"

"Sure, Patrick. Let me just take another look at them."

Nikos slowly picked up the contents of the envelope and examined them closely. He couldn't believe it as he studied the photographs of Maria walking Anastasia in a baby carriage and read the note.

"We're watching you and your entire family. Drop the charges. By the way, the baby's cute."

The Island of Rhodes, Greece . . .

Nikos carried his bag through Diagoras International Airport toward the taxi stand and waited his turn.

"Next," the attendant said.

The driver exited the taxi and put Nikos's bag into the trunk and asked, "Where to, sir?"

"Lucky's Café, in Sianna, please."

"Yes, sir."

Nikos had never been to Rhodes before but had heard nothing but beautiful things about it. The driver drove through the winding hills, trying to make small talk.

"American, I presume?" the driver said in Greek.

"Yes, sir, I'm American."

"You speak Greek very well. What part of Greece is your family from?"

"My family's from Cyprus."

"Ahhh, Cyprus, a beautiful island. It's a shame the Turks invaded and still illegally occupies 38 percent of the island since 1974. Did you know there are still 1,587 men, women, and children still missing and unaccounted for? A real shame."

"Actually, sir, I've never been there. But I do know the history. Every Cypriot American is taught that, either by their parents or by their grandparents. I plan on staying in Rhodes for a day or so. Then I'm booking a flight to Cyprus. I have grandparents there."

"Good for you. I'm sure your grandparents will appreciate it."

Ninety-nine percent of all Greeks and Cypriots considered themselves one. Although separate countries, they shared the same language, religion, music, foods, and national anthem.

"Sir, do you have business in Sianna?"

Nikos knew the taxi driver wasn't trying to be nosy. All people on the Greek islands were always extremely friendly. The driver was just trying to be friendly with conversation.

"How much farther, sir?" Nikos asked.

"Just on the other side of the hill."

As they approached the village of Sianna, Nikos smiled. It was just as beautiful as it had been described.

"Well, sir, here it is—Lucky's Café."

* * *

Nikos stood outside Lucky's Café for a few seconds and entered. As he entered the café, it was exactly as he had imagined—seven or eight men sitting around, smoking while drinking Greek coffee and talking politics. When they noticed Nikos enter the café, they all stopped and stared at the handsome muscular stranger.

"Welcome to Lucky's Café," said one of the men as he lit a cigarette.

"Thank you, sir," replied Nikos as everyone continued to stare.

"Are you looking for anyone in particular?" another man chimed in as he sipped his coffee.

"Yes, sir. I'm looking for Tommy, Tommy Two-Fingers."

* * *

Tommy Two-Fingers and Nikos went way back to Glastonbury, Connecticut. Tommy got the nickname Two-Fingers because he was rumored to have shot several people. Tommy was advised to move to his native land of Rhodes the year before Nikos had moved to the Bronx. Although he was never convicted of any crime, Nikos knew Tommy's many secrets of being a young enforcer. One day, after Tommy finished a job that consisted of eliminating a man who had raped the young girl of a wealthy businessman from Hartford, Connecticut, Nikos served as a witness to Tommy's whereabouts. Nikos would have done anything for Tommy as Tommy would have done anything for Nikos, but when the grand jury did not indict Tommy based on Nikos's testimony, Nikos advised Tommy to move back to Rhodes before any other witnesses came forward. So Tommy moved back to Rhodes, but the name of Tommy Two-Fingers stayed with him.

* * *

"Holy shit," Nikos heard coming from the opposite end of the café. "I don't believe it. Nikos, Nikos, my friend. What are you doing here? Why didn't you call me? I would have met you at the airport."

Nikos could only smile as Tommy approached him and gave him a tight hug that lasted for a full fifteen seconds. When Tommy attempted to withdraw, Nikos could only hold him tighter. After a few more seconds, Nikos let go. Tommy stared at Nikos a few seconds as he noticed Nikos's eyes water. Tommy sensed something was wrong. He had never seen Nikos's eyes water.

"Nikos, my friend," Tommy said, breaking the ice, "when did you get in?"

"I landed about two hours ago and took a taxi straight here. Is there a hotel in this town or what?"

"Nothing doing. You're staying at my house. I can't wait for you to meet my family."

"You have a family? How long have you been married?"

"Five years now. Kathy and I have two beautiful children."

"Wow, congratulations! I'm so happy for you."

"What about you? Are you married with a family, or are you still playing around?"

"Come on, Tommy. I'm getting old. I'm not at your point yet, but I am engaged to a wonderful woman named Georgia."

"Georgia? Georgia from Sunday school?"

"Nooo, not her!"

"Nikos, it's been a long time."

"How long has—"

"Too long," Tommy interrupted. "Too long. Anyway, Nikos, how's the family? You're parents doing well, I hope? And Lilly? She had to have landed a guy. She was always beautiful."

"Tommy, we need to talk—"

"What's wrong, my friend?" Tommy interrupted as he noticed Nikos's eyes water again. "Let's go. Let's go to my house so we can talk."

"Tommy, I'm tired and hungry. I noticed a hotel at the beginning of the village. Can you drive me there? I want to get a bite to eat, and I need some sleep. We can talk tomorrow."

Tommy knew something was up with Nikos and didn't want to push it.

"Okay, Nikos. I'll take you to the hotel, and we'll get a bite to eat together. Then you can sleep through the night, and we'll talk in the morning."

"Thanks, Tommy. Thank you for understanding."

"I understand, but you're only spending one night in the hotel. Tomorrow night you're staying at my house."

"Maybe."

"No maybe."

* * *

Tommy drove Nikos to the hotel and parked up front.

"Some things never change," said Nikos.

"What do you mean?"

"What do I mean? Just look at where you parked. You parked in the no-parking zone."

Tommy could only laugh as he looked at Nikos.

"What's so funny?"

"Nikos, it says 'no parking' because I don't want anyone parking here. It's my hotel and restaurant."

"Holy shit, you've done well for yourself."

"Yes, I have. But we can talk business some other time. For now, let's eat."

Nikos let Tommy do all the talking as they ate. Tommy explained to Nikos how he had come back to Rhodes and started working at various different sites, painting buildings. Before he knew it, he was buying up most of his village.

"Tommy, is this a new hotel?"

"Yes, it is. It's only two years old, and I'm booked solid."

"Shit, man, where am I going to stay?"

"I have a private suite on the top floor I never rent. I keep it exclusively for friends and family. It's yours for tonight or for however long you keep refusing my hospitality," Tommy joked.

"Tommy, thank you. But right now, I need to get some sleep."

"Okay, my friend. We'll talk tomorrow."

* * *

Nikos watched Tommy leave the hotel as the manager escorted him to his suite. When they reached his suite, Nikos went into his pocket to tip the manager.

"No, sir. Mr. Tommy insisted your money is not welcome here. No charge for anything."

"You're not charging me, nor am I paying you. I'm tipping you. Do you hear me? I'm tipping you. Now please take the money."

"I'm sorry, Mr. Nikos, but Mr. Tommy said not to accept any money from you. Please do not insist. I cannot afford to lose my job."

"Okay for now. But believe me when I tell you, you're going to receive something from me before I leave."

"Mr. Nikos, is there anything else I can do for you?"

"Just the Wi-Fi password, please. That's all I need for now."

"Yes, sir."

As Nikos stepped inside his suite, he was immediately impressed. *Tommy Two-Fingers has done well for himself,* he thought.

Nikos immediately showered and sat at the desk that overlooked the valley straight to the mountains with his iPad. *What a beautiful view,* he thought as he started to tap away. Within seconds, he was Skyping with Maria.

"Mom, it's seven in the morning there, isn't it?"

"Yes, it is."

What time is it in Rhodes?"

"Midnight."

"How was your flight?"

"It was fine, Mom. Are you doing all right? Are you careful?"

"Careful? I feel like the president of the United States with your secret service here."

"Who's there now?"

"Everyone."

"Who's everyone?"

"Who's everyone? Let me see. Richie and Vinny are in the basement. Gary's with Lenny in the living room. Lilly has Anastasia in your room and John sleeping in Lilly's old room. I can't go anywhere without your secret service."

"Good. Anyway Mom, I'm fine but very tired. I'm going to bed now. I'll speak to you sometime tomorrow."

"Okay, Nikos. Take care of yourself, and don't make any commitments with Tommy."

"Good night, Mom. I love you. And be careful."

Nikos next Skyped with Georgia for thirty minutes. Georgia explained her plans for the week planning their wedding. Nikos was as excited as Georgia.

"Anyway, Nikos, tomorrow morning I'm going to see two houses. One in Country Club and the other in Scarsdale."

"Great. Now just sit there and let me look at you."

"Oh, really?" Georgia smiled. "Just sit here like this? Okay, I'm here. Do you like what you see?"

"Very much."

Georgia smiled and kissed her screen. Nikos immediately joined in.

"Ahhh man," said Georgia. "I smudged my screen. I need to clean it." Georgia then took her iPad and cleaned it with her breasts as Nikos sat smiling. After a minute of Georgia attaching and reattaching her breasts to her screen, she stopped and said, "There, that's better."

"Are you sure your screen is completely cleaned?"

"I'm sure."

"I don't know. I think you should give it the white glove test."

"White glove test? I don't have a white glove."

"Come on, beautiful. You have to have *something* white."

Georgia smiled and adjusted her iPad so it didn't show her face. She tilted the camera toward her breasts and removed her shirt.

"The only white I have is my bra. So I guess I'll have to *white-bra* the screen."

"That will do just fine."

Georgia put on a show for Nikos that drove him crazy. Finally, Georgia put her shirt back on and raised the camera toward her face again and said, "Good night, my love. I'm guessing you're going to take matters into your own hands."

"Good night, Georgia. Gotta go."

53

Nikos slept through the night without remembering if he had tossed or turned even once. He was tired, depressed, and worried for his loved ones back home, although he knew the Bronxmen had everything under control.

At 8:00 a.m., Tommy was already in his office at the hotel. Over the last several years, Tommy had accumulated several millions of dollars in his hotel businesses. Every morning he had breakfast at home with Kathy and his two beautiful children, but today he was worried about Nikos. He always knew Nikos was a strong person both physically and mentally. Physically, Nikos looked as he always had, but mentally, Nikos looked disturbed, and Tommy knew Nikos had come to Rhodes needing his help.

Tommy instructed his hotel staff to keep an eye on Nikos. "I want to know when he comes and goes."

At 9:00 a.m., Tommy phoned Nikos's room.

Nikos answered on the second ring.

"Hello."

"Good morning, Nikos. You going to sleep all day?"

"No, Tommy, I'm awake. This jet lag thing is making me feel a little tired. That's all."

"I hear you. Anyway, you coming down for breakfast?"

"I'll be down in five minutes."

"Great. You still like bacon and eggs?"

"Oh yeah."

"Then get your Cypriot ass down here."

"Five minutes."

* * *

Downstairs, Nikos and Tommy hugged each other like they had the day before. Finally, they sat in a private dining room.

"Demitri," Tommy said to the waiter after he had served them their breakfast, "close the dining room door and stand outside and make sure no one comes in. I don't want to be disturbed. If we need anything, I'll call your cell phone. Understand?"

"Yes, Mr. Tommy."

"Good. No one comes in here. If anyone asks, I'm in an important meeting and cannot be disturbed."

"Yes, Mr. Tommy."

* * *

"Okay, Nikos, start talking."

"Tommy, you're the only guy I know who might be able to help me."

"What's going on?"

Nikos started talking as Tommy absorbed everything like a computer.

He started with the move to the Bronx and about his first day of school. He went through everything, from befriending Irving to Gary, Richie, Vinny, and Lenny moving to the Bronx.

Tommy sat staring at Nikos as he explained his father's murder. He did speak briefly about his partnership with the Bronxmen just to let Tommy know he wasn't hurting for money. Tommy showed sympathy for Michael's death and the fight he had had with the large man when he was opening the diner early one morning. He showed extra concern when Nikos told him about the pictures Maria had received in the mail.

"Nikos, how can I help you?"

"Tommy, I know you know how to get inside organizations. Us Bronxmen, we're fighters. We can handle ourselves—except for Irving.

Although Irving has a pair of balls just like we do, he just can't back it up. But you, you've always been good at getting in and out quickly."

"Nikos, what exactly do you think is going on? Level with me."

"I think it could be organized crime. Deep down, I was hoping you could use some extra money and would help me. But from what I can see, money is something you don't need. But I'm afraid I'm asking you to risk everything."

"I don't understand. Risk what?"

"You have a family now. A successful business—"

"Hold it right there," interrupted Tommy. "I owe *you*. I owe *you* big time."

"Tommy, you don't owe me anything."

"I owe you my life, and you know it. If you didn't vouch for me, I would have gotten life without parole, and you know it. I owe you, and I owe you big time. Now I'm going to ask you—what do you need from me?"

"Tommy, I need to find out who killed my father. Because the guy who killed my father is probably connected to the person who sent my mother the pictures."

"Nikos, can you give me a week or so? I need to tie up some loose ends here before I come to America."

"Tommy, take your time. And again, I'm sorry. But you're the only one I can turn to right now."

"No problem, my friend."

* * *

Nikos wanted to get back home as soon as he could, but for Tommy, he stayed an additional two days and visited Kathy and their beautiful children. Two days later, Tommy drove Nikos to the airport, where he boarded a plane to Athens. After a two-hour layover, Nikos boarded a plane to Cyprus to visit his grandparents.

* * *

In Cyprus, Nikos's grandparents catered to him hand and foot and cried every day as he reminded them of Michael. Although Nikos was bigger than Michael, he resembled his father very much.

Nikos toured the small village of Vavla, which had a population of twenty-eight.

"This is where your father would have gone to school if we didn't move to America when he was three years old," said his grandfather, Nikos. Nikos was named after his grandfather.

"And this is our church, Saint George." His grandmother pointed. "As you can see, it's falling apart. It's so bad, we can't have church services on Sunday. The roof needs repair, and the village doesn't have enough money to pay a priest."

"Yiayia (Grandma)," said Nikos, "how much is needed to repair the roof?"

"The mayor said it would cost the village €50,000 to do all the repairs needed. But even if we raised the money, we still need €50 every Sunday to pay a priest. It's a lost cause. The government cannot subsidize the churches anymore."

Every village in Cyprus has always had their own church and was always fully subsidized by the government, but since the recent economic crisis, many villages were forced to close their churches. Vavla was one of them.

That afternoon, when Nikos's grandparents took their afternoon siesta, Nikos walked to the mayor's house. Although he was the mayor, his job consisted of virtually nothing. When Nikos knocked on the mayor's door, it took him several minutes to answer. After all, mayors needed siestas too.

Mayor Constantinou explained to Nikos in detail how the church was in desperate need of money.

When Nikos left Mayor Constantinou's house, he immediately took out his cell phone and called Irving.

"Nikos," said Irving, "how's it going? You're still leaving tomorrow?"

"Yes, I am. Is everything all right there? You still holding down the financial fort?"

"You know I am."

"Good. I need a favor."

"Sure."

"I'll put it all in an email, but I want to explain to you what I need."

"Go ahead."

"I need you to wire €50,000 to the Bank of Cyprus. The account number will be in the email—"

"Can I ask what for?" interrupted Irving.

"Sure. My grandparents' church needs repairs. So besides the €50,000, I'm also going to need €50 wired every week to pay a priest—"

"Nikos," Irving interrupted again, "it's going to cost $40 for the wire. I'll just wire a year's worth at once. But let me get this straight—€50,000 plus €2,600, correct?"

"Correct. Wait a minute. Wire €55,000. There are many holidays here in Cyprus that are celebrated. So €50,000 for the repairs and €5,000 for a year's worth of priests and some flowers for the holidays. After that, I need the €5,000 to be automatically sent every year for the next twenty years."

"Nikos, are you in your father's village?"

"Yes, I am."

"I take it you want the money wired from the Michael Ioannis Memorial Foundation and have the donation in your father's name?"

All Irving could hear was Nikos crying hysterically. After a full minute, Nikos finally answered.

"Sorry, Irving. It's a little emotional here. But yes, that's what I want."

"I'll take care of it tomorrow."

That evening, Nikos explained to his grandparents how he earmarked the money from the Michael Ioannis Memorial Foundation for the next twenty years to supply a priest and about having the money wired for all the necessary repairs for the church. It was an emotional evening as they all knew it might be the last time they would ever see one another.

54

Once Nikos returned home, he was back to his routine. Every morning he opened the diner but was never alone. One of the Bronxmen was always there. Maria continued to babysit Anastasia but was never alone either.

Two weeks later, Tommy came to America alone. He felt it would be better to leave Kathy and the children home. Nikos rented Tommy a fully loaded car, including GPS since he had never been to the Bronx, and put him up in one of the three-bedroom apartments with brand-new furniture. One of the spare bedrooms were for the children should he decide to send for his family, and the other was an office for Tommy to run his various businesses in Rhodes.

Once Tommy settled in, Nikos had a meeting in his mother's basement. He made sure it was a night that Maria was sleeping at Lilly's, although Nikos did tell her that Tommy was here in America on business.

"Just be careful, Nikos. Okay? Just be careful and stop trying to bullshit me."

"Mom, what are you talking about? I'm not trying to bullshit anyone."

"Yeah, okay, Nikos. You're not trying to bullshit anyone. Tommy Two-Fingers is really here on business."

* * *

That evening, Tommy got reacquainted with his friends from Glastonbury. They all sat together as though they were teenagers again. They laughed and reminisced their teenage years of drinking and getting into trouble. They talked for hours.

"Hey, Tommy Two-Fingers," said Vinny, "Nikos said you've done very well for yourself in Greece."

"Not bad. I've been working hard ever since I moved to Rhodes. Plus, I married a good girl who keeps me in line. I bet you thought that would never happen."

"No, I didn't. I don't think any of us did."

"Yeah, Tommy," said Lenny. "The way we were going, we should all be in jail or dead."

"That's enough," interrupted Nikos. "Let's focus on why Tommy's here."

"I agree," said Irving.

"Irving," said Tommy, "I'm glad these guys found you. Nikos tells me you're the finance guy. I could use a guy like you in Rhodes."

"Tommy, I'm not familiar with the tax laws in Greece, but if ever you need any advice, just ask. I can always read up on your tax laws."

"Irving, I just might take you up on that."

"Okay, guys," said Nikos. "Tommy has a plan."

"We're all ears," said Richie.

"Go ahead, Tommy," said Nikos.

"Okay, guys, listen up. Nikos filled me in on what's been happening around here, and I thought about it. I have the picture of Caramooso, and Irving already looked up his address. I'm going to follow him. If he is involved in some sort of organization, I need to know. But before anything, I need to distance myself from you guys. We know the Ioannises are being watched. Or at least *were* being watched. I cannot be seen with you guys. We'll communicate with our cell phones. I can't be seen anywhere near where you guys are—"

"But what's the plan?" interrupted Richie.

"Well, if possible, I would love to befriend Caramooso. And if we do become friends, then I can learn something about him. But first, I'm going to have to follow him."

"What are you going to do if you do become friends with him?" asked Irving.

"Look, we all know he's involved somehow with the pictures that were sent to Maria. Someone wants the charges dropped. If Caramooso acted alone, it'll be easy as pumpkin pie. But if he's involved in some organization, it's going to get risky. From what Nikos told me, he's our man. We already know he attacked Nikos. I need to find out who he works for—if there even is someone he works for. So, guys, this is it. If I'm going to do this, it has to be done my way."

"Tommy," said Nikos, "you have my complete support and resources. You do what you need to do."

"Okay, tomorrow morning I'm going to Caramooso's house and waiting for him to leave. I will follow him for a week."

"Won't he spot you?" asked Irving.

"No. If I do this, I'm going to do it right. I have disguises. I could be blond or brunette. I can dress like a business man or a bum. He'll never notice."

* * *

For the next few weeks, everyone's life was back to their routine, with extra focus on Maria. The Bronxmen always had her in their sights. For two weeks, Tommy watched Moose at different hours of the day. He first watched him every morning get into his car and drive to what looked like a waterfront mansion in Country Club four times that week. The other times, Tommy never saw him leave his house, but Tommy left Moose's block at 3:00 p.m. After all, he was human. He couldn't stay awake day and night, but in the evening, he went to Arthur Avenue and sat across the street from where Gary had taken his picture.

Finally, one evening Moose showed up with a beautiful young lady. Tommy sat across the street with a crew-cut wig as he watched them for an hour before they left.

Two nights later, Moose showed up again at the same restaurant, but this time, he was with several men who looked mob connected.

After a few more weeks, Tommy needed to alter his plan. Befriending Moose wasn't going to happen.

He called someone he knew years ago in Hartford, Connecticut, hoping he was still around. When he discovered his old friend was still in business, he smiled to himself and thought, *It's going to be all right.*

* * *

"Tommy, how's it going?" Nikos said as he answered his cell phone.

"It's going. That's all I can say for now."

"Good."

"I need to get away for a few days. I need for you guys to be careful. You're on your own."

"Tommy, what happened? Are Kathy and the kids all right?"

"They're fine. I'm going away for a few days. That's all."

"Where you going?"

"To the old neighborhood."

"Glastonbury?"

"Kind of. I'm going to Hartford."

"What's in Hartford?"

"Someone."

"Who?"

"Angelo."

"Angelo? Who's Angelo?"

"Garuccio."

"Angelo Garuccio? Holy shit. I completely forgot about him. What's the deal with him? I heard he was in jail."

"You heard correct. He *was* in jail. He's been out for a few years now, and I think he could help us."

"How could he help us? He's never been anything but a wannabe."

"True. He was always a wannabe. And what happens when you are a wannabe?"

"You become a *be*?"

"Exactly. Angelo Garuccio is very connected. In the old days, we would have referred to him as a made man."

"Holy shit. How do you know that?"

"Believe it or not, ten years ago, Garuccio had a problem with some Greek pedophile who ran away to Athens. Garuccio needed him taken care of, so he contacted me. Remember, ten years ago, I was still struggling, so when Garuccio called me, I needed the work." Tommy giggled. "And besides, I hate pedophiles. Nikos, if what we think is going on here with organized crime, Garuccio could help us."

"Hey, what did I tell you? You have my complete support. Just be careful."

"Thanks, pal. See you in a few days."

55

Hartford, Connecticut . . .

"Holy shit," said Angelo Garuccio. "Come on in here, Tommy—or do you still go by Tommy Two-Fingers?"

"Tommy's fine."

"Okay, Tommy it is. Tommy, it's so nice to see you. How long have you been in America?"

"A few weeks now."

"Are you back for good?"

"Nah, I'm here only for a couple of months. Kind of like business."

"Really? I had no idea you've had business ties here in the States."

"Well, not really. No businesses like that. It's more of the business of helping a friend."

"Well, I don't know what kind of help your friend needs, but I'll tell you one thing—your friend has a loyal friend in you. Anyway, I have a feeling this isn't much of a social call, is it?"

"You were always good at reading people."

"Tommy, I'm reading you right now, and I see some concern in your eyes. How can I help you?"

"Who said I needed any help?" Tommy smiled.

"Tommy, have a seat. You know I'm indebted to you. I'll never forget what you did for me with that Greek pedophile."

"I know, Angelo, I know. You know I would have done anything for you. I just wish I could have done what you really wanted me to do."

"What was that?" Garuccio asked, confused.

"You forgot? You wanted me to bring him back to America so you could handle it yourself."

"Oh yeah. I knew that was impossible. But you doing what you did was good enough."

"Angelo, I wish I could have refused to accept payment. But as you know, I was really struggling at that time. Remember, although I was acquitted, I had to leave America just in case."

"Tommy, I'll never forget what you did for me, and it was worth every penny. Do you need any money now?"

"No, no, no, I'm fine. Money, I have. But help, I do need."

"Talk to me, Tommy."

"All right, Angelo. Like I said, I need your help."

"Ask away."

"You remember Nikos? Nikos Ioannis."

"Yeah, how's he doing? I heard he moved to New York."

"He's doing fine and not so fine."

"What's going on?" Angelo asked, concerned.

"Well, it sounds like you have no idea what happened to his father."

"No, I don't."

"Okay, I'll try to give you the short version. His father lost his restaurant in Connecticut because of Eminent Domain. He ended up opening a diner in the Bronx with his brother. Nikos ran into some problems in high school and ended up kicking some ass."

"Nikos was a tough guy. I'm surprised anyone would fuck with him."

"Yeah, well, he was fucked with. But anyway, his father was murdered one night while locking up the diner. They never found the guy. Nikos thinks he knows who it might be but isn't sure.

"Now listen to this. Shortly after Nikos's father was murdered, as Nikos was opening the diner, a man named Anthony Caramooso stood at the back door where Nikos always opened. At the time, Nikos didn't know his name. Now nothing happened. This Caramooso guy was just sizing him up. After that, no one saw him again for a few years until the day of the wedding of Nikos's younger sister. You do remember Nikos's younger sister, Lilly, don't you?"

"Oh yeah. Good-looking girl, like her mother. But tell me about the murder."

"Angelo, the way Nikos described it, his face was totally destroyed. He died a painful death. They even had to have a closed casket."

"Holy shit."

"Anyway, several months ago, again, as Nikos was opening the diner, Caramooso and some guy who's nicknamed Fat Sal—who, by the way, was one of the guys who gave Nikos a problem on his first day in high school, whom Nikos beat the living shit out of—was standing at the door of the diner at five thirty in the morning. With Fat Sal distracting Nikos, Caramooso attacked Nikos. But Nikos was able to beat the shit out of both of them. Caramooso, as big as he is, ended up in the hospital and then got arrested."

"Nikos was always able to handle himself."

"To give you a little history, Caramooso did spend ten years in jail years ago for manslaughter after plea bargaining."

"I see."

"But the scary thing is this. After Caramooso was bailed out of jail, right after that, many pictures were taken of Nikos's mother and niece, Lilly's daughter. They were taken on many different occasions to show they were being watched. One day Nikos's mother opened a large envelope that was mailed to her with, of course, no return address that contained pictures of her and the baby with a note telling her to tell Nikos to drop the charges against Moose and Fat Sal.

"Ordinarily, as you remember, Nikos could handle himself. But this, as you can imagine, is scaring the shit out of him. He came to Greece to ask for my help. He knows he could trust me and my ability to get inside.

"So the first thing I did was check out Caramooso by following him. As it turns out, several mornings a week, the first place he goes is to some house that's in the name of Antonio Giovanni. I understand Giovanni is some small fry. Do you know him, and can you help me?"

"Tommy, this sounds like some serious shit. Where are you staying tonight?"

"I don't know. I was thinking of checking into a hotel in Glastonbury and checking out the old neighborhood. Why?"

"I think that's a good idea. Why don't you stick around a day or so and let me see what I can find out?"

"Angelo, I really appreciate anything you can do. Thank you again."

"No problem. I have your cell phone number. I'm sure by tomorrow, I'll have some sort of answer for you."

Angelo Garuccio watched Tommy leave and thought for a few minutes, thinking how he would handle this. Finally, he took out his phone and called.

After the second ring, there was an answer.

"Mr. Garuccio, how are you?"

"Giovanni, we have a problem."

56

Tommy stuck around Glastonbury for a day and a half, visiting some old friends. He was surprised how little the town had changed and how many of his old friends had never left their small town. Everyone was extremely friendly to him.

While having lunch in the Glastonbury Coffee Shop, Tommy's phone rang. It was Angelo Garuccio.

"Angelo," said Tommy, "thanks for getting back to me. Do you have any news?"

"As a matter of fact, I do."

"Great. Can you talk on the phone?"

"Tommy, you should know the answer to that."

"You're right. Do you want me to come to your office?"

"Can you?"

"I'll be there in forty-five minutes."

* * *

"Tommy, come in. Enjoying your old neighborhood, I hope."

"Somewhat. It does bring back some good memories. But I'm here to do a job for Nikos. Then I need to get back to my family."

"Well, if getting back to your family is what you really want to do, I have some good news for you."

"Great. Then you can help us."

"Well, not really."

"I'm not sure what you mean," Tommy said, confused.

"I don't know what the fuck you're not sure of," Garuccio said arrogantly.

"Angelo, what the fuck—"

"Don't 'what the fuck' me. You heard me. I can get you back to your family—"

"Angelo—"

"Don't interrupt me, you Greek fuck."

Tommy sat looking at Garuccio, confused. He knew something was up.

"I asked you a question, you Greek fuck. Now answer me."

"The fuck did you ask me?" Tommy yelled.

"Don't raise your voice at me! I asked you if you heard me."

"Angelo, what the fuck has gotten into you?"

"Listen to me—and listen to me good. I'm going to say this one time and one time only. Go home. Go home to your family. Get on the next plane and fly back to Greece. That's all I have to say to you."

"Angelo, I need your help. Nikos needs your help. We go back a long way. You said you would look into helping me. What happened in the last two days to make you change your attitude toward me?"

"Tommy, go home."

"I'm not going home!" Tommy screamed as he stood and walked over to Garuccio's desk with fire in his eyes. "Do you hear me? Huh? Do you hear me? I'm not going home! I came here the other day looking for your help, and you told me you would help me if you could. Well, it looks like you changed your mind all of a sudden. What the fuck happened? Did you forget what you told me yesterday? 'Oh, Tommy! Thank you for taking care of that guy in Greece! Oh, Tommy, I owe you! Oh, Tommy, I'll never forget what you've done for me!' Now it's 'Tommy, go back to Greece! Tommy, get on the next plane out of here!' Well, fuck you, Angelo, I'm not going anywhere! Do *you* hear *me*? I'm not going anywhere unless you explain to me what the fuck is going on!"

Garuccio sat smiling at Tommy, thinking how he was going to react.

"The fuck are you smiling at?" asked Tommy.

Tommy's last sentence was all Garuccio needed. Garuccio opened his desk drawer, took out his nine millimeter, stood, and pointed it at Tommy's face. Tommy turned white but still had fire in his eyes, and Garuccio knew it. He knew Tommy too well to take him lightly.

"Sit down," Garuccio said firmly. "Sit the fuck down."

Tommy knew he had no choice but to sit and listen.

"Now listen to me, Tommy. I do owe you. I owe you big time. And now I'm going to pay you back by letting you walk the fuck out of here—"

"Angelo, what the fuck—" Tommy interrupted.

"Just listen to me, and listen to me good," Garuccio said as he now pushed the nine millimeter against Tommy's temple. "You will leave here and go straight to the airport. You will purchase your ticket and wait until the next available flight. You will not go back to the Bronx. You will not call Nikos or anyone else. Do you understand?"

Tommy could only nod as Garuccio pushed the nine millimeter against his temple even harder.

"Now, Tommy, do you hear me? Do you feel me?"

Tommy could only nod again.

"Angelo, please, please put down the gun. Can you at least tell me what's going on, for old times sake?"

Garuccio slowly withdrew the nine millimeter from Tommy's temple.

"What is it you want to know?" Garuccio asked softly.

"I want to know why you're acting this way toward me."

"Tommy, Tommy, Tommy. I'm in charge here and in New York. Giovanni works for me. Giovanni doesn't make a move without checking with me first. And Moose works for Giovanni."

"Who's Moose?"

"Moose is Anthony Caramooso."

"Are you telling me you're behind everything that has been going on in the Bronx?"

"I'm telling you Giovanni works for me and I approve everything Moose does."

Tommy slowly looked into Garuccio's eyes and cautiously asked, "Nikos's father . . . Did you approve Nikos's father's death?"

Garuccio smiled as he put his nine millimeter to Tommy's temple again and said, "Tommy, Tommy Two-Fingers, I also have *two fingers*. Just leave before I use them."

Tommy was furious as he sat in his car, trying to decide what to do. *Who the fuck does that guinea bastard think he's talking to? Telling me he has two fingers. I'm the one who has two fingers. I'm Tommy Two-Fingers. Fuck him,* he thought.

Tommy started his car and headed toward the Interstate. The first thing he did was make a call to his friend Steve Margarites. After a few minutes, he called Kathy in Rhodes.

"Tommy, how are you? We miss you so much. When are you coming home?"

"Kathy, listen to me—"

Kathy knew Tommy too well. She immediately recognized trouble in his voice.

"Tommy," Kathy interrupted, "what's wrong? Something's wrong. I can hear it in your voice."

"Kathy, something *is* wrong here in New York. But I need for you and the kids to be safe. I want you to tell everyone you are going to America—"

"America?" Kathy interrupted. "Why do I have to go to America?"

"You're not. You're not coming to America—"

"Then where am I going, and why do I have to lie about going to America?" Kathy interrupted again.

"Kathy, just listen to me. After you tell everyone you're going to meet me in America, I want you to go see Steve Margarites. I already called him, and he's expecting you. He's the only person I trust. He's going to take you to your parents' house in Nisyros with his boat."

"Tommy, you're scaring me. What's going on?"

"Nothing. Absolutely nothing. But I need for you and the kids to get out of the house and off Rhodes for a while. I'll continue to run all our businesses from here. You just enjoy spending time with your parents. Besides, I'm sure they miss the kids."

"Okay, Tommy. I'll do what you ask, but I'm still worried."

"There's nothing to worry about."

"Tommy, I love you."

"I love you too, Kathy. Kiss the kids and tell them I love them."

"Will do."

As soon as Kathy hung up the phone, there was a knock at the door. Kathy casually opened it and saw Steve Margarites.

"Kathy, we need to get going."

"I can't. I need to pack. Steve, what's going on? What's wrong? Tommy told me to go see you, and you're here the second I hang up with him. What's going on?"

"Kathy, we need to leave immediately. That's all I can say. Please, Kathy, let's go."

"I said I need to pack."

"Kathy, pack only what you need for the trip. You can buy anything you need in Nisyros."

Kathy started to cry. She knew someone was after them. Tommy never would have arranged anything like this unless there was something terribly wrong. Then she really got scared when Steve grabbed her firmly by the arm, looked her dead in the eyes, and told her with authority, "Now."

Kathy quickly packed a few things, grabbed the children, locked all the doors, and followed Steve to his car. Unknown to Kathy, there was another car following behind with two armed passengers for her protection.

When they reached Steve's boat, Steve hesitated a minute until the car following him pulled alongside of him. When Kathy saw the three men exit the car, she knew their lives were in danger.

"Let's go, Kathy," said Steve. "We need to get going."

Kathy didn't even answer. She knew she needed to get onto Steve's sixty-five-foot boat for the three-hour ride to the island of Nisyros.

When they finally reached Nisyros, there were two cars waiting for them. Kathy got into one of the cars with Steve and the children. The three other men followed behind to the house of Kathy's parents. When they reached the house, Kathy's parents were already running outside.

After Kathy's parents greeted Kathy and the children, Steve ushered them all inside. Once the children were put to bed, Steve sat with Kathy's parents, Peter and Desi.

"Steve," said Peter, "Tommy called me right after he called Kathy. He didn't say much, but it sounds real serious. What should I expect?"

"Well, Peter, Tommy told me it could be nothing. But as we know, he always overkills when it comes to anything regarding his family, especially for their safety. So I'm spending the night, although it's not necessary. My three friends will sleep on the boat—"

"No way," interrupted Desi. "They're staying here. We have plenty of room. Besides, you all must be hungry. I started cooking when Tommy called Peter to tell me you were all coming. Please, Steve, call your friends inside."

Within five minutes, they were all eating a meal that Desi had prepared. It was enough to feed an army.

After everyone ate, Steve's friends left for his boat; although Desi had given them a hard time, they wanted to see some of the nightlife on the docks.

Once Kathy and Desi were sound asleep, Peter asked Steve to sit with him outside on the porch.

"Steve," said Peter, "what's going on? Tommy told me it's probably nothing but could be serious. He told me he needed to take precautions."

"That's exactly what he told me—"

"Bullshit," interrupted Peter. "You are his most trusted friend in the world. I'm sure he told you something."

"Believe me when I tell you, Peter, I know what you know."

"Can you at least answer me one question honestly?"

"If I can."

Peter looked Steve straight in the eye and asked, "Are Desi and I in any danger?"

"None of you are in any danger as long as my men and I are around." Then Steve looked Peter in the eye and said, "And we're not going anywhere unless Tommy tells us it's safe to bring Kathy and the kids back to Rhodes."

As Tommy drove south on Interstate 95, he knew Garuccio would know his every move. Garuccio would either have him followed or, at the very least, take down his license plate and tracked his rent-a-car.

Tommy knew he had to outsmart Garuccio. He knew what he had to do. He called Nikos and explained everything to him.

Nikos was shocked. He couldn't believe Garuccio would do this to Tommy. *Me, I could understand. Garuccio doesn't owe me like he owes Tommy*, he thought.

"Tommy," said Nikos, "are you sure you want to do this?"

"I'm sure as the sun will rise tomorrow. I know what I'm doing, so please have confidence in me."

'Tommy, maybe Garuccio's right. Maybe you should just go home."

"No way. What I did for him with that pedophile—he should be kissing my ass."

"Tommy, if you don't go home, you could start a war that would include all of us."

"Don't pussy out on me."

"Not me. I'm in if you're in. And I'm sure the rest of the Bronxmen are in too."

"That's what I want to hear, my Cypriot friend."

* * *

Tommy crossed the Whitestone Bridge and headed toward Kennedy International Airport. At the airport, Tommy went straight to the car-rental return section. At the car-rental return, Tommy exited the car and signed the appropriate paperwork. Because the car-rental place was off airport property, Tommy was then taken to the airport by shuttle.

Tommy then entered the terminal knowing he wouldn't actually be followed into the terminal, but as a precaution, he approached the security line, turned, and walked in a different direction. He felt Garuccio might have him followed to the airport but also knew no one would follow him into the airport terminal, but Tommy was overkilling his precautions. He left nothing to chance. He went into one of the airport souvenir shops, purchased a sweatshirt and a New York City baseball cap, and put them both on. Then he exited the airport terminal, headed toward the passenger pickup area, and, jumped into a taxi.

"Where to, sir?"

"Times Square, please."

"Sure thing."

With rush-hour traffic, it took two hours, but Tommy didn't care. He needed a diversion in case he was followed.

Overkill—that's the name of the game, Tommy thought.

From Times Square, Tommy walked down the first subway steps he came across, took the subway one stop, and exited. Once upstairs, he took another taxi to his apartment in the Bronx and immediately called Nikos.

Once Nikos received his call, he dropped everything and met Tommy at the apartment. Upon entering the apartment, Nikos hugged Tommy tight for several seconds. Then Tommy briefed Nikos about Steve taking Kathy and the kids to her parents' house in Nisyros.

"Tommy, will they be safe in Nisyros?"

"Don't worry, Nikos. With my friend Steve guarding my family, they will be as safe as the gold in Fort Knox."

"That's great."

Within thirty minutes, the rest of the Bronxmen were in Tommy's apartment.

"We have to get these people," said Vinny. "I never did trust Garuccio growing up."

"Yeah," chimed in Richie. "Garuccio was a real piece of shit."

"Hold on, guys," said Tommy. "This isn't anything you guys have ever come across."

"We can handle it," said Gary.

Lenny jumped in with arrogance. "Tommy, there isn't anything we can't handle."

"Lenny," said Tommy, "shut up. Do you hear me? If not, I'll say it again. Shut up. You think because you could bench-press three hundred pounds, it makes you bulletproof? Huh? Is that what you think? You think you're going up against Fat Sal? Is that what you think? Because if that's what you think, you might as well start digging your own grave. And that goes for all you tough guys. So shut the fuck up and listen to me."

Before anyone had a chance to open their mouths, Nikos spoke.

"Listen up, guys. You all know Tommy knows his shit. And besides, if you don't remember, I'll remind you. *I* brought Tommy here to help *me*. It's *my* problem, not yours—"

"How dare you say such a thing!" yelled Vinny. "We're all in this together. Don't ever say it's your problem and not ours."

"I'm sorry," Nikos said, teary-eyed with emotion. "Vinny's right. Whatever problems any one of us has concerns all of us. It's just that . . ." Nikos paused for a few seconds to get his composure. When he started to speak, that was when he broke down completely.

"Nikos," said Tommy, "that's enough. Stop crying like a baby. We need to concentrate. We have some serious shit about to go down."

During this entire time, Irving never said a word. This was totally out of his comfort zone.

"Okay, guys," said Nikos. "Let's listen to Tommy. And keep in mind—*I* brought him here. And the deal was it has to be done his way, with no questions asked."

Everyone nodded.

"Now listen up, guys," said Tommy. "The big guy that Nikos put in the hospital, as you all know, is Anthony Caramooso. They call him

Moose. He spent ten years in jail for manslaughter, that should have been life without parole. It was, without a doubt, murder in the first degree.

"Also, Antonio Giovanni controls all five boroughs. Don't look at me like that, guys. Don't look so surprised. This is organized crime. Giovanni gave Moose the order to kill Nikos's father."

As soon as Tommy said that, everyone looked at Nikos.

"Come on, guys," said Nikos. "Don't look at me. Pay attention to Tommy."

"Anyway," Tommy continued, "my friend in Connecticut whom you all happen to know, who happens to owe me big time, just shoved it up my ass. That's right. My friend who called me in Greece to take care of someone in Greece is now fuckin' me. He put a gun to my head and ordered me to go straight to the airport and get on the next plane back to Greece. Well, guess what? I'm still here.

"Guys, these people are the worst of the worst. I had my family moved from my home for their safety. We all need to be careful."

All the Bronxmen just sat and stared at Tommy.

"What do you need us to do?" asked Vinny.

"Right now, I'm not sure. I have a cousin in Maryland who can get me some guns—"

"Guns?" Irving interrupted. "Are you kidding? Guns?"

"That's what it's going to take," said Tommy. "This is not half-assed. What do you think this is, a rumble in the schoolyard? If you're not in it all the way, Irving, you have to let me know."

"What is it you want us to do?" asked Richie.

"Okay, hear me out," said Tommy. "We are dealing with top organized crime people. We need to play into their hands. It's important we make them think they have the upper hand. The first thing I want Nikos to do is drop the charges against Moose and Fat Sal."

Nikos could only stare at Tommy. *I don't believe this guy. He wants me to drop the charges against the man who killed my father?*

"Nikos," said Tommy, "you heard me, didn't you?"

"Yes, I did."

"Good. Now listen up. Once Giovanni discovers the charges are dropped, they will definitely look at it as a sign of weakness. After that, they will definitely put on the pressure. But we'll be prepared. They won't be able to touch us."

"Why's that?" asked Irving.

"Just listen. I know how these people work. Nikos, the very first thing you must do is to convince your mother to get out of here—"

"Where do you expect her to go?" interrupted Nikos.

"I suggest you send her to Cyprus to visit your grandparents. Make sure she takes Lilly and Anastasia. Do you think Lilly's husband, Dennis, would go?"

"Dennis is a doctor. He can't just pick up and leave."

"He could end up dead. Try to get him to leave too."

Irving," said Tommy, "is your fiancée still working for you?"

"Yes, she is."

"She has to go too."

"Oh, come on, Tommy. What am I supposed to tell her?"

"I don't care what you tell her. Break up with her or fire her ass for all I care. You just might save her life. And you other guys, send your families on long vacations. And, Nikos, something needs to be done with Georgia."

"What do you want me to do with her?"

"I don't give a shit. Just get her out of here. Any other questions?"

They all had questions, but unfortunately, they all knew the answers.

The Bronxmen sat listening to Tommy's strategic plans for three hours while he refused to listen to any advice. He rattled on and on. Finally, after a group hug, everyone left, knowing what they needed to do.

They knew they would be safe for a day or so.

Tommy remained in Nikos's apartment with a new rented car.

When Nikos arrived home, Maria was cooking dinner with Georgia. *Ahhh, look at this—my mother and soon-to-be wife working hand in hand in the kitchen. What a beautiful sight. And here I come to fuck it all up.*

"Nikos," said Maria, "I hope you're hungry. Georgia and I have been slaving in the kitchen all day. I'm teaching Georgia how to make traditional Cypriot food."

"Come on, Mom, you're going to scare her away."

"Nikos," said Georgia, "it was my idea. And besides, I'm not going anywhere. I'm here for good."

"That's right," said Maria as she hugged Georgia. "She's not going anywhere. She's now part of the family. Now come over here and give us both a hug."

After several seconds of the group hug, Nikos kissed Maria on the cheek as she walked away. Then he looked at Georgia with his glistening eyes and said, "I love you," as he cupped her breast.

"Stop it," she whispered. "Your mother's right over there."

Ten minutes later, Maria and Georgia were serving the food.

"Nikos," said Maria, "you seem to be preoccupied about something. Is everything all right?"

"Everything's fine."

"No, it's not, Nikos. I can read you like a book. What's wrong? Is everything all right at the restaurants?"

"The restaurants are fine."

"The apartment buildings?"

"The apartment buildings are fine."

"The McDonald's restaurants in New Jersey?"

"The McDonald's restaurants are fine."

"Nikos," said Georgia, "what's wrong?"

"You too?"

"Yes, Nikos, me too."

With that, Nikos put down his fork and looked up at his mother and Georgia as tears dripped down his cheeks.

"Nikos, what's going on?" asked Maria, concerned, as Georgia sat confused.

"Mom, Georgia, things are not good. As a matter of fact, things are terrible."

"Talk to me, my son—"

"Do you want me to leave?" Georgia interrupted.

"Absolutely not," said Maria. "You're family. Whatever Nikos has to say concerns you too. Isn't that right, Nikos?"

"Yes, it is."

"Good. Now please tell us. What's wrong?"

"I know who killed Daddy."

"What?" yelled Maria.

"You heard me."

"Who did it?" asked Georgia in a much softer concerned tone.

"Both of you, listen to me and please don't interrupt. It's hard enough for me to talk about this, let alone with interruptions. Okay?"

Both women nodded.

Then Nikos stood and walked over to his mother, sat next to her, and held her hand.

"The man who killed Daddy is the same large man I put in the hospital—"

"Oh my God!" cried Maria. "Oh my God. Why? Why did he do it? He was going to kill you too—"

"Are you sure, Nikos?" interrupted Georgia.

"I'm sure. Now let me finish—"

"Do the police know?" Maria asked, interrupting.

"No, Mom, the police don't know. And I'm not going to tell them—"

"Why?" asked Georgia.

"Because our family is in danger. That's why."

"What are you talking about?" cried Maria. "We need to call the police."

"Please, Mom, let me finish."

"Okay," said Maria as she continued to cry.

"Mom, you were right about Tommy. Tommy isn't here on business. Well, he isn't here on his business. I sent for him. The man I put in the hospital is Anthony Caramooso. He is known around as Moose. He takes his orders from a man named Antonio Giovanni. Mom, as you may or not know, Tommy has always been connected with the right people. Mom, please don't look at me like that."

"Like what?"

"Like the way you're looking at me."

"Are you talking about the look I gave you for saying Tommy has been connected with the *right* people? What *right* people? Tommy has always been connected with the *wrong* people. Just finish your story," Maria said as she blew her nose.

Nikos looked at both women and continued while wondering if all this could end his engagement with Georgia.

"Tommy came here to help me get to the bottom of this. Mom, do you remember Angelo, Angelo Garuccio?"

"Sure, I do. He was always bad news. Why? What about him?"

"Giovanni is mob connected, and Moose works for him. Tommy went up to Hartford to ask Garuccio for help. Well, as it turns out, over the past several years, Garuccio has become a big boss in organized crime, and Giovanni reports to him. It was Garuccio who gave permission to Giovanni to have Moose kill Daddy."

"Why?" cried Maria. "Why, why, why? What did Daddy ever do to deserve it? Why?" Maria kept repeating over and over as she cried.

"Anyway, let me finish. When Tommy went to Garuccio to ask for his help, he was turned down with a gun to his head—"

"Oh my God," said Georgia. "You're scaring me."

"Let me finish. Garuccio instructed Tommy to stay out of it and leave America. But, Mom, you know Tommy. Tommy's still the same Tommy. A few years ago, Garuccio got in touch with Tommy in Rhodes because he needed a big favor—"

"What kind of favor would Garuccio need from Tommy in Rhodes?" interrupted Maria.

"Don't ask. But it was a big favor that Tommy took care of, which ended up with Garuccio telling Tommy that he would basically be indebted to him for life. So you can imagine how pissed off Tommy became when Garuccio put a gun to his head. So Tommy had no choice but to tell Garuccio he would go back to Rhodes, but of course, he didn't. He's hiding out in one of our apartments."

"What's he hiding from?" asked Georgia.

"Now listen closely," Nikos said, ignoring Georgia's question. "Tommy has a plan. He doesn't trust the police. He thinks some of the police might be on the take, and I agree. I'm giving it to you guys straight. Tommy feels I should drop the charges against Moose—"

"I agree," interrupted Maria. "We'll get him on murder charges."

"No, Mom. No murder charges. They're too connected."

"I don't understand. You're going to let them get away with killing Daddy?"

"No, Mom. That's why Tommy's sticking around. This is the plan. Number one, no police. Number two, I'm going to drop the charges. Now once I drop the charges, Tommy feels they would take it as a sign of weakness, and then they'll come after us to really teach us a lesson. Mom, Georgia, you're not safe here. You need to leave."

"Where am I supposed to go?" asked Maria.

"Yeah," chimed in Georgia. "Where do you want us to go? Witness protection? Not me."

"No, no, no, nothing like that. I'm not going to ask any of you to go away forever. But I need to help Tommy get rid of these terrible people. Irving is sending his mother and his fiancée to Israel for a long vacation. Mom, I also want you to take Georgia on a long vacation to Cyprus. Yiayia and Pappou would love to see you—"

"Nikos," interrupted Maria, "what is it you plan on doing?"

"Not me, Mom. Not me alone. I have the entire Bronxmen behind me, including Tommy. But I need you to take Lilly and Anastasia with you. I'm sure Dennis is going to give us a hard time, but we need to somehow convince him to go too."

"Oh my God, Nikos, Lilly's married. Why do we have to involve her? Besides, Dennis is a doctor. He can't just pick up and leave."

"And I'm a nurse. I can't just pick up and leave either," said Georgia.

"Mom, Georgia, everyone goes. It's not safe for you to be here. I have some Cypriot friends who have contacts in Cyprus. Dennis and Georgia can work at the hospitals in Cyprus. Mom, it has to be done. Georgia, I'm so sorry to involve you, but there's nothing else I can do at this point. Both of you, please stop looking at me like that."

Georgia stood, walked to Nikos, wrapped her arms around him, and asked, "Will we be safe in Cyprus?"

"Tommy's going to send some of his friends from Rhodes to protect you. You'll never be alone."

"Will you send for me when it's safe to come home?"

"Of course, I will."

"Will you still marry me when I come home?"

"Of course, I will."

"Will you escort me home to pack?"

"Yes, I will."

Nikos texted Lenny and Vinny to come spend the night with Maria, knowing he would be spending the night at Georgia's.

Within three days, Maria and Georgia were on a plane to Greece. In Greece, they spent two days in Athens doing the tourist thing. After that, Margarites took them to Cyprus on his boat. Nikos requested it that way since Margarites knew where and when he could dock in Cyprus to avoid the customs agents. This way, if they were ever traced, they could only be traced to Greece and not Cyprus.

A day later, Lilly, Dennis, and Anastasia followed. It was such a happy time for Nikos's grandparents. In Vavla, they all stayed at the beautiful bed-and-breakfast called Our House, run by George and Donna-Marie Pavlou, although every night one of them stayed with the grandparents. Margarites had three of his men rent a house in Vavla to guard the family.

Meanwhile, Silvia and Bess decided to take a cross-country trip to California, stopping at many different sites before boarding a plane to Israel.

The Bronxmen got in touch with their families in Glastonbury and sent them all on trips to relatives throughout the country. Everyone was safe.

After two weeks, Nikos reached out to his lawyer and dropped the charges against Moose and Fat Sal. Meanwhile, Tommy laid low while in constant communication with the Bronxmen and, of course, Kathy and Margarites.

* * *

As expected, one afternoon the harassment started when Fat Sal knocked on the diner door while Jackie was sweeping. Nikos recently starting closing the diner between the hours of 3:00 p.m. and 4:00 p.m. for cleaning and preparing for the dinner rush.

"Hey, Nikos, what's going on?" Fat Sal asked as Nikos unlocked the door.

"Nothing much, Sal," Nikos answered, trying to act as though he wanted to let bygones be bygones. "Can I get you something to eat?"

"Sure. How about a couple of cheeseburgers and some fries?"

"Something to drink?"

"Yeah, I'll have a Coke."

"Sure thing. Coming right up."

Nikos called Jackie over and instructed her to place Fat Sal's order into the kitchen.

"Hey, Nikos, give me piece of that chocolate layer cake over there. I'll eat it while I wait."

"Sure thing, Sal," Nikos said as he started to slice the cake. Within thirty seconds, Nikos brought the cake to Fat Sal.

"Where's my Coke?" Fat Sal asked arrogantly.

"Sorry, Sal. I thought you might want it with your cheeseburgers."

"Next time, don't think."

"Sorry, Sal."

A few minutes later, Nikos brought Fat Sal his cheeseburgers and fries. To his surprise, he noticed Fat Sal hadn't touched his cake.

"Here you go, Sal."

"Hey, Nikos, where's your mother?"

The second Fat Sal mentioned Nikos's mother was when he almost lost it.

"Nikos, I asked you a question. Where's your mother? I'm in the mood to stare at her tits. I mean, really, she's a real-live MILF."

"Come on, Sal, that's my mother you're talking about. Please stop."

The way Nikos said "please stop," Fat Sal took it as a sign of weakness. He would continue making sexual comments toward Nikos's mother.

Meanwhile, Nikos excused himself from Fat Sal and went into the kitchen, where Jackie was having a bite to eat.

"Jackie," said Nikos, "why don't you go home?"

"Now?"

"Yes, please. Now."

"Okay."

Nikos then asked his short-order cook, Carlos, to also go home. Nikos watched them both walk out the back door and locked the door behind them. Within minutes, Nikos was back with Fat Sal in the diner.

"Hey, Nikos."

"Yeah, Sal?"

"Come over here a minute."

Nikos tried holding back from attacking Fat Sal. *Just another few minutes. Then I'll be rid of your fat ass for good*, he thought as he approached Fat Sal.

"Yeah, Sal. What else can I get you?"

"Nikos, do you remember, years ago, your first day at Lehman?"

"I'm not sure what you mean."

"What are you, stupid or something? The first day of school. Don't you remember the fight we had in the cafeteria, you stupid Greek?"

You're damn right, I remember. I kicked all three of your asses.

"I remember," said Nikos. "It was a long time ago. I'm really sorry about that."

"Well, I also remember. I remember the way you shoved the chocolate cake in Capo's face and shoved the hamburger in my face, and let's not forget the way you spilled the Coke in Carmine's face."

"I said I was sorry."

"Yeah, well, that's not good enough. I need my revenge." A second later, Fat Sal shoved the cake and cheeseburger in Nikos's face and poured the Coke on his head. "Now I asked you before where that mother of yours is with the beautiful tits. I want to see her tits."

"Come on, Sal, mothers are supposed to be off limits," Nikos said as he grabbed a towel to wipe his face.

"Where the fuck is she?"

Nikos took a deep breath and said, "She's downstairs in the basement doing paperwork in the office."

Fat Sal immediately started walking toward the back of the diner into the kitchen as Nikos followed.

"Come on, Sal, please. That's my mother."

Fat Sal took a moment and found the stairs leading to the basement and started walking down the stairs. Within seconds, Nikos was right behind him and gave him a swift kick that sent Fat Sal flying face-first onto the concrete floor.

Once downstairs, Nikos grabbed Fat Sal by the hair and put him on a chair. After a minute, Fat Sal looked up at Nikos as his nose bled.

"I'm going to ask you a few questions," Nikos said. "And you're going to answer me. Do you understand?"

"Fuck you. You're going down, along with your entire gang, including your mother and sister."

Nikos punched Fat Sal so hard, he fell off the chair. After several more punches, Nikos called Vinny and asked him to pull one of the work vans around to the back of the diner. When Vinny pulled up with the van, Nikos went to town on Fat Sal, punching him into unconsciousness. Once he was unconscious, Nikos and Vinny dragged him up the stairs and threw him into the van.

"Vinny, I'm going to take out the trash. Can you cover the diner for me?"

"Sure."

"Thanks. Also, I had to send Jackie and Carlos home. Do me a favor and call them back. And I'm going to need you to open the diner in the morning too."

"You got it."

"Thanks."

Nikos then entered the back of the van and tied up Fat Sal with duct tape.

"Where you taking him?"

"To my cabin upstate."

"Be careful. Make sure you obey the speed limit. You don't want to get pulled over."

"Don't worry, Vinny. I'll drive like a Boy Scout."

"You do that."

It took Nikos nearly three hours to get to his cabin. Once there, he drove the van around the back and parked. He exited the van, dragged Fat Sal into the house, and threw him into the basement. Nikos then tied his hands together at the wrists and pulled a rope around an exposed pipe in the ceiling. He then tied the rope around Fat Sal's wrists and hoisted him up.

"Wake up, motherfucker," he said as he threw cold water on him. "Wake the fuck up."

"I'm sorry, Nikos. They made me do it. They made me do everything."

"I know, but you still did it. You still tried to set me up so Moose could kill me, didn't you?"

Fat Sal hung there in silence, afraid to answer.

"Answer me!" Nikos screamed.

"Yes. It's true."

"Did they send you to the diner today?"

"Yes."

"Are you supposed to report back to them?"

"I don't know."

"What do you mean you don't know?"

"They told me to go fuck with you. They want to humiliate you."

"Who?"

"I can't tell you. They'll kill me."

"*I'm* going to kill you if you don't tell me."

"Will you let me go if I tell you?"

"I promise."

"Nikos, I hear you're a stand-up guy. I believe you."

"I am a stand-up guy. Now tell me before I really do kill you."

"Okay, can you first cut me down? I'm in a lot of pain."

"Tell me first."

"Moose sent me."

"Did Moose get the order from Giovanni?"

"That, I don't know. I hardly ever see Giovanni. Me going to the diner came from Moose."

"Now I'm going to ask you a question, and you better answer me."

"I don't want to die. I'll answer your question because I believe you when you tell me you're going to let me go."

"That's right. Now all that shit you were saying about my mother—what were you going to do if she really was in the basement of the diner?"

Fat Sal could only cry in fear.

"Answer me, you fat fuck."

Fat Sal lowered his head.

"You motherfucker. What did my mother ever do to you, you piece of shit?"

"I'm sorry, Nikos. I'm truly sorry."

"Well, you piece of shit, at least you're not lying. I have one more question for you, you fat bastard."

"What is it?"

Although Nikos knew the answer, he needed to hear it from Fat Sal. He looked Fat Sal square in the eye and asked, "Did Moose kill my father?"

Fat Sal could only nod.

With a fury of violent rage, Nikos grabbed a two-by-four that was up against the wall and swung it at Fat Sal's legs, breaking them both. Nikos then cut him down, dragged him up the stairs, and pulled him deep into the woods. He then stripped him naked and left him there to be eaten by the animals. Nikos knew his three hundred acres were surrounded by thousands of state-owned acres. The place was loaded with coyotes and bears. He knew the bears would leave nothing for anyone to find.

He then rolled up Fat Sal's clothes and threw them into the van. At the first local shopping center, he threw the clothes into a garbage can. Nikos then returned to his cabin and went to sleep. When he awoke the next morning, Fat Sal's body was gone. There was only a puddle of blood that he knew would be eaten away by other smaller animals and washed away with the rain.

One down, I don't know how many to go, he thought.

The next day, Nikos went to see Tommy and explained what he had done.

"Holy shit, Nikos. Do you think it was a bear that ate him?"

"Probably, but I'm not sure. There have been lots of bears in that region. I hope it was a bear and not a coyote. A coyote wouldn't be able to crush and destroy the skull."

"I wouldn't worry about it."

"Do I look worried?"

"Not at all. Now I hope you don't think it's going great."

"Well, we do have one down."

"Come on, Nikos. He barely even counts. We have a few heavy hitters to go up against."

"Tommy, do you have a plan?'

"Of course, I do."

"You want to share it with me?"

"Sure. The next thing we need to do is to eliminate Giovanni."

"What about Moose?"

"Moose?" Don't you want to save the best for last?"

"All I know is I want to kill him with my own bare hands."

"You will, my friend. You will. But for now, we need to sit with the other Bronxmen and devise the plan."

* * *

That evening, Tommy sat in his apartment along with all the Bronxmen. Step by step, he explained exactly what he wanted done as they all looked on eagerly. They were there for two hours.

The next morning, they were all ready to go at nine o'clock. The first thing Irving did was drive over to Moose's house and give him two flat tires. Tommy, Nikos, Richie, Lenny, and Vinny drove over toward Giovanni's house. They parked seven blocks away, and together, they exited the car. They all had on jogging suits and started jogging separately throughout the neighborhood while constantly looking at their watches. Lenny, of course, was in the best shape of them all. One by one, as they approached Giovanni's house, they hid in all parts of his property. Richie, being the technical guy, disabled the wires along the house for the telephone and internet.

Giovanni always had his breakfast on the back patio, overlooking the Long Island Sound, with City Island in the background. That was his ritual.

Lenny approached the front door and rang the bell.

"Can I help you, sir?" Roberta asked.

"Yes, ma'am. I was jogging through the neighborhood, and I somehow twisted my ankle. I'm going to be running a marathon next month, and I was wondering if you can give me a bag of ice because my ankle is starting to swell."

Roberta looked at the handsome muscular man and smiled. "I'm sorry, sir. This is private property, and you're going to have to leave."

"Please, ma'am. My ankle is swelling, and I'm going to need to ice it."

"Sir, I told you this is private property, and you must leave. If you do not leave, I'm going to be forced to call the police."

"But, ma'am, if my ankle swells up, I'm not going to be able to run in the marathon next month."

"Goodbye, sir," Roberta said as she started closing the door.

As Roberta was closing the door, Lenny pushed the door open, grabbed Roberta by the throat, and threw her onto the floor. Before Roberta had a chance to scream, Lenny kicked her several times and hit her over the head with an object he had seen on a shelf.

"Listen, bitch. Don't open your mouth. Do you hear me? If you open your mouth, you're dead." Lenny then removed plastic ties from his pocket and tied her wrists together. Then he gave her several more kicks in the ribs.

"Roberta!" yelled Mrs. Giovanni from the kitchen. "Who's at the door?"

When Roberta didn't answer, Mrs. Giovanni strolled through the living room toward the foyer to the front door and saw Lenny standing over the battered Roberta.

"Sir, I suggest you leave if you want to stay alive," Mrs. Giovanni said.

"Ma'am, shut your mouth and come over here and let me tie you up. Because if you resist, you will end up like your friend here on the floor."

Mrs. Giovanni looked at the battered Roberta and admitted to herself how happy she was to see her husband's mistress beaten up the way she was.

Lenny was running out of patience, so he grabbed Mrs. Giovanni, tied her hands with the plastic ties, and put duct tape on her mouth. By the time Lenny had reached the back porch, Giovanni was almost finished with his breakfast. Simultaneously, Nikos, Gary, and Vinny surrounded Giovanni on his patio.

"Who the fuck—"

Without letting Giovanni finish his sentence, Richie grabbed him by the hair and smashed his face onto the table. Nikos then took out his knife and slit his throat.

"That's from my father," Nikos whispered to Giovanni as he watched him bleed.

"Come on, guys," said Vinny. "Let's go."

They all left and jogged their separate ways.

* * *

That evening, the Giovanni house was surrounded by police. Mrs. Giovanni was hysterical and had to be sedated. Roberta, on the other hand, was only worried about her future. All she knew was she was a black mistress to a white man who had controlled the Bronx. Among her own people, she was disrespected.

Now she would be another unemployed black housekeeper with a reputation of degrading herself for a white gangster.

Both Mrs. Giovanni and Roberta knew the routine. The only thing they were worried about at this point was their own lives.

So when they were asked if they had seen anyone, their replies were identical. Four black men had come into the house and overtaken them.

If, for a second, they knew it was a bunch of nobodies who had killed Giovanni, they would have spilled the beans, but living in the world they lived in, they felt it was 100 percent a mob hit, and if they would describe anyone in the mob hit, they knew they would be dead too. So as all gangsters did, they said it was a bunch of black guys.

* * *

That evening, everyone met in Irving's office upstairs from the pizza place.

"So, guys," said Tommy, "I saw on the news some gangster got killed by a bunch of black guys."

"Yeah, I saw the same thing." Gary laughed. "That's pretty messed up. I can't believe a bunch of black guys are coming into our neighborhood and killing us. We better keep our heads up and be observant of our surroundings for now on."

"That's exactly right," said Tommy sarcastically. "We better keep our heads up and constantly look over our shoulders. Because there might be a bunch of black guys who might even come after *us*. Our next problem is figuring what Garuccio's next move is. Right now, I doubt very much if he suspects any of us. Let's not forget we still have Moose to contend with. Because as much of a scumbag Giovanni was, Garuccio's a thousand times worse. If Garuccio suspects us, he'll have Moose kill every one of us. Besides, Garuccio has a lot more people behind him."

"Tommy," said Nikos, "I know you're calling all the shots. But please save Moose for me. Don't get me wrong, guys. If Moose comes after any one of you guys, you do what you need to do. Don't let up on this guy because he *will* kill you."

"Don't worry about Moose," said Lenny. "I can handle him."

"He is big," said Gary. "I'm not sure if I can handle him one on one. But you guys know me, I'll never back down."

"Vinny," said Nikos, "what do you think? You think everything went well? I think it did."

"I agree. I think everything went well today. I am a little concerned about the housekeeper and the wife possibly identifying us—"

"Don't worry about them," interrupted Tommy. "This is the way these people live. They all know sooner or later, something like this could happen. Giovanni's wife is set for life. She will definitely be taken care of. The black housekeeper is going back to the projects where she belongs. She'll have to go back to sucking some black cock. Like the saying goes, once you go white, you always go back."

They all laughed and made jokes for a full minute.

"Hey," said Gary. "How about we hire the black lady for ourselves? We all got little white dicks."

"Speak for yourself," said Nikos.

63

It wasn't long ago when Lilly and Dennis had spent part of their honeymoon in Vavla. The joy of having baby Anastasia, who was now running around in her great-grandparents' house, was overwhelming for Michael's parents.

Every evening Nikos Skyped with Georgia. They spoke about their upcoming future and the beautiful life they planned on having together. Nikos also Skyped with Maria.

"Nikos, I'm worried about you," said Maria.

"Mom, please don't worry about me. I'm fine. It's important for me to have my mind free of worrying about you worrying about *me*. I promise you. I'm fine. Nothing will happen to me."

"Nikos, how much longer is this going to take? I want to come home. I miss you. I miss my house. I miss my church . . ."

"Soon, Mom. Real soon."

"Nikos, I don't mind being here temporarily. I don't mind waiting until things cool down. I'm worried about you getting killed."

"Mom, I promise you. No one's getting killed."

* * *

Every few days, Nikos also spoke with Lilly.

As Cyprus's economic problems continued, Dennis was doing lots of volunteer work at some of the clinics. Getting to see a doctor in Cyprus could actually take months.

Lilly was getting scared that Dennis was actually loving this type of work. He would come home every night and say, "Lilly, this is what a doctor is supposed to do."

"And what is that, Dennis?"

"Help people. Not worry about insurance payments. Not worry about affordable health care. These people are human beings. They have no money. They have no insurance, and the government here doesn't want to pay anymore. We need to do something."

"And that something is what, Dennis?"

"I'm not sure, but I definitely want to spend a few months a year on this beautiful island where your ancestors come from."

"That would be wonderful, Dennis, but we're Americans."

"I know, my love, but I have an idea."

"And what is your idea, Dennis? Do you want to open a hospital? We have money, but we don't have that much money."

"No, you gorgeous piece of woman you. I want to make another baby, and I want to do it here in Vavla."

* * *

Three months had gone by since Tommy told everyone their families should go on long vacations. The Bronxmen continued looking over their shoulders. Nikos went back to his upstate cabin several times since Fat Sal had been left to die in the woods. He walked what felt like miles of his property looking for any signs of Fat Sal's remains and found nothing. Meanwhile, Tommy was keeping as low a profile as he possibly could.

* * *

Early one morning, Steve Margarites called Tommy, informing him Kathy was starting to become uncooperative with his security.

"Steve," said Tommy, "what's going on with her? Why isn't she cooperating?"

"Tommy, we've been friends a long time. You know me. You know how I work."

"I know, Steve. You're the only one I trust to protect my family. Why isn't she cooperating?"

"I guess she's tired."

"Tired of what?"

"Come on, Tommy. She's tired of being followed around. She's tired of living with her parents. Tommy, she wants to go home."

"Don't worry, Steve. I'll talk to her."

"Please do."

* * *

That evening, Kathy called Tommy, all frantic.

"Kathy, what's going on?"

"Don't ask me what's going on. You know what's going on. And I'm tired of it. I want to go home. Do you hear me, Tommy? I want to go home."

"Kathy, listen to me. You are going home. But not now—"

"When?" screamed Kathy. "When am I going home?"

"Kathy, listen to me. I need you to calm down. There are people looking for me. And if they come to Rhodes, they might hurt you and the children. Please trust me. I know what I'm doing."

Kathy cried as she understood what Tommy was trying to tell her.

"Tommy," she said, lowering her tone, "I trust you. And I know you know what you're doing. It's just that I'm getting tired. I want to go home."

"I know, Kathy. I know."

"Do you have any idea how much longer?"

Tommy knew he had no idea, although he knew the minimum would be a few more months.

"Kathy, I'll call you tomorrow."

"Tommy, please be careful."

As the weeks passed, Maria was getting extremely restless in Cyprus. Finally, she called Nikos and told him she was coming home.

"Come on, Mom. Please, please give me some more time. I need more time."

"Take all the time you need. I'm still coming home."

"You can't come home. Do you hear me? You can't."

"I not only can. I am. I land five o'clock tomorrow afternoon."

"Tomorrow? Where?"

"Kennedy Airport. You picking me up, or should I take a taxi?"

"Mom, where's Georgia?"

"She's at the hospital, working with Dennis."

"Does she know you're coming home tomorrow?"

"No, she doesn't. If she did, I'm sure she would have called you."

"She better have."

"Don't worry about Georgia, she's dedicated to you. She definitely would have told you. I didn't tell her because I want to keep her out of it."

"Mom, please. Please reconsider. It's too dangerous."

"I'm coming home, and that's final. Are you picking me up or not?"

"Okay, Mom, I'll pick you up."

* * *

That evening, when Nikos Skyped with Georgia, he tried to convince her to talk Maria out of returning home.

"Sorry, Nikos, I can't do that."

"Why not?"

"You know why not."

"No, I don't."

"Come on, Nikos. I need to stay out of it. And to tell you the truth, I'm thinking of coming home too."

"Oh no, not you too."

"Yes, me too."

"Why?"

"Why?" Georgia snapped. "Did you ask me why?"

Nikos remained silent as he looked at his future bride. "I'll tell you why. First of all, my Greek is terrible, and no one here speaks English. Second of all, although your grandparents are wonderful people, their English is as bad as my Greek.

"At the hospital where I'm working with Dennis, none of the patients speak English either. I'm scared shitless driving on the left side of the street. And I miss my parents. Do you want to know something else? Huh? Answer me. I asked you if you want to know something else."

"Yes, I do want to know something else," Nikos said, afraid to ask.

"Well, I'll tell you then. I miss you. Do you hear me? I miss you," she said as she broke down crying.

"Georgia, listen to me—"

"No, Nikos, you listen to *me*. I don't like it here. I don't like being afraid for my life—"

"There's nothing to be afraid of," Nikos interrupted.

"Don't tell me there's nothing to be afraid of. Why did you send me here? Huh? What am I doing here?"

Nikos knew she was at her boiling point.

"I'm tired of this place. And do you know what the worst thing about all this is?"

Nikos knew he had no choice but to say, "No. What is the worst thing about that place?"

"I am sick and tired of having cybersex. I'm sick and tired of rubbing my tits on the screen while you jerk yourself off—"

"Georgia, stop it. I don't jerk off."

"The hell you don't. For now on, my tits are off limits to you unless you grab them and bury your face in them in person. Good night," she finally said as she slammed her laptop shut.

* * *

"Tommy," said Nikos, "I just got off the phone with my mom. She's coming home."

"When?"

"Tomorrow. She lands at five o'clock tomorrow afternoon—"

"Are you out of your mind?"

"Tommy, what was I supposed to do? She already bought a ticket. I can't stop her."

"Does she have any idea how dangerous it is?"

"Of course, she does."

"Nikos, don't tell me she knows how dangerous it is because if she knew, she would stay far away from this place. You have to call her back. You have to tell her to stay right where she is. She cannot come home. Do you hear me, Nikos? She cannot come home."

"Tommy, I've tried. I don't know what else to do."

"Don't tell me you don't know what else to do!" Tommy screamed.

"Tommy, watch your tone with me. Do you hear me? You watch your tone."

"Nikos, don't go there. Not with me. I'm here for you. Remember, you came to me. I could be in Rhodes right now getting laid three times a week instead of jerking off every night for you. So *you* better watch *your* tone."

"I'm sorry, Tommy. It's just that sometimes I feel like I'm losing my mind. Georgia is even starting to break my balls. She wants to come home too. I don't know how much longer I can keep her there."

"Well, you better keep her there, and you better keep your mother there too. They cannot come here. Do you hear me, Nikos? They cannot come here. Keep them there."

"Okay, Tommy. I'm going to call my mother right back."

"Good. And, Nikos?"

"Yes."

"I'm sorry I yelled at you."

"Come on, Tommy. We go way back."

"I know, Nikos. I know."

Nikos called Maria back and stayed on the phone with her for thirty minutes but to no avail. She was coming home, and that was the end of it. After hanging up with her, he called Georgia but got no answer. When Georgia didn't answer, he called Maria back, and Maria informed him that Georgia was asleep and she would not disturb her because she had just completed working a double.

"Nikos," said Maria, "Georgia is exhausted."

"Okay, Mom."

After hanging up with Maria, Nikos called Tommy to inform him of Maria's refusal to remain in Cyprus.

"All right, Nikos. We'll deal with it."

"Tommy, thanks for understanding. By the way, what are you doing right now?"

"Right now? I was about to go to the liquor store and buy a bottle of scotch. Why do you ask?"

"I was thinking of doing the same thing. Stay right where you are. I'll be right over."

Twenty minutes later, Nikos showed up at Tommy's apartment with a bottle of Johnny Walker Blue.

Meanwhile, that same morning, Moose drove to Hartford, Connecticut, to meet with Garuccio. Garuccio was furious with what had transpired in the Bronx.

"Moose, come in here," Garuccio said arrogantly. Before Moose had a chance to respond, Garuccio started in with him. "What the fuck happened down there?"

"I don't know, Mr. Garuccio. I have no idea. The news said it was four niggers—"

"Four niggers, my ass. Don't give me that nigger bullshit. All right? Fuck that nigger shit. Who was it? Could it have been a bunch of wannabes who wanna take over the Bronx?"

"I don't think so, sir. I know all the wannabes. None of them have the balls or the ambition."

"Where were you when this happened?"

"I was home."

"What were you doing home?"

"I was with a lady friend."

"A lady friend? Don't you meet with Giovanni every day?"

"No, not every day."

"Then when *do* you meet with him?"

"Four days a week."

"Four days a week? The fuck am I paying you for?"

"I'm sorry, Mr. Garuccio, but that's all Mr. Giovanni required of me."

"No wonder that stupid fuck got killed. Now listen to me, you dumb ox. I want you to think. Who—and I want you to think real hard—who do you think had it in for Giovanni? And don't give me any of that nigger bullshit."

"Look, Mr. Garuccio, there is one person who might have it in for *me*. But he has no idea the connection I have to Mr. Giovanni."

"You are a real asshole. You know a guy who could possibly be behind this, and you're telling me now? You stupid asshole. I oughta put a bullet in your head right now, you dumb fuck."

"Please, Mr. Garuccio. I didn't realize it until now."

"That's because you're an asshole! Now who is this person you think might be involved?" Garuccio screamed.

"Well, Mr. Garuccio, there is this guy named Nikos—"

"Nikos?" Garuccio screamed again. "Don't tell me it's Nikos Ioannis!"

"Yes, Mr. Garuccio. Do you know him?"

"Of course, I know him, you stupid fuck. I grew up with the guy. His friend Tommy Two-Fingers came here looking for help against Giovanni. It's all starting to make sense now. Do you know his friend Tommy Two-Fingers?"

"No, I do not, Mr. Garuccio."

"Tommy Two-Fingers came to my office to ask for help against Giovanni. I sent his ass outta here and told him to go home. I told him to go straight to the airport and get the next plane. I even had him followed to the airport. Do you know if he's still around?"

"I'm sorry, Mr. Garuccio, but I don't know Tommy Two-Fingers. But I will ask around. If I do find him, what do you want me to do with him?"

"I want you to bring his Greek ass to me. Do you understand? Bring him to me. Alive."

"Yes, Mr. Garuccio. I understand."

"Good. Now get the fuck outta here before I put a bullet in your head, you piece of shit."

The next morning, Nikos awoke in Tommy's apartment. They were both hungover. The two of them put away the entire 1.75-liter bottle of Johnny Walker Blue.

"Holy shit, Tommy, I'm fucked up. I mean really fucked up," said Nikos.

"You're fucked up? How do you think I feel? I kept drinking long after your ass fell asleep."

"Shit, man, look at the bottle. It's empty. We really put that shit away."

"We sure did. Did you ever think two kids from Glastonbury would ever be able to afford a $235 bottle of scotch?"

"What are you talking about? I paid for the shit."

"True." Tommy laughed.

"Tommy, what am I supposed to do? My mother's coming home today. I'm scared for her."

"To tell you the truth, Nikos, I'm scared for her too. We just can't let her out of our sight. You have no idea how dangerous these people are."

"Come on, Tommy. How could you say that?"

"Say what?"

"Say I don't have any idea how dangerous these people are. They had Moose kill my father. He almost killed me . . ."

"I'm sorry, Nikos," Tommy said as his eyes watered. "Don't worry. They're all going to get what they deserve. As personal as it is to you, it's also personal to me with Garuccio."

"I know, Tommy. I know. I just feel so bad asking you to leave your family the way you did."

"Nikos, don't worry about my family. They're fine. My friend Steve will never let anything happen to them. Besides, I have a feeling this is going to be over with real soon."

"I hope so, my friend. I surely hope so."

* * *

Nikos left Tommy's apartment and stopped by the diner a little before noon. As usual, the place was packed. Irving was there, working the register.

"Nikos," said Irving, "you look like shit."

"Yeah, well, I feel like shit."

"What's going on?"

"Nothing much. I got drunk with Tommy last night."

"Come on, Nikos. We need to stay on our game. We need to be sharp, not drunk and hungover. What's the matter with you?"

"I know, Irving. By the way, how are your mother and Bess doing?"

"Are you kidding? They're living a dream. They drove cross-country, and now they're in Israel, living it up on my dime."

"They breaking your balls to come home?"

"Not at all."

"Well, let me tell you this. Against my will, my mother is on a plane right now, and I'm picking her up at five o'clock."

"Are you kidding?"

"I wish I was."

"Does Tommy know?"

"Yeah, Tommy knows."

"What did he say?"

"What do you think he said? He's pissed. But he knows my mother. He knows how stubborn she can be. And another thing—Georgia's also pissed. I wouldn't be surprised if she follows right behind. Anyway, I'm going in the kitchen and getting some breakfast to bring home. Then I'm taking a shower and a nap."

"Go ahead, my friend, and be careful."

"Thanks, Irving."

The minute Nikos left, Irving took out his cell phone and called Tommy.

"Hey, Irving, what's going on?"

"Tommy, don't ask me what's going on. You tell me what's going on."

"What are you talking about?"

"What am *I* talking about? Nikos just left the diner and basically stumbled out of here."

"Yeah, I know. We got a little drunk last night."

"A little?"

"Okay, a lot."

"We're supposed to be on our guard. What's going on?"

"It kind of got away from us."

"And why is Maria coming home tonight?"

"I know. Nikos is really pissed."

"I know he is. He's even worried Georgia might want to come back real soon too." "We need to keep an extra eye on Maria."

"I know that, but you guys better keep sharp. You were brought here to make sure we're on our game, and you guys are getting drunk. You know what these guys are capable of doing more than we do."

"Okay, Irving. I hear you, and I feel you."

"Don't feel me. I'm starting to get worried."

"You're right, Irving."

"I know I'm right."

"Irving."

"What?"

"Thank you."

* * *

When Nikos returned home, he sat at his kitchen table and ate his breakfast out of the aluminum plate. After he watched television for a few minutes to wind down, he went upstairs, showered, and crawled into bed. As he fell asleep, he was trying to plan what his reunion with his mother would be like.

He had to protect her.

He would not let her out of his sight.

But who was he kidding? He knew he couldn't stay with her twenty-four hours a day. He had to get the Bronxmen to take turns staying with her.

* * *

Nikos woke up at 4:00 p.m., still somewhat hungover. He quickly went downstairs and grabbed a quick bite to eat. When finished, he went back upstairs, brushed his teeth, and showered again. Maria's plane was landing at 5:00 p.m. Nikos knew by the time she went through customs, he wouldn't have to leave his house until five thirty.

As Nikos approached Kennedy Airport, he received a text from Maria that she already had her luggage and was waiting for him outside. Three minutes later, as he approached the arrival platform, he couldn't believe his eyes. There was Georgia, standing right next to Maria. He didn't know what to do. He knew if he started screaming, it would only make matters worse. So he did what he needed to do, which was to greet them both with open arms.

During the ride back to the Bronx, Nikos slowly asked Georgia, "So, Georgia, what made you decide to come home with my mother?"

"Well, Nikos, you knew I wasn't happy there and knew I would be coming home soon. So I figured I'd just jump on a plane with your mother."

"You could have let me know."

"I know, Nikos. But I didn't want to hear it."

"Enough, Nikos," said Maria. "I don't want to hear about this anymore. Drop me off at home. Then you can take Georgia back to her apartment and discuss it with her in private. I don't want to hear it."

"Okay, Mom, but first, I have to make a phone call and make sure someone stays with you at your house."

"No way, Nikos. I don't want a babysitter. Do you hear me? I don't want a babysitter, and that's final."

"Mom, I can't leave you home alone, and *that's* final."

"Don't tell me what's final. I'll tell you what's final. I don't want a babysitter, and I don't want a bodyguard. I need to get on with my life."

Against everything Nikos believed in, he took his mother home and walked her to the door, while Georgia waited in the car.

"Mom, I'll be back in a little while."

"Don't 'little while' me. Spend some time with your fiancée before you lose her."

"Mom, I'm not going to lose her."

"Nikos, stop being stubborn. Georgia's a good girl, and you're going to lose her. Do you hear me? You're going to lose her."

"All right, Mom. Just lock all the doors."

"Okay, my son," Maria said, lowering her tone. "I know you're worried about me. But please try to understand. I cannot and will not live in fear. Whatever God has planned for me, he has planned for me. I will be careful, and I will always keep my doors locked. Now go. Go to that beautiful fiancée of yours and take her home."

"Okay, Mom. And, Mom?"

"Yes, my son?"

"Welcome home."

"Thank you, Nikos. I love you."

"I love you too, Mom."

"Now go."

* * *

For the first few minutes, the car ride to Georgia's apartment was so quiet and tense, you could cut the tension with a knife.

Finally, Nikos spoke.

"Georgia, it's great to see you. You're looking as lovely as ever. Cyprus must have done wonders for you."

When Georgia turned to look at Nikos, he felt the tension even more, but he knew they needed to talk.

"Nikos," she said, "what is it you want from me?"

"Georgia, I want nothing but the best for you."

"Nikos, I know that. But sending me to Cyprus for such a long time was not the best thing for me or for our relationship."

"Yes, it was, Georgia. It's dangerous here. And with you in Cyprus, I knew I didn't have to worry about you."

"Nikos, if my life's in danger, I'm calling the police right now."

"Please, Georgia, we've been through this before. No police. There are some bad people around, and I just need to make sure they don't bother you. Do you understand me?" Nikos said, raising his voice. "You must listen to me and be careful."

"Be careful how?" Georgia screamed. "What do you want me to do? Walk around with bodyguards looking over my shoulder? I cannot and will not live like that. Do you understand me? I'm not living like that. If you love me and still want to marry me, let's get the hell out of here. We'll move far away, where no one will touch us. I am willing to do that to spend the rest of my life with you."

"Georgia, I can't just pick up and leave."

"Don't tell me you can't. Be honest with me and tell me you won't. I picked up and left and went clear across the globe to work at some witch-doctor hospital for *you*."

"Come on, Georgia. I own two restaurants, two McDonald's, and a bunch of apartment buildings. I can't just pick up and leave."

"Bullshit. You can manage all your business from anywhere in the world, and you know it."

"Can we talk about this tomorrow?"

"Fine, but don't think this problem is solved."

Nikos walked Georgia into her apartment to make sure it was safe.

"My apartment needs to be dusted. It's a mess."

"Georgia, if I knew you were coming home, I would have gone to the store and stocked your refrigerator and had someone freshen up the place."

"Yeah, right. If I told you I was coming home, that's exactly what you would have done. You wouldn't have said anything else," she said sarcastically.

"Yeah, I guess you're right."

"I know I'm right," she said this time, lowering her tone as her eyes watered. "Nikos, I'm scared. I'm scared not only for myself but also for you and your mother."

"Georgia, I love you—"

"I know you love me," she interrupted. "But none of us can live like this."

"I know, Georgia. And like I promised you, I'll take care of it."

"That's what I'm afraid of."

"Georgia, I will never put you in danger. Nor would I ever let anything happen to you."

"I know you won't. Now I haven't taken a shower in almost twenty-four hours. Can you help me by washing my back?" She smiled.

* * *

Nikos carried Georgia into the shower fully clothed. They stood in the shower for ten minutes, hugging and kissing as they reacquainted themselves with each other's bodies. Finally, Nikos started undressing her slowly. Georgia stood naked under the hot shower with goosebumps, watching Nikos soap up the washcloth. She knew what was next. Nikos slowly started washing her breasts with circular motions.

"Always starting with the tits," she whispered.

"That's right, beautiful."

"You love my tits, don't you?"

"You know I do."

After Nikos washed both breasts, he slowly worked his way up toward her neck. He stood there washing her neck and shoulders for several minutes. Then he started working his way back down and stopped at her breasts again, where he spent another several minutes making circular motions while fondling them.

As he approached the area between her legs, he dropped to his knees and spent several minutes there as she moaned in pleasure, but Nikos was a master at pleasuring her. He left her moaning as he lowered his way to her toes.

They both knew he would return.

When Nikos stood, they kissed for several minutes as she felt his manhood against her. Then he turned her around, started from the top of her neck, slowly kneeled, and worked his way down to her buttocks. He spent several minutes rubbing the washcloth in and around her rectum area as she moaned in pleasure. While still on his knees, he turned her around again and used his tongue to pleasure her until she reached her moment of climax.

Finally, he stood, and Georgia started undressing him.

She washed him from head to toe except for his manhood. She was saving that for last, although she accidentally on purpose, brushed up against it several times to make him erect.

Finally, when she was on her knees, Nikos took the shampoo and applied it on her hair as she washed his manhood. As she soaped his manhood, he shampooed her hair. When they both felt they had had enough, Nikos again lifted her and carried her into the bedroom. There, they made love into the night.

Two nights later…

While Nikos was having a late dinner with Maria and Georgia, there was some small talk about their situation, but most of the dinner was quiet. Maria looked fine. It was as though she had a renewed confidence in her life being back home. Nikos really noticed a difference in her.

On the other hand Georgia looked miserable. She wasn't happy the way her life was going. She ended up getting her job back at Jacobi Hospital, which she was grateful for, but she was not happy to have to spend the night with Nikos at his mother's house. She moved out of her own parent's house to become independent and had to move in with her fiancé in his mother's house. *Here I am; moved out of my parent's house and my fiancé is still living with his mommy,* she thought. Finally, Nikos spoke:

"I had a good day at the diner," he said.

"That's nice Nikos," said Maria.

"Yeah, that's real nice," said Georgia.

"I was talking with Irving today and we are thinking of purchasing a nineteen family building on Manhattan's lower East Side."

"That's wonderful Nikos," said Maria. "Can you guys afford it?"

"Yeah Mom, Irving's really good at figuring these things out. With a minimum down payment of 20% we should be able to handle it…"

"How much is the building," interrupted Georgia.

$17,000,000. It's a great opportunity for all of us."

"Will the numbers cover?"

"Yes they will. Irving calculated everything. As long as we average $4,500.00 an apartment we'll break even," Nikos answered happy that Georgia started to take an interest in his businesses. "We have the 20% to put down. The rents are astronomical in Manhattan as you know. All the apartments are small three bedrooms. But little by little we are going to start converting them into luxury two bedroom apartments. We're going all out with stainless steel appliances and granite countertops. The bathrooms will be made of marble. We'll definitely get between $7,000-$8,000 a month for each renovated apartment..."

"That's crazy," interrupted Maria. "You have to be out of your mind to pay $7,000 a month for an apartment."

"Mom, that's what people do in Manhattan. It's different than what we're used to. We think it's nuts to live in the city. But let's not forget they'll all be professionals. Two bedroom apartments for $7,000-$8,000 a month will be split among four people. They'll easily be able to afford it."

Suddenly the doorbell rang. Maria looked up and smiled as Nikos cautiously walked to the door. He slowly looked into the peep-hole and saw it was John Pappas.

"How are you John?" said Nikos as he opened the door. "It's great to see you," as he wondered what Pappas was doing there.

"Nikos, is that John?" Maria yelled from the kitchen.

"Yes Mom, it is."

"Great, tell him to come in. I'll be right there."

"Okay Mom," Nikos yelled back confused as to why Pappas was there.

"How are you John?" Maria said as she approached Pappas and gave him an affectionate hug and kiss as she lifted her left leg.

"I'm great. Are you ready?"

"You bet I am. Just give me a second. I need to get my bag."

"Sure, take your time."

Thirty seconds later, Maria came down the stairs carrying a small overnight bag.

"Mom, what are you doing?"

"What does it look like I'm doing? I'm going to spend the night at John's."

"Mom, do you think that's wise?"

"Nikos, don't worry. She'll be fine," said Pappas.

Reluctantly, Nikos didn't say anything. But thought to himself; *I'm losing control. No one's listening to me anymore.*

"Good night Mom."

"Good night Nikos. Good night Georgia."

"Good night you two. Have fun," said Georgia.

"John," said Nikos.

"Yes Nikos?"

"Please take care of her. Please don't let anything happen to her."

"Don't worry Nikos. She'll be fine."

All Nikos could do was hug his mother tight and tell her he loved her.

Nikos stood in silence watching his mother leave with Pappas. He then turned and looked towards Georgia.

"Hey big boy," she said. "You going to stand there and cry because you miss your mommy or are you going to come over here and show me what you got?"

"Come on Georgia. That was uncalled for."

"What was uncalled for?" Georgia asked arrogantly.

"Come on Georgia, how could you say something like that? You know exactly what's going on. I'm worried about her."

"Don't worry about your mommy. It looks like John is going to take really good care of your mommy tonight," she smiled.

"Fuck you." he said.

"Fuck me? How dare you talk to me like that!"

Nikos caught himself. He knew what he said was totally out of line.

"I'm sorry Georgia. I think I'm losing it."

Georgia looked at Nikos totally confused. She has never seen that side of him, nor has he ever spoken to her like that. But she knew he had a lot on his mind.

"Forget it Nikos. We all have bad moments when we say things we wish we never said. Don't give it a second thought. I never should have said what I said. Now come over here and give me a hug."

Nikos cried in Georgia's arms like a five-year old.

68

Meanwhile in Hartford, Connecticut Garuccio sat in his office with four of his top men.

"Guys, I still can't get to the bottom of what happened in The Bronx. I'm getting calls from my men in Brooklyn and Manhattan and as far away as New Jersey. They want to know if they should be worried about these niggers that we all know don't exist."

"Do you have any idea who it could have been?" asked one of Garuccio's men.

"Yes I do as a matter of fact. There's this guy in The Bronx who I know since childhood. He's building an enterprise buying up all kinds of real estate and opening restaurants and shit. But I'm not totally sure it's him. Right now I have Moose looking into it."

"You mean the big guy?" someone asked.

"Yes, the big dumb ox."

Everyone laughed at Garuccio's comment about Moose.

"I had a meeting with Moose recently. Hopefully he'll be able to give me some information. I told him to do whatever it takes to get to the bottom of what happened. So guys, I need you to stick around. I'm not saying anyone's coming after me, but I need to be surrounded."

"So that story about the niggers has to be bullshit, isn't it?" another asked.

"Of course it's bullshit," said Garuccio. "You know the way we are; we always blame the niggers."

"But what about Giovanni's housekeeper? Isn't she a nigger?"

"Yeah," laugh Garuccio. "She's sucking real dick now instead of the little Italian dicks we all have." Everyone laughed hysterically at Garuccio's comment.

* * *

The next morning Nikos drove over to Tommy's apartment.

"Nikos," said Tommy. "I spoke to my cousin Ronnie. Each of us will have a 9mm with plenty of rounds. We need to get up to Garuccio's place and teach him a lesson; otherwise Garuccio will kill us all if given the opportunity. Ronnie tells me his connections tell him Garuccio's preparing for a war. Garuccio has plenty of bodyguards and we need to take them all out at once."

Just then Tommy received a text message from Ronnie in Maryland.

"Tommy, give me a call."

"*Sure thing,*" Tommy texted back.

Tommy excused himself and went into the next room and called Ronnie.

"Ronnie," said Tommy. "What's going on?"

"I just got word that tomorrow some of the heads of families are going to meet Garuccio at his mansion in Hartford."

"What time?"

"I'm not sure, but it's sometime in the afternoon."

"Ronnie, we need the guns tonight. We need to surprise them."

"Shit, I really don't feel like driving five hours."

"Ronnie, I need the shit tonight."

"Okay Tommy, you know I'll do anything for you. I'll bring you whatever you need and then some."

That evening, Ronnie showed up at seven o'clock at Tommy's apartment. This time, they were all there except for Irving. Nikos didn't trust Irving to do what was needed to be done.

"Listen up, everyone," said Ronnie. "These are the nine millimeters. You guys know how to use them?"

They all nodded.

"Good," said Ronnie as he distributed the guns. "You have plenty of ammo. Now this is the aerial of Garuccio's home—"

"What are you, NASA?" interrupted Lenny.

"No, I'm not, tough guy."

Before Lenny had a chance to answer, Tommy jumped in.

"Okay, guys, let's calm down. Let's focus on who the bad guys are, and remember, we're all on the same side. Lenny, Ronnie's a technical genius. He's ex-military intelligence. He went to the Google Earth site and took as many pictures as he could of Garuccio's home. He has this thing planned out perfectly."

"Thanks, Tommy," said Ronnie. "But I got this. Don't let the muscle guy intimidate us."

"Hey, fuck you," said Lenny.

"Lenny!" screamed Nikos. "Listen to Ronnie. He knows his shit."

Lenny could only look at his lifelong friend and close his mouth.

"Don't worry about it," said Gary. "Tommy's right. Let's focus."

"I'm sorry," Lenny said to Ronnie. "You really seem to know your shit."

"Yes, I do."

The five Bronxmen sat in the apartment and listened to Ronnie speak for three hours. They knew what they had to do.

"So, guys," said Ronnie, "we're all going to drive up to Connecticut in separate cars. I will be in constant communication with each of you. I will call the shots as I track each and every one of you through the Google Earth satellites."

They sat there, shocked, looking at Ronnie, wondering how he could possibly know how to do this.

"I know what you're thinking," said Tommy. "Believe it or not, according to Ronnie, all you need is half a brain to be able to do all this. It's all about tracking devices in the cars."

"What's in the boxes?" asked Vinny.

Ronnie opened one of the three boxes and pulled out a drone. "These drones have cameras on them. I will be monitoring and controlling them high above Garuccio's home. I will be watching the house as everyone gets inside. I might not even need any of you. As I'm watching the house, I might pull an ace out of my sleeve."

"What are you talking about?" asked Richie. "What ace out of what sleeve?"

"Don't worry about the ace. I'll take care of the ace."

"Come on, Ronnie," said Nikos. "No secrets here. We need to all be on the same page, and we all need to know what page we're all on."

"Ronnie's got this covered," said Tommy. "That's all you need to know. You guys have to be ready in case you're needed. That's all I'm saying for now. So, everyone, go home and get some sleep. We leave tomorrow morning at eight."

"All right," said Gary. "Where do you want us to meet you tomorrow morning?"

"We don't meet. You all live relatively close to one another. Just leave your homes at eight o'clock, and I'll monitor you all. Now take these tracking devices and leave them in your cars. I'll worry about the rest. Just obey the speed limits because each and every one of these nine millimeters aren't legal." Ronnie smiled. "Tommy and I are leaving tonight and checking into a local motel in Hartford. Good night, everyone. Sleep tight, and don't let the bedbugs bite."

That evening, Nikos arrived at Georgia's apartment.

"Nikos," said Georgia, "how was your day?"

"Come on, Georgia. You should know by now—"

"Let me guess," Georgia interrupted. "All your days are good, just some days are better than others." She laughed.

"You know it."

Since Georgia and Maria had returned home, he never let either one of them spend the night alone. Maria, by now, had totally moved on with her life with John Pappas.

She no longer felt she was disrespecting Michael by having another man sleep in her bed. She did end up renovating her bedroom—new paint, new curtains, new carpeting, and, of course, an entirely new bedroom set that was arranged in an entirely different manner than what she had when she had shared the room with Michael.

That evening, Nikos knew Pappas was spending the night with Maria. Although Pappas was in excellent physical condition, Nikos wasn't totally happy with Pappas protecting his mother. He wanted to do it himself, but Georgia did not want to move into Maria's house either. So he did what he had to do to make everyone happy.

Maria had her privacy with her new lover, while Nikos and Georgia shared her apartment. "I'm so glad you moved in with me," said Georgia.

"I'm glad I'm here too, my love. I can't wait until our wedding day and return from our honeymoon and moving into our own home."

By now, Nikos and Georgia had already purchased a home in Westchester County in the exclusive area of Purchase, New York. It was an older home they were totally restoring to its original state in the period of 1910.

"What time are you waking up tomorrow?" asked Georgia.

"I need to be up by seven."

"What happened? You're not opening the diner tomorrow?"

"No, not tomorrow. I have some business up in Connecticut."

"Connecticut? What's going on in Connecticut?"

"Well, as you know, Georgia, I'm from Glastonbury, and I still have some connections there. I'm going to look at a shopping center."

"A shopping center? You just said you're buying an apartment building in Manhattan."

"Georgia, I've told you so many times. Business is better than good. The diner is doing great, and the pizza place is even doing better."

"Well, good luck to you."

"Thanks, Georgia, and thank you for your support."

"How can I not support all your business ventures?" Georgia laughed. "I take it I'm marrying a rich man."

"Yes, I am rich in dollars and cents. But I am even richer in love. Now give me some of that beautiful body you possess."

Georgia stood there looking as beautiful as ever. Before Nikos came home, she had showered off her day from the hospital and freshened herself up. Nikos looked at her beautiful face and body as she stared at him.

"You like what you see?" she said as she put her hands on her hips.

"Oh yeah."

"Well, my big man, you want this beautiful body? Come get it."

That evening, for some reason or another, Georgia sensed an extra bit of love coming from Nikos. She knew he loved her, but there was something different about their lovemaking. He was gentle and at times rough, the perfect combination for Georgia to receive her multiple orgasms.

* * *

"John," said Maria, "this steak is delicious. What kind of flavoring did you use?"

"It really wasn't much, Maria. A good friend of mine sells these herbs and spices. It's called Big Papou's Mediterranean Rub. All I did was rub it on the steaks yesterday."

"That's it?"

"The important thing is rubbing it on the steaks and sealing it all in with cellophane and refrigerating overnight. Then I brought them to your house, cranked up your barbecue real hot, five minutes on each side, and bingo. We have the two most delicious rib-eye steaks. Does this mean I need to compliment you on your salad?" John laughed.

"Yes, you should. Anyone could make a salad, but it's a special oil and vinegar I added to make it taste better."

They smiled at each other as John stood from his chair, walked over to Maria, and licked some of the steak's juice off her lip.

"That tasted great," he said.

"What tasted great? The blood from the steak or my lips?" she asked, looking passionately into his eyes.

"I must admit to you, my love. It's a combination of both." Then John lifted Maria's chin slightly with his right hand, gently put his left hand behind her head, and locked lips with her as his right hand cupped her breast.

After several seconds, Maria unlocked lips and said, "Our steaks are getting cold. We have plenty of time for this later on this evening."

John smiled at her and gave her a peck on the lips.

Three quarters through dinner, the doorbell rang.

"I wonder who that could be," asked Maria.

"I don't know," answered Pappas. "I'll check."

The next morning . . .

"Let's go, Nikos. Rise and shine," said Georgia.

"What time is it?"

"Seven o'clock."

"Wow, I slept heavy last night."

"Did I knock you out?"

"You sure did."

"You kind of knocked me out too."

"Hey, I got an idea."

"Oh yeah? What could your idea possibly be?" she said as she removed her T-shirt.

"You guessed it."

* * *

At 8:00 a.m., Nikos kissed Georgia goodbye and left.

"What time should I expect you home tonight?" she asked.

"I shouldn't be too late. Irving already crunched the numbers. I just need to meet with the engineer as he goes over the building. I'm hoping to be home by eight."

"I'll be waiting."

* * *

The drive to Hartford was extremely stressful for Nikos. He knew what needed to be done and didn't feel guilty in the least. Although he knew nothing about Ronnie, he knew Tommy well. Tommy informed Nikos that Ronnie would never take on anything of this magnitude unless he was absolutely positive it would work.

Throughout the three-hour drive to Hartford, Ronnie was in constant contact with everyone.

"Guys," said Ronnie, "remember, watch your speed. You get pulled over by a Barney Fife, you could have a problem."

"I know," said Lenny. "You told us that yesterday."

"Yeah, well, I'm telling you again today. Watch your speed. Now no more talking. I want silence until you hear from me."

Ronnie sat in his motel room with Tommy, staring at three laptop screens while controlling several joysticks. Like a surgeon, his eyes were fixed as though he were repairing the heart of a premature baby. He was totally focused.

"How's it going?" asked Tommy.

"It's not. Not yet anyway. I'm just getting into position. Now let me concentrate."

"Okay, you're the boss."

"I know I'm the boss. Now listen to your boss and run across the street and get us some breakfast."

"You know, in Rhodes, I'm the one who sends people for breakfast."

"Dorothy, you're not in Kansas anymore."

"I guess not."

* * *

Ronnie sat staring at the three screens that were each split in four. The drones were high above Garuccio's house, not seen by anyone.

Garuccio was totally oblivious to what was flying overhead.

Meanwhile, the Bronxmen were still two hours away but in constant communication with Ronnie.

When Tommy returned with breakfast, Ronnie didn't even notice him. His eyes were fixed on all three screens.

"Earth to Ronnie. Earth to Ronnie," said Tommy to get his attention.

"Holy shit, Tommy, look at this shit."

"I'm looking, but all I see is a bunch of cars and a bunch of people."

Tommy sat staring at the three screens that were each split in four. Garuccio was still totally oblivious to the drones high above his house.

"Tommy, do you see all these people?"

"Yes, I do, and I'm a little concerned because it looks like there's a lot of them."

"Not a lot of them. I'm talking about all of them."

"What do you mean by 'all of them'?"

"Tommy, my friend told me there were going to be several members of the top families at this meeting. Look at these guys."

"I see them, but I'm not really sure what you're talking about."

"Tommy, these are not a few heads of the families. These are all the heads of the families. I had no idea all of them would show up at Garuccio's house."

"Ronnie, we need to get in touch with everyone and send them back home. There are too many of them. We can't handle them all. They'll kill us all."

"I got this under control, cousin. Do not worry."

"I hope so, Ronnie. I surely hope so."

"Listen up, guys," said Ronnie through the airwaves. "I want you guys to stop at separate rest areas and have a cup of coffee and wait for my call."

"What's going on?" asked Nikos.

"Yeah, what's going on?" almost everyone asked simultaneously after Nikos.

"Guys," said Ronnie, "just relax. I think I got this."

"The fuck you talking about?" said Lenny.

"Lenny, you and I need to talk a little later. You're beginning to piss me off."

"You know where to find me."

"Nikos," snapped Ronnie, "shut your friend up."

"Hey, Ronnie," said Gary, "are you kidding? You want us to just get off the highway and go for breakfast somewhere?"

"That's exactly what I want you to do."

"All right," said Richie. "Let's all get off an exit and wait for Ronnie's call."

"Good idea," said Nikos.

"Tommy," said Ronnie, "watch and learn from the master."

"I'm watching you, cousin. But so far, I'm not sure why you're so happy."

"Pay attention."

"I'm paying."

"Good. Now watch."

Ronnie pointed everything out to Tommy.

"See this guy?" Ronnie pointed to the screen.

"Yeah."

"That's Big Richie from Chicago."

Tommy watched Big Richie as he exited his limousine and went into the house. One by one, with the high-powered cameras attached to the drones, Ronnie was able to name all the heads of the families as they exited their limousines.

"Ronnie, do you think this meeting is about us?"

"I think so. My source didn't know for sure, but he did tell me it was definitely about Giovanni and the Bronx incident."

"Holy shit. I feel so important."

"Yes, holy shit. Now watch this."

Ronnie got himself in position as he scanned the screens, with his hand on one of the joysticks.

"Here it goes."

The first press of the joystick button dropped two C-4 grenades from each of the drones around the perimeter of the house, with two grenades behind all the limousines, making the drivers run toward the house. Once the drivers were close to the house, Ronnie clicked his joystick again as two more grenades dropped within feet of the limousine drivers, killing them all.

By now, everyone inside had to have been totally startled. With several more touches of the joystick, nine more C-4 grenades landed directly on top of the house, exploding it beyond recognition, killing everyone inside.

"How do you like them apples?" Ronnie said to Tommy.

"I generally don't like apples, but I'm starting to like them now. What's our next move?" "Very simple. I crash the drones into the flaming house, and they will all disintegrate. Evidence is fried."

"I can't believe it, Ronnie. I can't believe you did this. I owe you big time."

"Yes, you do. Now give me a second."

"Sure."

Ronnie made his call to the guys, informing them their services were no longer required and to return to the Bronx. Ronnie then called Nikos and asked to meet with him and Tommy privately. Within an hour, the three of them sat in a booth at a rest stop.

"Guys," said Nikos, "I just heard on the radio about the mob being wiped out in Connecticut. Is it done? Is it really done?"

"Totally." Ronnie smiled.

After leaving Ronnie and Tommy, Nikos called Georgia.

"Hey, Nikos. How did your meeting go?" asked Georgia.

"Not as well as I expected."

"I'm sorry to hear that."

"It's okay. That shopping center wasn't meant to be."

"I love your attitude."

"And I love you."

"And I love you back. What time should I expect you home?"

"I'll be in the Bronx by eight tonight. But I need to stop by Irving's office first to discuss the shopping center. Then I need to stop by my house to pick up a few things. Expect me at your house by nine thirty."

"I'm counting the minutes."

"Me too."

* * *

Nikos listened to the news as he drove. It seemed the blowing up of Garuccio's house was all over the radio. The news reporters were calling it a strategically planned massacre. No one could understand how something like this could have gone unnoticed. Many of the gangsters were under the radar of the FBI, but no one knew about this big meeting. It seemed Ronnie's contact was very connected with some of these people. But Ronnie's contact was also upset with most of them for various reasons. So he decided to drop a dime on them.

When Nikos reached Irving's office, Irving looked scared.

"Nikos, what happened?"

"What are you talking about?"

"Come on, Nikos, it's all over the news. You guys did that shit?"

"Me? I didn't do anything."

"Yeah, I know. You didn't do anything," Irving said sarcastically.

"Don't worry, Irving. It's all over now. They can't hurt us anymore."

"I know, Nikos. I know. And since it was that scumbag Garuccio who gave Giovanni the order to have your father killed, he got what was coming to him. Everyone else who was there, I'm sure, also got what was coming to them too."

"I agree."

"Nikos, was Moose there?"

"I don't know. There's a part of me that wishes he wasn't."

"Why's that?"

"Because I would have loved to kill him with my own bare hands."

"You know what, Nikos? You never know. You might've had a bad day and gotten yourself killed instead."

"I know, Irving. But I still would've loved to have strangled him slowly. Anyway, what about your mother and Bess? They coming home soon?"

"Are you kidding? They're still in Israel, living it up. I'm going to call them tomorrow and tell them it's safe to come home."

"Great. By the way, I'm looking forward to your wedding."

"I can't wait to have you there. But I need a favor."

"Anything."

"I would like for you to be my best man."

Nikos's eyes glistened as he said, "I would be honored."

"Great."

"Anyway, Irving, I need to get going."

"Okay, my friend."

Irving stood and gave Nikos a hug and thanked him for everything he had done for him since high school.

"Come on, Irving, I should be thanking you."

* * *

As Nikos was driving home, he was contemplating what he should tell Maria. By now, he was wondering if Maria had seen anything on the news about Garuccio and his people being killed. She knew Garuccio was behind Michael's death.

Chances are she hasn't heard anything. Because if she did, she would have called me, he thought.

As Nikos approached his house, he noticed Pappas's car still parked in the driveway. By now, he wasn't fazed in the least about his mother spending the night with another man. He decided he would tell Maria everything.

"Hey, Mom," Nikos said as he stepped into the house and almost fainted.

The night before.

Three quarters through dinner the doorbell rang.

"I wonder who that could be?" asked Maria.

"I don't know," answered Pappas. "I'll check."

* * *

Pappas opened the door and was met by Moose as he grabbed Pappas by his throat, threw him across the room, and kicked the door closed with his foot.

Maria was shocked as she stared at Moose.

"Please, please leave us alone. We've done nothing to you," she said as she sat frozen in her chair, wanting to go help Pappas.

"No, you haven't. Not *yet* anyway." Moose smiled.

Moose slowly walked over to Pappas as he lay helpless on the floor. Pappas looked up as he watched Moose bend down, lift him by his hair, and punch him in the face, breaking his nose.

"Leave him alone! Help! Help!" Maria screamed to no avail. "Help! Help!" She watched Moose continuously kick Pappas throughout his body as he lay helplessly on the living room floor.

"There we go, Miss Connecticut. I think he's out for the count. But just in case, let me make sure."

Moose then lifted the nearly dead body of Pappas by his neck and held him for several seconds before sending a kiss across the room to Maria and snapped Pappas's neck to his death. Maria screamed, watching Pappas's lifeless body drop to the floor.

"Why? Why? Why?" Maria cried hysterically. "We've done nothing to you! Haven't you've done enough to us? You've killed my husband! You've nearly killed my son! And now you killed John! Why? Why? What did we ever do to you?"

"Like I said to you before, Miss Connecticut, you've done nothing to me *yet*, but believe me when I tell you, you will do something real soon." He smiled and winked.

Maria saw the look in Moose's face and started to shake uncontrollably.

"Miss Connecticut, have I ever told you how beautiful you are?"

"Please leave me alone. Please. You've done enough!" she cried.

"There's one more thing I need to do before I kill your son."

"No, no, no!" she screamed. "No, not my son! Please leave him alone. Do what you want to me, but please leave my son alone. Please."

"I will leave him alone for now. But like I said, there is one more thing I need to do before I kill your son. And in case you're wondering what that is, we're going upstairs into your bedroom, and I am going to show you what I'm going to do before I kill your son." He smiled.

"Don't you come near me!" Maria yelled with fire in her eyes.

"Oh yeah, I'm real scared."

Moose then walked slowly toward Maria as she stood and tried to run around the table. Moose grabbed her by her hair as she screamed. Moose then smacked Maria in the face, which sent her flying across the room.

Moose then grabbed Maria by her hair again and whispered in her ear after he licked her face, "I could kill you right now, but I won't. We are going upstairs onto your bed where you made passionate love with Michael. And then you and I are going to make the same passionate love in the same spot."

Nearly unconscious, Maria said, "That's not going to happen."

"Oh yes, it is. And it's not going to be rape. I'm going to make you want it. I'm going to make you beg for it."

Still holding Maria by the hair, Moose dragged her as she followed him helplessly up the stairs.

"Let's see now. Which is *our* bedroom?"

Upstairs, there were three bedrooms and one bath. Moose continued dragging Maria by her hair as he went from room to room.

"Not this room," he said, banging her head against the wall. "It's the bathroom. This room looks like Nikos's bedroom. Look at this bedroom. This must be Lilly's. I really wanted to get a piece of your daughter, but what can I say? I never had the opportunity." Then he looked Maria in the eye and smiled. "Well, I haven't had the opportunity yet. But her day will come too. Here's our bedroom. I can see this is it. So this is where you fucked Michael."

Moose threw Maria onto the bed and ripped off her shirt and bra.

"I've always knew you had beautiful tits, Miss Connecticut. They are beautiful," he said as he aggressively squeezed them both with his massive hands, almost ripping them off.

Maria screamed in pain.

Moose then smacked Maria in the face several times as she lay in bed, nearly unconscious. Then he removed her pants and panties.

"Now, Miss Connecticut, as I fuck you, you're going to beg me to fuck you more and more. Do you hear me?"

All Maria could do was lie there.

"Now," he said to her, "tell me to fuck you."

"Please stop," Maria cried as Moose smacked her in the face.

"I'm gonna say it again. Tell me to fuck you."

"Please. I'm begging you. Please stop."

"This is the last time I'm gonna tell you. I want you to tell me to fuck you. Beg me to fuck you."

Maria knew Moose was going to kill her. She would not give him the satisfaction. "Drop dead," she said as she felt Moose penetrate her.

75

"Mom," Nikos said as he almost fainted as he saw Pappas on the floor.

"Mom! Mom! Mom!" he kept screaming over and over as he approached Pappas. When Nikos finally approached Pappas, he knew he was dead. He kept screaming for his mother.

"Mom! Mom! Mom! Mom, where are you?"

Finally, he had the courage to go upstairs to check her bedroom.

"Oh my God! God, please. Not you, Mom. Not you too. Please, God. Oh my God. Please, God. Why? Why did this happen? Why, Mom?" he kept screaming over and over.

He got his composure and stared at the bloody mess on his mother's bed as she lay completely naked, with her face totally bashed in, beyond recognition.

Her face was totally unrecognizable, just like his father's.

Finally, he had the strength to dial 911. When the police arrived, they were followed minutes later by an ambulance. Although Maria was dead, they still needed to secure the area before they could tend to Nikos. The paramedics knew they could not touch Maria's body until the coroner came.

"Please cover her," Nikos said to the paramedics.

"We have to wait for the detectives and the coroner to get here. We cannot touch anything. This is a murder scene."

"I know it's a murder scene!" screamed Nikos. "You think I'm stupid?"

"Please come downstairs, sir," said the paramedic.

After several minutes, the police and the paramedics were able to escort Nikos downstairs, where Pappas lay dead.

Several minutes later, one of the police officers came downstairs and told Nikos someone had left a note.

"Who left a note?" Nikos asked, confused.

"It looks like it was the murderer."

"How do you know?" asked Nikos. "Let me read it. Please let me read it!" he cried.

"I can't let you touch it, but I can let you read it."

The police officer left the note exactly where it was in Maria's bedroom but took a picture of it with this phone.

The note read,

> *Hey, Nikos. How does your mother look? I tried to make her face exactly like your father's after I killed him. How did I do? Did I do a good job? Was I able to duplicate it exactly like your father's? I must tell you this. Your mother was a great fuck before she died. She kept begging me to fuck her more and more. I wanted to kill her right away, but she kept begging me to keep fuckin' her, so I kept fuckin' her and fuckin' her and fuckin' her until I couldn't fuck no more. Then I had fun bashing in her face. By the way, after I do the same to your sister and your girlfriend, I'm coming after you.*

* * *

Nikos spent the next few weeks at Georgia's apartment. The bodies were not released to the families for six days. Then Nikos's house remained off limits for another two weeks as the place continued being inspected for evidence.

Lilly was devastated about the murders.

Nikos made sure Tommy returned to Rhodes.

"Come on, Nikos," said Tommy. "You need me now more than ever."

"No, Tommy. You've done enough. Go home. Go home to Kathy and your beautiful children. I got this. Moose is mine and mine alone."

"Do the police have any idea it was Moose?"

"No. And it has to stay that way. According to Ronnie, Moose has nowhere to go. Anyone who could help him is dead. Believe me, Tommy. I got this."

* * *

Two days after the funeral, Nikos still wasn't able to function. The Bronxmen didn't leave him alone for a second. Although Nikos spent most of his time at Georgia's apartment, the Bronxmen kept in constant touch with him.

Moose was nowhere to be found. He moved out of his house and seemed to have vanished.

Meanwhile, Lilly and Dennis, along with Anastasia, were in some type of routine, although Lilly was still numb. She couldn't believe both her mother and father were gone.

Because of the note left by Moose, the police monitored Georgia's and Lilly's every move.

The Bronxmen were unable to locate Moose, but they knew sooner or later, he would turn up. Moose knew his connections were now nonexistent. He literally had nowhere to go.

* * *

A month after Maria's funeral, Father Lou contacted Nikos.

"Hey, Nikos, how are you today?"

"Sorry, Father. The diner's real busy right now. I can't talk to you. I'll give you a call tonight if that's okay."

"That's fine. I'll be in the office working on the monthly newsletter until 1:00 a.m. Just give me a call when you close the diner. Or better yet, why don't you come by the church? I would love to see you."

"Okay, Father. No promises, but I'll try."

"Nikos?"

"Yes, Father?"

"Don't try. Guarantee me."

"Come on, Father. The only guarantees in life are death and taxes."

"Well, maybe death. But taxes? The church doesn't pay taxes." Father Lou laughed.

"True."

Little did Nikos know, Father Lou was actually at the diner when he had called Nikos.

* * *

For several months, Nikos was going through the motions of life but wasn't really focused on anything. The guilt he had leaving his mother alone with Pappas while going to Hartford was making him crazy. The other Bronxmen were always around in one way or another, but it didn't help him much.

* * *

Meanwhile, Georgia was starting to worry about her future with him. He was too distant.

One evening, while Nikos was at home, Georgia called.

"Nikos, what are you doing?"

"Nothing much. Just sitting around, watching TV."

"Why don't you come over? I miss you."

"I miss you too, but I'm really not up to it right now."

"Up to what?"

"It."

"What's *it*?"

"Seeing you."

The truth was Nikos had already put down five glasses of scotch. He knew he not only wouldn't be able to drive but also wouldn't even be able to stand.

"So you don't want to see me?" Georgia said, choking up.

"Come on, Georgia. Stop breaking my balls."

"I didn't know me wanting to see my fiancé was breaking his balls."

"Georgia, what do you want from me?"

"I don't want anything *from* you. I just want *you*."

"I'm sorry, but I don't want to be wanted right now."

* * *

Thirty minutes later, Nikos was awakened by pounding on the door.

"Who's there?" Nikos asked.

"It's Father Lou. Open the door."

"Go away, Father. I don't want to talk to you."

"Nikos, I said open the door. If you don't open it, I'm going to break it down. And if I break it down, I'm going to be so pissed off, I'm going to kick your ass."

"Go away, Father, before I forget you're a priest and kick *your* ass."

"Not on your best day. Now open the door before I break it down."

Nikos slowly stood from his recliner, stumbled to the door, and opened it.

"Whose ass you going to kick in the condition you're in?" asked Father Lou.

"Yours and anyone else's I need to kick."

"Bullshit."

"Father, I didn't know you curse."

"Well, now you know," said Father Lou as he grabbed Nikos by his ear and dragged him across the room to the couch. "Now sit your ass down and listen to me."

"Okay, okay, I'm sitting."

"You call that sitting? I call that collapsing. You look like shit, and you know it."

"Father, what do you want from me?"

"I want you to stop drinking and sober up."

"Do you see a drink in my hand at this moment?"

"Don't be a wise guy with me, kid."

"Father, I love this new tough guy side of you."

"I've told you many times before, Nikos. 'A monkey dressed in silk is still a monkey. And a tough kid from Brooklyn dressed in a collar is still a tough kid from Brooklyn.' So don't ever forget. This tough kid from Brooklyn will kick your ass."

"Okay, Father," said Nikos, lowering his tone. "But why are you here, and what can I do for you?"

Father Lou sat with Nikos for an hour, explaining to him how he needed to move on with his life and to let the law take care of things. He reminded Nikos about his upcoming wedding next year and how he needed to focus on that. "Georgia is scared. I mean really scared of the way you're acting and especially shutting her out. For God's sake, Nikos, she's going to be your wife. Treat her that way before you lose her."

Before Father Lou left, he looked Nikos in the eye and said, "Nikos, I know the last thing you want to hear right now is forgiveness—"

"Don't go there with me, Father," snapped Nikos. "Don't ever go there. If you think I'm going to forgive the person who killed my parents, you're outta your fuckin' mind."

Father Lou ordinarily would never allow anyone to speak to him like that, but he knew he needed to let Nikos vent.

"I can't believe you actually want me to forgive this motherfucker."

"I know you think you know who killed your parents. But you're not totally sure, are you? And even if you are, let the law handle it. Because even if this person did kill your parents and you kill him, you're going to spend the rest of your life in jail, and you know it."

"I know, Father, but don't ever use the word *forgiveness* with me when you talk about my parents' murderer. What do you expect me to do? Forgive the person and invite him over for tea?"

"No, and you know I don't. But you can still forgive someone with your soul without ever having to see them or ever having a relationship with them. Because if you don't forgive that person, that person will eat you up from the inside out. Understand?"

Nikos sat silent.

"I asked you a question. Do you understand?"

"No, Father. I don't understand. That's something I could never understand."

"I promise you, Nikos, one day you will."

Father Lou then took the nearly empty bottle of scotch and poured its contents down the kitchen sink.

"Yeah, that'll help. I don't have any more alcohol in this house." Nikos laughed.

"Nikos, I want you to stop drinking." Father Lou then took out his cell phone and called.

"Hi, Father Lou," said Georgia.

"Hi, Georgia. I think you should come over and spend some time with Nikos tonight. He seems extremely lonely and in need of some guidance."

"Oh, really? How come *he* hasn't called me?"

"Because *he's* too drunk to call. That's why. But he still needs you, and I think you should come over."

"I'll be right there, Father."

Six months later, Lenny was in Westchester County, working out with Glenn, his personal trainer, who specialized in strength training. While lifting weights, Lenny couldn't believe his eyes when he saw Moose walk into the training facility.

"Hey, Moose," said Glenn. "Did we have an appointment today?"

"No. We're scheduled for tomorrow morning."

"That's what I thought. Is everything all right?"

"Oh yeah. I have a heavy date tomorrow night. I need to save my energy for the evening, if you know what I mean."

"I know exactly what you mean." Glenn laughed.

"You have time for me now?"

"Give me a few minutes. I just need to finish up with Lenny."

"Sure. Take your time."

"Thanks. Hey, Lenny, I want you to meet Moose."

"Hi, Moose. Nice to meet you," Lenny said as he approached Moose while extending his hand to shake.

"Nice to meet you too, Lenny."

"Moose," said Glenn, "why don't you start on your stretching?"

"Sure."

Lenny continued working out with Glenn while keeping an eye on Moose as he watched him limber up and stretch.

"Hey, Moose!" Glenn called out across the room after a few minutes. "Why don't you work with the free weights until I finish with Lenny?"

"Okay."

"You know what, Glenn?" said Lenny. "I think I might've pulled something in my shoulder. Why don't you go work with Moose and I'll do a half hour on the treadmill?"

"Sure, but first, let me take a look at that shoulder."

"It's all right. It probably needs a little rest. What's today? Monday? I think I'll take the rest of the week off to give it a chance to heal. But for the rest of my session, I'll take advantage of your treadmill and elliptical."

"Sure, Lenny. Stay as long as you'd like."

Lenny did a medium pace on the treadmill as he watched Glenn work with Moose. Lenny couldn't believe the amount of weights Moose was lifting. His size had really increased.

This guy is strong, thought Lenny, thinking that Moose had to be on some sort of medically enhanced drugs.

Lenny needed any kind of information he could get. Finally, he was able to overhear Moose tell Glenn he was taking a twenty-two-year-old to Arthur Avenue tomorrow night.

No way is Nikos going to kick this man's ass, thought Lenny.

After thirty minutes, Lenny, wanting to keep a low profile, left the gym without saying goodbye.

As soon as Lenny entered his car, he called.

"Hello."

"Ronnie?"

"Hey, tough guy. How's it going? You still want a piece of me?"

"No, asshole. I need your help."

"What happened?" Ronnie asked, hearing the concern in Lenny's voice.

"It's Moose. I saw him."

"Where?"

"Believe it or not, in Westchester County, working out with the same strength trainer I use."

"Did he see you?"

"He sure did. My strength trainer actually introduced us."

"Holy shit. Were there any connections made?"

"Nope. None at all."

"It's a miracle."

"No shit."

"Okay, Lenny. All the tough guy shit aside, how can I help?"

"I'm not sure. But he's a really big guy. I'm not sure how any one of us could grab him without bringing attention to ourselves."

"I take it you want to bring him somewhere alive."

"Yes."

Lenny and Ronnie spoke for several more minutes. After Ronnie advised Lenny on what needed to be done, Ronnie jumped in his car and headed to New York. Lenny sat in his car for another hour and waited for Moose to leave. Lenny then followed Moose to a local low-end motel.

The next morning at four o'clock, Gary, Vinny, and Ronnie knocked on Moose's motel door. Moose stumbled to the door and opened it. As soon as he opened the door, Vinny and Gary Tasered Moose, but Moose was strong as an ox. He didn't go down until they Tasered him a second time. Once he was down, Vinny put plastic ties on his wrists. As Moose lay there, trying to get his composure, Ronnie gave him a shot of a sedative. After the sedative started to work on Moose, they quickly stood him up and quickly ushered him into one of their work vans outside.

Once Moose was in the van, Gary jumped in alongside of him, Tased him again, and tied his hands and feet with plastic ties as Vinny jumped into the driver's seat.

"Watch your speed," said Ronnie.

"Don't worry," said Vinny. "I'll drive like I'm taking my road test."

Ronnie then watched Vinny drive away as he walked to his car.

Fifteen minutes later, Vinny called Nikos.

"Talk to me, Vinny."

"We got him. We're on our way."

"Is everyone all right?"

"Everyone's perfect. Those Tasers Ronnie gave us could bring down a horse."

"Great. How's your passenger?"

"Hog-tied, with Gary babysitting him."

"Tell Gary to be careful."

"Don't worry about Gary. Every time Moose moves, Gary zaps him."

"Good. But please be careful. I don't want you guys killing him."

"Don't worry, my friend. That's a job for someone else."

"You better believe it."

79

Nikos sat patiently, eating his breakfast in his log cabin in Upstate New York, waiting for Vinny and Gary to bring him Moose.

He had it all planned. He knew what he was going to do to Moose. His only fear was losing his cool and killing him too quickly.

Whatever happens, remember to slow down. Do not let him make you end his suffering, he thought.

After breakfast, Nikos went into the basement to fantasize about what he was going to do to Moose when they arrived. Once Moose arrived, Nikos's fantasies would turn into reality.

Finally, at 11:00 a.m., while sitting on his front porch, calm and collective, he saw Vinny driving up his six-hundred-foot driveway.

"Hey, guys," said Nikos. "How's it going?"

"Great," said Vinny, exiting the van.

"Glad to hear it."

"What's Gary doing?"

"Gary? He's probably pouting."

"Why would he be pouting?"

"Because I took away his Taser. That's why."

"Why did you do that?"

"He kept Tasing Moose for no reason at all."

"So what?"

"Come on, Nikos. You gave us specific instructions to bring him to you alive. How many times can you Tase a guy before you kill him? I wanted to bring him to you not only alive but also healthy."

"Yeah, I guess you're probably right."

Nikos opened the back door of the van and noticed Gary sitting there, looking almost lost.

"Gary, you okay?" asked Nikos.

"No. My daddy took away my toy," Gary said as he motioned toward Vinny.

"Hey, you had your fun. Now I'm going to have my fun. Moosie baby." Nikos smiled. "How's it going, my friend?"

Moose looked confused before he realized who he was looking at.

"How was your trip upstate? I hope it was to your liking."

Moose was still out of it and unable to speak.

"Feeling a little fucked up?" asked Nikos. "Don't worry. I'm going to make you feel all better. I hope the stewardess treated you with love on your way up here. If not, I'll make it up to you. I promise.

"Now get this piece of shit into the basement." Nikos motioned to Vinnie and Gary. "And be easy with him. I don't want him getting hurt. Hurting him is my job."

Gary put an animal restraining leash with a long pole around Moose's neck and pulled him out of the van.

"Let's go, big boy. It's time for your walk."

Vinny cut the plastic ties that held Moose's ankles together to allow him to walk.

"I can hardly breathe," said Moose. "That thing around my neck is too tight."

"Don't worry, Moosie," said Nikos. "You'll get used to it."

From the van, they brought him several yards into the woods. Nikos removed a pair of industrial-sized scissors from his pocket and cut Moose's pants off. Then he cut off his shirt and underwear and had him stand there completely naked.

"First thing we're going to do," said Gary, "is have you *make* in the woods like a dog." Gary, under the watchful eye of Vinny and Nikos, paraded Moose around like a dog. "Come on. I want to watch you pee and shit."

"Fuck you," said Moose.

"Fuck me?" said Gary. "Not on your best day. But at this point, it's no big deal because in a very short time, you will be scared shitless."

With Moose's hands still tied behind his back, they led him with the restraining leash to the basement entrance.

"Watch you don't fall," said Nikos as he kicked Moose in the back and watched him fly down the stairs, reminiscing about what he had done to Fat Sal.

As Moose lay helplessly on the basement floor, all three Bronxmen stared down and smiled. Together the Bronxmen lifted Moose from the floor onto a large table that was prearranged for him. They tied him tight and used clamps to fasten him to the table; wild horses couldn't set him free.

"Comfortable?" asked Nikos.

"What are you going to do to me?" asked Moose.

"I'm not sure," said Nikos. "But I guarantee you it might not be so much fun for you, but it will be fun for me."

"Fuck you. Fuck your father. And by the way, I fucked your mother. I fucked her and fucked her and fucked her. And as much as I fucked her, she pleaded with me to fuck her more. 'Please, Moose, fuck me harder. Please, Moose, suck my tits,' she kept repeating. I got so tired of fuckin' her and so tired of her begging me to keep fuckin' her, I ended up having to kill her, the whore that she was. Were you able to recognize her? Did you see the way I bashed in her head? The newspapers said she was beyond recognition, just like your daddy. Man, did I enjoy fuckin' her."

Moose smiled as he watched tears drip down Nikos's cheeks.

"Have your fun, motherfucker," said Nikos. "Have your fun."

"I already did have my fun with your mother. Did I mention to you about me fuckin' her between her tonsils?"

"That's it. I'm gonna kill you, you piece of shit—"

"Quiet while I reminisce about fuckin' your mommy."

Nikos started punching Moose as he lay helpless on the table, but after a few seconds, Vinny and Gary pulled him off.

"No, Nikos. Not this way," said Vinny. "This is too quick."

"I don't know, Vinny. I think we just slit his throat," said Gary.

"No," said Vinny. "He has to suffer. Ain't that right, Nikos?"

"Damn right, he has to suffer. But, guys, I want you both to leave. I want personal time with my Moosie."

"Are you sure, Nikos?" asked Gary.

"Yes, I am. This is something I need to do alone."

"What about disposing of the body?" asked Vinny.

"Don't worry. I got this."

"Okay," said Gary.

Once Vinny and Gary left the basement, Nikos turned his attention back to Moose.

"Well, Moosie, it looks like it's just you and me."

"Yes, it is. Just you and me, along with the beautiful memories you have growing up with your mommy and daddy. How did that end up for you?" Moose smiled.

"Aren't you scared in the least of what's going to happen to you?"

"Nah, not at all. I know it's over for me. There isn't anything I could say or do that would entice you to let me live."

"No, there isn't." Nikos smiled. "No, there isn't."

"So I can have a little fun telling you about the fun I had with your whore mother."

"Knock yourself out. But while you're talking, take a look around. Do you see the blue tarp on your table along with the tarp on the floor?"

"Yes, I do, son of the best blowjob giver I've ever had."

Ignoring what Moose had said, Nikos continued. "The tarps are here to catch all the blood from your body as you bleed. I also have a wet Shop-Vac to soak up the blood. I'll show you."

Moose watched Nikos lift the hose of the vacuum and hold it with his left hand while he picked up a brand new butcher's saw.

"Moosie, see this saw?"

"Yes, I do, son of a whore."

"It's a butcher's saw. It cuts through bone like a hot knife through butter. And in case you're wondering what's going to happen, I'll tell you. You know what? On second thought, I'll show you."

Nikos then turned on the Shop-Vac as he started sawing off Moose's foot at the ankle. Moose screamed as the Shop-Vac sucked up most of the blood. Then he grabbed a towel and wrapped Moose's foot to stop the bleeding.

"Gotta stop the bleeding, Moosie. I need to keep you alive."

"Nikos, please listen to me," begged Moose.

"What? No joking about my mother? Are you changing your tune?"

"Look, Nikos. I know I'm done for. And I'm not going to try to convince you to let me live. I would kill me too if I were you. But I would like to make a deal."

"Fuck you!" screamed Nikos as he grabbed a fillet knife and started filleting Moose's other leg.

Moose screamed at the top of his lungs.

"Please, Nikos, please hear me out!"

"Fuck you," Nikos said as he sliced off his left kneecap.

Moose begged him to listen.

"I can give you money. A lot of money!" cried Moose. "Millions. Millions of dollars in cash."

"There isn't enough money in the world that could save your life," Nikos said as he sliced off a thick piece of his thigh.

"I'm not asking you to let me live!" Moose screamed. "I want you to put a bullet in my heart. I want to die instantly," he pleaded. "Please. Giovanni has millions in a mini storage. I've been stocking it in there for years. There's a combination code to open the door. I'll give it to you. But please. I can't take the pain." He cried. "Please put a bullet in my heart."

"Fuck you."

"Nikos, don't be stupid. If I die, the money will die there. The storage unit is paid up for the next ten years. Please take the money. It's my way of saying I'm sorry. Take the money."

"How much are you talking about?" Nikos asked, changing his tune.

"About thirty million."

"You're telling me there's $30,000,000 in this mini storage?"

"Give or take."

"What's the address?"

"I'm not telling you shit unless you guarantee me you'll put a bullet in my heart."

"And you'll believe me?"

"Yes."

"After the way you murdered my parents, do you really expect me to let you die peacefully?"

"Yes, I do. Because if there's anything I do know about you, it's that you're a stand-up guy."

Nikos thought a moment as he sliced off Moose's bicep as Moose continued screaming. "Okay, I'll let you off the hook. You have my word I will shoot you in the heart so you can die instantly. But I need the address, unit number, and combination code to enter the unit. I will then go there and see if you're lying. And let me tell you something, you piece of shit. You better be telling the truth. Because if you're lying, you will suffer even more than I planned."

"I'm not lying."

"Okay, Moosie, here we go."

Nikos then put on a pair of disposable gloves, took Moose's penis in his hand, and cut it off with a box cutter as Moose screamed.

"You motherfucker! You fuckin' cocksucker! Your mother sucked my dick!"

"Back to the mother jokes, I see."

"Please, Nikos. I want you to have the money."

"Okay, you piece of shit. For $30,000,000, I'll end your suffering," Nikos said even though Moose deserved to suffer much more, even though he himself was ready to vomit. "Let's go. Give me the information I need, and I'll put a bullet in your heartless heart for you."

Moose knew Nikos couldn't continue, so he gave Nikos the information he needed as he watched him take a gun off the shelf, but right before Nikos pulled the trigger, Moose said, "Your mother can really suck cock."

"You spoke too soon," Nikos said as he put the gun back on the shelf. "Now you're really going to suffer."

"Please, Nikos. I just gave you $30,000,000."

Ignoring him, Nikos grabbed his fillet knife and started filleting Moose's chest by starting at his nipples, but within another minute, Moose had lost too much blood and passed out, never regaining consciousness. So Nikos continued to carry out his original plan.

He took his butcher's saw and started cutting away. He cut Moose into thirty pieces and disposed of him in ten heavy-duty black plastic bags. He then took the plastic tarps and rolled them up. Within an hour, Nikos was in his van, traveling south on Interstate 87 toward the Bronx, with Moose cut up and distributed into the ten bags, along with the rolled-up tarps and the bloody Shop-Vac.

When Nikos returned to the Bronx, Vinny and Gary jumped into Nikos's van and headed south to see Ronnie in Maryland. Once they arrived, with the help of Vinny and Gary, Ronnie put the bags, tarps, and Shop-Vac onto his boat.

Within twenty minutes, they were headed to deep waters and dumped the bags, tarps, and Shop-Vac into Chesapeake Bay, knowing the tide would bring them out to sea.

Then they quickly returned to shore.

The next afternoon, the Six Bronxmen met for a board meeting in Irving's office. As always, Irving ran the meeting. He told everyone about the $30,000,000 Moose had told Nikos about.

Nikos made it perfectly clear he was going to split everything that was found in the storage unit equally among the Bronxmen.

"No way, Nikos," said Richie.

"I agree," said Lenny. "That money belongs to you, Nikos. Your family paid the ultimate price."

"That's true," they all said, agreeing with Lenny.

"Hold on, guys," said Nikos. "I appreciate what you're all saying, but no fuckin' way. We're all partners in this. Nothing would be the way it is without you guys. None of us need the money. But since it's coming our way, it's going to be split equally, and that's final."

"Well, guys, you heard it," said Irving. "Nikos said equally, so it's equally."

"Okay then," said Gary. "Let's go check out the storage unit."

"Yeah, guys," said Vinny. "Let's get going. I always wanted to be like those guys on TV checking out storage units."

"Hold on, everyone," said Irving. "We should trust Moose like we would trust Garuccio."

"What are you talking about?" asked Vinny.

"I don't trust him," replied Irving. "He told Nikos it's a simple six-digit code. You guys should know how those codes work. There could be two codes. One code to unlock the storage unit and another code to set off some sort of explosion."

"Holy shit," said Gary. "I never thought of that. What are we going to do?"

"We're *going* to take a vote. That's what we're *going* to do," Irving said sarcastically.

"What kind of vote?" asked Richie.

"First of all, no one's going to open the storage unit. We're going to bring Ronnie here to check out the keypad. If he thinks there's the slightest chance of a bomb, we're going to have to take other measures."

"What kind of measures?" asked Vinny.

"Well, first of all, I want you guys to know I checked out the mini storage place this morning. As it turns out, it's a prime piece of real estate. I'm thinking it could be a good investment for us. I mean, let's face it. We have restaurants and apartment buildings. A mini storage could be perfect for us to diversify."

"Guys," said Nikos, "Irving thinks it's a good idea. What do you guys think? I think it might be worth looking into."

"How do you know if the storage unit is even available for sale?" asked Vinny.

"I don't," said Irving. "But I already tried looking up the owners. As suspected, it's owned by a corporation."

"Who owns the corporation?" asked Richie.

"I'll look it up. That's the easy part. The difficult part is getting them to sell."

"Why would it be difficult to get them to sell?"

"Come on, Richie. It's a storage unit. The place runs on autopilot. And besides, it's in an up and coming area. In ten years, the property value could triple."

"Shit, man—"

"Look, Irving," said Lenny, interrupting. "You know we're all in if you think the numbers work. But what are we going to do if Ronnie thinks there's a bomb attached to the code?"

"First things first. Let's see what Ronnie has to say."

81

Two days later, Ronnie met Nikos, Irving, and Lenny at the storage unit.

"So what do you think?" asked Lenny.

"I don't think. I never think. I either know or don't know."

"You starting your shit again, wise guy?"

"I guess I am, tough guy."

"Children, let's cut the shit," said Nikos.

"Yeah, cut the shit," said Lenny.

"Enough!" screamed Nikos. "This is serious. So you both better cut it out before I kick both your asses."

"Okay," said Ronnie. "I need a couple of minutes." Ronnie examined the keyboard for several minutes. "Well, guys. Here's the story. Without a doubt, this keyboard is multifunctional. What that means is this. You can assign multiple codes to it so the owner knows who has been here and for how long. It also has a detonating function. But it is impossible to know if anything is connected to it unless I can get inside. And I can't get inside."

"What do you suggest?" asked Nikos.

"We need to get inside."

"Any ideas?"

"Yeah."

"Speak."

"Okay. But keep in mind I have no idea what's inside. But my guess is to *not* trust Moose. So if it was totally up to me, I would not touch the door to get inside. What I would do is somehow get inside either one of the units adjacent to this one and not go through the wall but tunnel underneath."

"Holy shit," said Lenny. "Do you think the walls could be rigged?"

"Yes, I do. I also think the roof could be rigged too. It might be overkill, but that's what I would do."

"Okay, guys," said Nikos. "I've heard enough. No one touches this unit until we all meet and decide."

"Good idea," said Ronnie.

* * *

The next morning, the Six Bronxmen met in Irving's office. Irving explained how he had looked up the owners of the storage units and would contact them that afternoon to ask if they would consider selling.

"What if they don't want to sell?" asked Gary.

"If they don't want to sell, they don't want to sell. There's nothing we can do but try to find out who rents the units on both sides of Giovanni's unit and take them over. There's nothing else we *can* do."

* * *

Within the next six months, the Bronxmen owned the storage unit. Three months after that, Irving was able to contact the people renting the units on both sides of Giovanni's. He offered them both larger units for the same price if they moved. Of course, they took the deal. Once the units were empty, Irving called everyone into his office.

"Okay, guys," Irving started. "I called you to my office for a meeting, but in actuality, Ronnie's going to speak. It's his meeting."

"Listen up, guys," said Ronnie. "Both units are empty. We know they're not rigged because the previous renters were able to get in and out without any explosions. So this is what we need to do. First, we need to get jackhammers and start tunneling through. Irving has the engineer reports, and after examining them, he says there are no pipes or electrical wires under the units. So we're able to dig. We will first jackhammer through the concrete floor. Then after digging approximately ten feet, we're going to dig sideways and then up into Giovanni's unit.

"It's going to take some time. It must be done slow as to not attract any attention—"

"What do we care about attracting attention?" interrupted Lenny. "We own the place. We can do whatever we want."

"There you go again, tough guy," said Ronnie. "Just calm down, take a deep breath, follow my instructions, and no one will get hurt—I hope. Now are there any real questions?"

"No, there aren't," Nikos jumped in. "Just tell us our next move."

"There really isn't anything else I can say. We need to purchase jackhammers, picks, shovels, and large crowbars to lift the broken pieces of concrete as the jackhammers break up the concrete. We also need to purchase sledgehammers. The units aren't large enough to house all the debris. So we're going to either need a dumpster or, what I think is a better idea to keep a low profile, get a bunch of five-gallon pails and load them into one or two of your vans and get rid of the debris little by little."

"How long do you think this would take?" asked Irving.

"Honestly, it's going to take weeks. There's a bunch of work that needs to be done. But we all can't work at the same time. We'll only get in one another's way. I don't suggest more than two guys in each unit. We work four or five hours filling the pails and load them into the vans and get rid of the shit. Then another shift takes over."

"I have to tell you," said Irving. "We took a vote yesterday and decided to cut you in as an equal partner."

"That's great," said Ronnie. "Thanks a lot. But what about Tommy? He's part of this shit too."

"You're right," answered Nikos before anyone could say a word.

Everyone nodded.

"Okay then," said Irving. "Since Ronnie's in charge, I think he should purchase all the equipment we need, and we'll begin as soon as he says so."

Everyone agreed.

"Guys," said Ronnie, "I want to work with Lenny. That's if he could keep up with me."

Everyone laughed, including Lenny.

Two days later, the digging began. In one empty unit were Richie and Vinny. The other empty unit was Lenny and Ronnie. Everyone decided it was best for Nikos to stay away. They thought it would be too emotional for him. The first day, they broke up the 6' x 6' concrete slab in the middle of each unit. There was plenty of room around because each unit was 12' x 12'.

"Come on, Lenny. Swing that sledgehammer." Ronnie laughed.

"You better be careful." Lenny giggled. "I might miss and swing it on your head."

"Not on your best day." Ronnie laughed.

In the other unit, Richie and Vinny were basically having their noses to the grindstone, no laughing or joking, only hard work. The first day was the most difficult day of all. The breaking up of the concrete into small enough pieces to put into the five-gallon pails was backbreaking. Once they were loaded into the pails, they were taken into the two vans parked outside.

The next morning, they went to the local dump to dispose of the concrete. The second day, they started digging out the dirt and gravel. Ronnie felt they should dig a hole ten feet deep. At first, Nikos questioned why they would dig two tunnels, but Ronnie explained to him it was important in case they needed to make a run for it when they finally got inside Giovanni's unit.

By the third day, they reached ten feet deep. The next morning, they started tunneling toward Giovanni's unit. They knew they would have to tunnel approximately ten feet sideways. Ronnie equipped them with precut 2' x 6' boards to use as support in case of a cave-in.

By the fifth day, as they were tunneling directly under Giovanni's unit, Lenny and Richie's shovels touched. They ended up working until eleven o'clock that night.

The next morning, when they arrived, both tunnels were secure except for a five-foot square above. Little by little, they used small hand shovels and picks to loosen the dirt above. They knew they had to go ten feet high while the dirt kept falling on top of them. Then they shoveled the dirt into buckets and took turns taking them out to the vans. The most difficult part of the dig was going straight up. After a week and a half, they finally hit the concrete up top. The next morning, they all met at Irving's office.

"Okay, guys," said Ronnie. "I have a large powerful drill. We know the concrete is six inches thick. We're going to drill holes into the concrete below Giovanni's unit. Once we weaken the concrete slab, we will then chip away at it. Let's keep in mind once we break through the concrete, we don't know what lies above."

Two days later, Lenny broke through. Shortly afterward, Lenny, Ronnie, Richie, and Vinny were standing inside the storage unit, staring at a transparent cylinder with two transparent tubes within it. Both inner tubes were filled with two separately colored liquids: red and blue.

"Holy shit," whispered Ronnie. "You guys see that?"

"Yes, I do," whispered Richie. "What is it?"

"It's highly explosive liquid."

"So what are we still doing here?" asked Lenny.

"Don't be afraid, chickenshit. They're harmless. Harmless unless the two hug and kiss. See the wires coming from the junction box?" Ronnie motioned toward the box. "It's connected to the alarm box. See the wires running up and down the walls? There're all booby-trapped. You put in the correct code, and it releases the red and blue liquids into the center tube. Once the two colors combine and turn purple, you get the boom." He smiled. "Good thing we didn't go through the ceiling either. It's also wired."

"Okay, let's look for the money," said Vinny, "and then get the hell out of here."

"Yes, that's what we should do."

It didn't take them very long. There were several boxes scattered about the unit. One by one, everyone nervously examined each box. To their surprise, they were filled with twenty-seven standard small safes that could be purchased at any home improvement store. All the safes had the keys in their locks.

"Hey, Lenny," joked Ronnie, "do you want the honors of opening one?"

"No way." Lenny laughed. "How about you?"

"Not on your life."

"So what are we going to do?" asked Richie.

"We're going to take the safes and put them into the vans. Then then we're going to bring them upstate to Nikos's house."

"What for?" asked Lenny.

"I understand in about a month or so, hunting season starts upstate."

"What's that have to do with anything?" asked Lenny.

"We're going to wait until hunting season starts. Then we're going to take the safes and line them up on Nikos's property. Then we're going to take a rifle, probably a .30-30, and shoot holes through them. Keep in mind it'll be hunting season. The gunshots won't bring attention to the area. If they blow up, then we know we did the right thing by testing them. Since I was in the military and I'm actually considered an expert marksman, I'll do the shooting. The bullet will upset anything inside the safes. Once we shoot through them, we'll know if there are explosives inside. If there are no explosives inside, very little of the money would be damaged. That's what we're going to do."

"I have to tell you," said Lenny, "you are a genius."

"I know I am." Ronnie smiled. "Now let's get the safes into the vans."

"What about the explosives?" asked Richie.

"The liquid is totally harmless if left separate. So this is what we're going to do. Once we have all the safes in the vans, I'm going to come back and remove the canisters containing the liquid—not together." He smiled. "Then I'll take the red canister and put it in one van. Then

I'll take the blue canister and put in the other van. We will spill them separately in the Westchester Square Creek. Remember, as long as we do it separately, nothing will happen."

Once the twenty-seven safes were loaded into the vans, Ronnie went back into the storage units and removed the canisters one by one.

"When are we going to dump this shit into the creek?" asked Lenny.

"I think the first thing we should do is safeguard the safes. Don't worry about the canisters. They're harmless. I would throw them in separate garbage bins, but I'm afraid they may end up at the same incineration plant. So how about this? Let's spill one of them right here on the grass. The other one, I'll spill in the creek."

83

The next day, Nikos and Irving drove to his house upstate with all twenty-seven safes in the van. When they finally reached the house, they unloaded half the safes into the basement and the others into two separate outside sheds. They wanted to keep them separated.

When finished, Nikos cranked up the barbeque and waited fifteen minutes for the grill to get white hot. Then he took two two-inch rib-eye steaks out of the large cooler and said, "Hey, Irving, why don't you pop open a couple of beers?"

"Sure thing, Nikos, and remember, three minutes on each side. I like mine rare."

"As do I, my friend. As do I."

That evening, while they both ate, they reminisced their high school days.

"Nikos, did I ever tell you how happy I was when you first moved to the Bronx?"

"Yes, you have. You were the first friend I made."

"Yeah, and you were the only friend I *ever* made."

"Now look at us. We're millionaires with millions more in cash, I hope." Nikos laughed.

"I hope so too. I really do."

"But you know what, Irving? Even if the safes turn out to be empty, we have plenty of money. Besides, we got you. And because of you, we'll have more."

"Thanks for the pressure." Irving laughed.

"Irving, all kidding aside, what do you think? Do you think there really is money in the safes?"

"Come on, Nikos. You know I never *think*. I either know or don't know," Irving joked, reminding Nikos of what Ronnie had said. "So I'm going to ask *you* two questions."

"Shoot."

"There were highly explosive liquids rigged up to the door of the storage unit. Why was that? There were twenty-seven safes in the unit. Why were there twenty-seven safes in there?"

"Obviously, there's something in those safes."

"Obviously. But if I *had* to think, this is what I would think. I would think there is something in those safes. What, I don't know. But it has to be important enough to kill anyone who tried to get inside."

"Do you think the safes could be rigged?"

"No. Not a chance."

"Why's that?"

"Because I asked Ronnie if the safes were lined up exactly the same. And he told me there was no particular order. If they had the same liquid explosives, they would be lined up in a certain way in case of leakage. I know what you're thinking. You're thinking they could be placed that way so someone would think the way I'm thinking. Correct?"

"You're a mind reader."

"I wish. But anyway, if that were the case, they would have to mark each safe. If they ever needed to empty the storage unit in a hurry, it would never have worked for them. So the answer to your questions is this. I don't know if there is money in the safes. But I do think there is something valuable in all of them. I just don't know what. And no, I do not think the safes are rigged. But then again, what do I know? I'm just an accountant."

"An accountant and my best friend."

Hunting season, opening day . . .

"Let's go, guys," said Ronnie. "Let's line this shit up."

One by one, the Bronxmen lined up the safes forty yards from the house on the open land.

"Stand them up longways and line them up a foot apart!" yelled Ronnie. "Put them on their sides. If there is any type of mechanism attached to the locks, that's where it will blow. I'm going to shoot right through the locks."

Once all the safes were lined up the way Ronnie wanted them, they all looked at one another in silence.

Finally, Nikos spoke. "Guys," he said, tearing up, "we've come such a long way together. Whatever is or isn't inside the safes means nothing to me compared to the friendship and bonding we have endured together. Nothing inside the safes can ever bring back my mother and father."

At this time, the 6'-5" 235-pound he-man broke down and cried like a five-year-old. The rest of them looked at him and started crying with him.

After a minute, Nikos stopped. "Come on, guys," he said. "Let's go. Let's do this."

Then they all stood in a circle and put their arms around one another in a group hug.

"I love you, guys," said Nikos. "I really do. So, Ronnie, start shooting."

Ronnie lay down on the ground with his high-powered scope attached to his Marlin .30-30 rifle that rested on a small stand. His sights had already been adjusted the day before at a rifle range. "Well, guys," said Ronnie, "it's now or never."

Ronnie closed his left eye and looked through the scope. Six seconds later, he shot the first bullet right through the lock of the first safe. Nothing happened.

One by one, all twenty-seven safes were shot right through the locks with no explosions. As Ronnie suspected, the safes did not open, but that was not a problem for him.

"Let's go take a look," said Lenny.

All the safes' locks had considerable damage. One by one, they brought the safes into the house. With all the shooting that was going on in the distance, Ronnie's gunfire only blended in.

"Okay, guys," said Ronnie. "We have a bunch of hammers and chisels. All we need to do now is bang the chisels into the seams, and the safes will open. Who wants to do the honors?"

"I'll do it only under one condition," said Nikos.

"What's that?" asked Richie.

"We still don't know if there are any explosives, although everyone seems to doubt there are any. I will open the first one as long as you guys wait outside."

"No way," said Gary. "We're all in this together. You blow up, we blow up."

"Not on your lives. Everyone outside. Now."

Once everyone was outside, Nikos got on his knees, put the chisel into the seam, hit hard three times, and watched the safe open. As suspected, the safe was full of money.

Nikos hurried to the door and yelled, "Holy shit, guys, come in here! There's money in the safes!"

They all ran inside as Nikos had the safe opened. It was filled with $100 bills. As suspected, some of the money was damaged from the gunshot, but most were intact. One by one, they opened all the safes, but not all were filled with money. Some of the safes had gold Krugerrands. Others had extremely valuable jewelry. One safe was filled with first-edition comic books. All in total, there was $32,700,000 in cash. They had no idea what the jewelry was worth, but Irving had several accounts in the jewelry district in Manhattan who could help. Nor did they know how much they had in gold with the Krugerrands. Again, Nikos broke down and cried. He was happy about the money, of course, but it brought back memories of his parents.

It took a few days to separate the money equally among the Six Bronxmen plus Ronnie and Tommy. The jewelry was worth an additional $2,000,000. Irving got them a great cash deal from one of his clients; although they knew the jewelry had to have been stolen, they had no way of getting it back to its original owners. The several thousands of dollars that were destroyed with the bullets, they shredded. Finally, Irving called a meeting.

* * *

"Hey, guys, listen up," said Irving. "I want to let you know I appreciate you all coming here, especially Ronnie and Tommy. It's important for all of us to be present for the division of the money. The bottom line is this. Everyone's share is $4,087,500. The jewelry was worth an additional $2,000,000. For my guy to fence it, I had to let it go cheap. I had no choice. So I got $500,000. The Krugerrands were worth another $1,500,000. I suggest we do not cash them in. Gold has been stale for a while. I'm thinking we should hold on to them until the price of gold climbs a little. But that's up to you guys. I'm just telling you what I'm going to do with my share. Now as far as the comic books go, they *are* worth some money. But they are also easily traceable. So my suggestion is to donate them anonymously to the Smithsonian. Are there any questions?"

Irving looked at everyone and smiled. He knew there wouldn't be any questions because he had discussed all this with them secretly the previous day without Nikos.

"Since there are no questions," Irving continued, "there is something I want to add." Irving turned to Nikos and started to speak. "Nikos, we had a meeting yesterday without you and came up with a few conditions—"

"What kind of conditions?" Nikos interrupted.

"Just listen and don't interrupt me. Now at our meeting, we decided we are not going to keep our entire share of the $4,087,500. We are going to keep $3,000,000 and donate back to you $1,087,000. And that's final. The rest of the money from the jewelry, we'll donate to your church in the Bronx. Sorry," Irving joked. "The gold, we're going to keep—"

"No way, guys. No way."

"Yes way," said Irving. "You're the only one who lost anything. So take the money. It's yours."

85

The following year, Nikos and Georgia were married. Father Lou, as always, performed a splendid wedding. At his wedding, Nikos decided not to have any ushers. Instead, he had seven best men: the five Bronxmen along with Tommy and Ronnie. It was the first time Father Lou had performed a wedding with seven best men, but there was nothing in the rule book that said otherwise.

Since all the others wanted to give Nikos $1,087,500, he decided to also kick in $1,087,000, which totaled $8,700,000. The first thing he did was give John Pappas's two children $1,000,000 apiece. Then he set aside another $1,000,000 for his grandparents in Cyprus. Then he put an additional $1,000,000 in trust for Saint George Greek Orthodox Church in Vavla, Cyprus.

The final $4,700,000, he put into the Michael Ioannis Memorial Foundation and then changed the name to the Michael and Maria Ioannis Memorial Foundation.

The End

CPSIA information can be obtained
at www.ICGtesting.com
Printed in the USA
BVHW032229300519
549770BV00018B/6/P

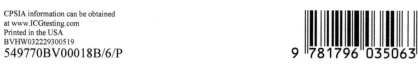

9 781796 035063